WHAT'S YOUR ST@TUS?

Also by Katie Finn:

Top 8

WHAT'S YOUR ST@TUS?

A TOP 8 NOVEL

KATIE FINN

Point

Library of Congress Cataloging-in-Publication Data Available

ISBN 978-0-545-21127-7

Text design by Steve Scott

12 11 10 9 8 7 6 5 4 3 2 1   10 11 12 13 14 15/0

Printed in the U.S.A.   40
First printing, July 2010

FOR AMALIA,
Partner in crime

ACKNOWLEDGMENTS

Many thanks to Finn's Ten:
Amalia Ellison, Jane Finn, Aimee Friedman, Abby McAden,
Laura Martin, Jason Matson, Sarah Milligan, Steve Scott,
Rosemary Stimola, and Siobhan Vivian.

"Look, we all go way back.
I owe you from that thing with the guy in the place,
and I'll never forget it."
—Ocean's 11

"Same song, second chorus."
—Bowling for Soup

STATUS Q
What's your status?

mad_mac/
Madison MacDonald

Song: 4ever/The Veronicas
Quote: "There is nothing funny about a prom." — Kittson Pearson

Age: 16
Location: Putnam, Connecticut

Followers: 300
Following: 45

About Me: I heart: my friends, old movies, new music, Stubbs lattes. TEAM JACOB! Currently trying to pull together a junior prom. So you know: I update my status a LOT. You've been warned!

Taken by: N8/Nate Ellis

mad_mac Trying to find appropriate prom music. Suggestions welcome.

 mad_mac iTunes is being remarkably unhelpful in the prom music quest.

 mad_mac WHO LISTENS TO MICHAEL BOLTON?! iTunes prom music epic FAIL.

 mad_mac Thinking it's time for the prom DJ to take some initiative.

 N8 Getting very familiar with the inside of the headmaster's office these days. I think that's not a good sign, right? Probably not.

 La Lisse Finally settled on a prom dress! J'adore cette robe! Victoire!

 Shy Time I'm updating my status! I think. Why is this phone so COMPLICATED?

 DJ Tanner → mad_mac Um, excuse me, Mad. What "initiative" do you want me to take? Just tell me and I will. It's not MY fault you didn't want the all-death-metal playlist. I'm just sayin.

Dave Gold You know, *American Pie* is actually a pretty good movie.

 N8 → Dave Gold Dave, you really want to go there? SERIOUSLY?

 Grounded_Brian Another weekend spent at home. Siiiiiiiiigh . . .

 the8rgrrl Am I the only one who misses *Dane* rehearsals? It's SO sad when a show closes. Parting is such sweet sorrow. . . .

 Roth Mann → the8rgrrl I don't know about you, Sarah, but I'm glad to be done speaking in a British accent for a while.

 Gingersnap → Roth Mann That was supposed to be a British accent?

 Roth Mann → Gingersnap Um. Yes.

 Gingersnap → Roth Mann I knew that. Great job with it!

 Shy Time Did my status work before? It just disappeared. Argh.

mad_mac → Shy Time It worked, Shy!

 KitKat I think that teachers ought to recognize the importance of the prom and give us class time to work on it. Because this is WAY more important than school. I mean, right?

 Glen → KitKat Absolutely, babe. Want me to mention it to Dr. Trent the next time I'm called into the office?

 KitKat → Glen Would you? Thanks, sweetie! xoxox

 Shy Time Now I can't see anyone else's status. HELLO? IS THIS WORKING??

 mad_mac → Shy Time YES.

 La Lisse → Shy Time OUI.

 Dave Gold → N8 Nate, I'm not saying it's the BEST movie ever made, but I think it gets a worse rep than it deserves.

Connor A. ➜ Shy Time Hi sweetie! I think your phone is working, but want me to take a look at it at lunch? Miss you! xoxo

 N8 ➜ Dave Gold You're going to regret that statement in 20 years when it's still on the interwebs and you're incredibly embarrassed by it.

 Jimmy+Liz Trying to speed-read James Bond before class. Kind of sure this is actually making me *less* intelligent. (this is jimmy)

 Jimmy+Liz Nothing could make you less intelligent, baby. You're too brilliant for that! (this is liz)

 Glen I tried to fight the Man, and all I got was detention. I think it's time for a regime change.

 La Lisse ➜ Glen Um, Glen, you know Dr. Trent has access to our Q pages, right?

 Glen ➜ La Lisse WHATEVER! We need to speak truth to power!

 Glen ➜ La Lisse In fact, should the ASSistant headmaster be reading these things at all? I think that's wrong, and—

 Glen THIS ACCOUNT HAS BEEN TEMPORARILY DISABLED.

Shy Time → Connor A. Thanks, honey! You're the best!! xoxo

 KitKat → mad_mac Mad, we need to talk about the Hayes crown. And DON'T FORGET we have a committee meeting this afternoon. Also, I think we should petition to get class time to work on prom stuff. Can you draw one up by this afternoon?

 La Lisse → mad_mac Mad, avons-nous un plan? Are we getting coffee this afternoon?

 Dave Gold → mad_mac Mad, your boyfriend is being completely ridiculous. Not to mention elitist. Help me out here?

 Shy Time → mad_mac Mad?

 KitKat → mad_mac Hello?

 La Lisse → mad_mac Bonjour?

CHAPTER 1

Song: Our Song/Taylor Swift
Quote: "Life is what happens to you while you're busy making other plans."—John Lennon

"Hi," I whispered to Nate as he tightened his arms around my waist.

"Hi yourself," he said, smiling down at me. And then, in one smooth movement, he spun me around and pressed me against the brick wall that was the back of Putnam High School.

"Wow," I said, leaning my head back against the bricks and brushing that one lock of hair away from his forehead. "Impressive."

"Oh, I've got some moves," he said, arching an eyebrow, which made me laugh. But I didn't laugh for very long as he started kissing me again, and the rest of the world faded away.

I had been going out with Jonathan Ellis—known to me and everyone else as Nate—for almost two months now. Before him, I'd thought I'd known what having a boyfriend was like. But being with Nate was like nothing I'd ever experienced. We fit. It just felt right, and it was *easy*. We always had something to say to each other, and he could make me laugh like nobody else. And I could make him laugh, something I tried to do as often as possible. I was, as my friend Schuyler Watson was constantly saying, a smitten kitten. Basically, I couldn't stop thinking about him, and had the plunging AP history grade to show for it.

Oh, and the kissing. The kissing was amazing. Making out with Nate could cause three hours to pass in what I could have sworn was ten minutes, tops. When we were kissing, I completely forgot about where I was and what else was happening; nothing else existed except Nate. This had led to several near accidents in crosswalks, run-ins with dog walkers, and so far, I had missed curfew eleven times. But I didn't care. Kissing Nate was worth it. It wasn't like when I'd been going out with my ex, Justin Williamson, and all we did was make out because we didn't have anything to say to each other. I wanted to talk to Nate as much as I wanted to make out with him, and it seemed to be mutual. But when we *were* making out, it was incredible.

We broke apart for a moment, and Nate traced his finger down my cheek, then kissed me softly. I wrapped my arms around his neck and was preparing to start round two of the makeout session when I caught sight of my watch and sighed. "I have class in ten minutes," I reminded him.

"Nope," he said, leaning down and kissing me again.

Unable to argue with that logic, I kissed him back, only to be interrupted when my phone chimed, letting me know that someone had just sent me a message on Status Q.

Status Q had really taken off last month. It was part of Friendverse, the social networking site that *everybody* used. But rather than showing people's favorite bands and their fake gardens and constantly asking you to take quizzes (Friendverse really had gotten out of hand with that kind of stuff in recent months) Status Q showed *just* status updates. Which, really, were the most important part. On my homepage, I could see my updates, but also all the updates of the people I followed. Everyone had started using it, and I used it a lot now in place of texting, as it let me reach the essential people without having to text each of them individually. If you wanted, you could post pictures with your updates, and there was also an optional GPS feature that, if you clicked on it, revealed your location along with your status. This was really helpful, especially when you were running late to meet people and could see, despite their outraged French posts, that they were actually running late as well. I'd gotten really into Status Q, and I updated my status a *lot*. But I only wrote stuff about myself, never about other people. I'd learned my lesson as far as that was concerned.

I didn't take out my phone to check the Status Q message, but it had startled me out of the moment, and now there was no denying the fact that I was going to be late for class. "Argh," I said, breaking away again. "I'd better go."

"You don't need to go," Nate said. He kissed me just under my ear, then slowly began kissing down my neck.

Okay, that was just not fighting fair. With a strength of will that, before that moment, I had not been aware I possessed, I moved away slightly and looked up at him. "I do," I said. "Not all of us are second-semester seniors, you know."

Watching Nate in action had convinced me that suffering through the hellish first semester of senior year might actually be worth it. I'd been able to see him a *lot,* as it seemed that once you'd been accepted to college and May rolled around, nobody was really keeping track of whether you showed up for class or not.

He smiled at me. "True." He lifted my arm off his neck and looked at my watch. "Huh. Would you look at that. Apparently, I also have class in ten minutes."

Considering that Stanwich High was a twenty-minute drive away, this didn't seem feasible. "I have a feeling you're not going to make it," I said as I tried to smooth down his hair in the back where I'd messed it up.

"Probably not," he said, seeming completely unconcerned. "But I actually should get back. I have to see the headmaster later."

I straightened up a bit and leaned back so that I could see him more clearly. "What for?"

"Oh, nothing," Nate said, giving me one of his half smiles, the kind that always made me feel like I was melting a little bit inside. "More stuff about the prank."

From what everyone had been saying, Stanwich's recent senior prank had been epic. Nate refused to tell me any details, or even confirm that he'd been involved. Whenever I asked him about it, he just said that the less he told me, the less likely it was that I would be deposed. But from what I'd heard, the prank had involved a cow, a staircase, a thousand Super Balls, and the mascot costume of Hartfield High. Hartfield High was the rival of both Stanwich and Putnam, and every time there was a prank, part of it always seemed to involve doing something to Hartfield.

"What about the prank?" I asked, hoping he'd forget that he'd declared—repeatedly—that the details were strictly need-to-know.

"Nothing," he said, smiling at me. Clearly, my intention had been obvious. "I guess I'm just now officially a Person of Interest. Specifically regarding the streaker."

This caused me to take a full step back. "Streaker?"

He laughed, probably at my expression. "It wasn't me," he said. "But they're now alleging that I had something to do with orchestrating it."

"So did you?" I asked casually.

"Nice try," he said with a smile. "But I will tell you one thing. Streakers make for the ultimate diversion. Nobody quite knows what to do or where to look. If you ever need an exit strategy, call in a streaker."

I couldn't help laughing at that. "I'll keep that in mind."

"You busy later?" he asked.

"Yes," I said sadly, knowing that *later* referred to immediately after school. Whenever we both had this window free, we took it, and it was great—at least three hours to make out, or hang with his friends, or my friends, or watch a movie on my laptop in the back of his truck, or go to our rock wall by the beach and sit together and look out at the water. But today, none of that would be happening. "I have to deal with prom stuff."

"Prom stuff," he said, running his fingers through my hair. "Yikes. You guys all set?"

"More or less," I said vaguely. The state of the junior prom these days was definitely falling into the *less* category. And it was being held at the Putnam Hyatt—the nicest hotel in town—this Saturday night. And Saturday was only five days away, a fact I was trying—without success—not to think about too much. But Nate and I were going to the prom together, and he seemed really excited about it—maybe because it was his last chance at one.

The Stanwich High prom had been put on hiatus after the prank in an attempt to get the people who had pulled it to come forward and confess. Needless to say, that hadn't worked, and the prom had been canceled. So I was feeling a lot of pressure about our prom. Not only to make it good—or at least disaster-free—but also to make it good for Nate.

But while I wanted it to be a success, I was annoyed that it was taking up so much of my time. Kittson Pearson, the head of the prom committee (who was also bound and determined to be crowned prom queen), had been transferring more and more work to me as the date got closer, to my mounting frustration. But I didn't want to burden Nate with these details and spoil what had been a really nice lunch—even though, technically, I hadn't gotten any food.

"Well, I'm looking forward to it," he said. "I can't believe it's here already."

"Mmm," I said noncommittally, pressing my lips together so that I wouldn't be tempted to tell him all about the drama with the DJ and the gift bags and my litany of issues with Kittson.

"If there's anything I can do to help," he said, "just let me know."

"Actually," I said, seizing my opportunity and smiling up at him, "there is."

There was only one thing about my relationship with Nate that had been bothering me—and that was our song. Or, actually, lack thereof. My Francophile friend, Lisa Feldman, insisted that it was *tres* bad luck for a couple not to have a song, and that it signified an underlying lack of commitment.

I'd been trying to bring this up with Nate for a while, turning up the volume when certain songs played in our cars and telling him how much I liked them. He hadn't gotten any of these hints, however, and had usually just started discussing discography and influences, and after a while of this, it was usually too late to bring the conversation back around to whatever song had been playing. Not to mention that by then, I could barely remember why I'd liked it in the first place, now that I knew what the lyrics symbolized.

But we were in zero hour. The prom was five days away, and we had to have a song so that we could dance to it together. And whatever we picked, I would just insist that Tanner—the sophomore DJing the prom and the current bane of my existence—play it for us.

"What's that?" Nate asked, tucking a lock of hair behind my ear.

"Well," I said, "I've been thinking that we need a song. And that it would be fun to pick one before the prom." I smiled up at him, but he just stared down at me. "You know," I said after a moment, "so that we can dance to it. . . ."

Nate smiled. "No, I get the concept. I just don't really do that."

I blinked at him. "Dance?" I asked, trying not to panic but thinking that it was a bit late for him to be telling me this.

"No," he said. "I dance. I mean have songs with people. I just don't think it's such a good idea."

I took an involuntary step back, and my hands fell down from his neck. But I wasn't "people." I was his *girlfriend*. "Well," I said, trying to understand, "why wouldn't it be a good idea?"

Nate shrugged and stuck his hands in his pockets. "I've just had some issues with it in the past. And then if something should happen, the song is tainted forever. So I just think it's better not to have one."

I nodded as though I was considering this, but really,

I was just trying to process. What did he think was going to happen? And was Nate talking about some issues with a specific person? Who?

It hit me that Nate and I had never had the ex talk. This wasn't a big deal for me, as he'd already known about Justin, and the rest of my relationships hadn't been serious enough to merit any kind of discussion. And I knew that Nate had gone out with his friend Melissa until last summer. But I hadn't thought it was a serious relationship—they were still really close. She was in his Friendverse Top 8, after all. I hadn't met her yet, but there had been lots of talk about us all getting together and hanging out. But now, I wasn't sure I wanted to do that. Suddenly, I felt like there was a lot to Nate I knew nothing about, even though five minutes earlier, I would have laughed at that idea.

"What," I said, trying to keep my voice light, "what kind of issues? And, um, with whom?"

Nate smiled at me and put his arms around my waist again. "We don't have to talk about this now."

"But—" I started, as Nate leaned down and kissed me. "But I wanted to—" I managed to say before he kissed me again. "That is—" But he kept on kissing me, and really, it was a lot more fun than talking about exes. I pulled back for a moment. "We're going to talk about this later," I promised as I reached up and kissed him back.

Some time later, the penultimate bell sounded, startling me. Apparently, lost in makeout land, I'd managed to miss the warning bell. "Argh," I said again, realizing that I was now going to be late for English.

"I know," Nate said, cupping his hand underneath my chin. "I wish you didn't have to go."

"Well," I said, dying to stay but knowing that every minute that was passing most likely meant a minute I'd have to spend in detention, "just wait until Saturday night. We can . . ." I paused. I was about to say "keep making out," or "make out some more," but both of those seemed kind of crass. So I just made a vague gesture with my hand. "You know." I smiled up at Nate, who blinked down at me.

About a second later, the implications of what I'd just said came crashing down on me. Oh, no. *Oh, God.*

"Wait," Nate said, his brow furrowing. "What?"

"Oh," I said. "Um." I wasn't sure what to say next. Saturday night was *prom night.* Prom night was when couples traditionally had sex for the first time. What had I just done? Had I just suggested to my boyfriend that we sleep together on prom night? With a *hand gesture*?

The final, Seriously-Get-To-Class-NOW bell sounded, and I looked over at the building, torn. Should I go to class, even though I was already late? Stay and try to explain to Nate what had just happened? What *had* just happened?

"You'd better go," Nate said, looking a little bit dazed.

"Right," I said. I looked at him, trying to figure out what *he* thought had just happened. "Okay." I shouldered my bag and stretched up to kiss Nate just as he leaned down to kiss me, and we bumped noses. We tried again and managed a quick kiss, but it was really more like a peck. It was awkward. And we never had awkward kisses. "Talk to you tonight?"

"Definitely," he said. He gave me a smile but still seemed confused.

"Bye," I said, turning and heading to the school building. When I pulled open the doors and turned back for a moment, Nate was still standing in the same spot, looking lost in thought.

What had I just done? As I hustled down the now-deserted halls of Putnam High School, I made a mental note to talk to Ruth about this as soon as possible.

As reality hit a second later, I slowed my steps and shook my head. Of course I wasn't going to talk to Ruth about this. Not anymore.

Ruth Miller had been my BFF for the past nine years, ever since third grade. But two months earlier, everything had changed. I'd come back from spring break to find my Friendverse profile hacked into. Pretending to be me, the hacker had said terrible things, and had even broken up me and Justin—which, in retrospect, I was actually thankful for. After much sleuthing—and realizing that the hacker had mostly been reporting secrets I'd promised not to tell anyone—I'd found out, to my shock, that the hacker had been Ruth. She'd been helped with the technical part of the hacking by Frank "Hold the Frank" Dell. Dell had been the school's go-to computer expert and had set up most of its databases. He had also kept copies of a lot of them and had been using this information to break into people's lockers. I had found out about this, and his role in the hacking, and had exposed him to Dr. Trent, the assistant headmaster. As a result, Dell had been expelled. From what I heard, he was now finishing junior year at some boarding school in New Hampshire that, coincidentally, also had a new auditorium. Ruth had been suspended for two weeks, and I had resolved never to share with other people what was said to me in confidence. But the hacking, and the subsequent fallout, had been the end of our friendship.

Ruth and I were now cordial to each other in the halls and in PE, the only class we had together. But somehow, that made it even worse. The superficial *Hi, how are you*s that we exchanged in passing only reminded me that we'd once been really close and had told each other everything. Now all we said to each other was *Fine, how are you?*

And with prom looming, I was thinking about Ruth, and our broken friendship, even more than usual. In fourth grade, the two of us had dressed up as prom queens for Halloween, and we had always said that when we went to the prom for real, we'd re-create the picture. But it was clear now that was not going to happen.

And while I had Lisa and my friend Schuyler Watson, and was close with both of them, Lisa and Schuyler were really best friends with each other. Life without your own best friend, I had found in the past two months, was just very lonely. And I couldn't get used to the situation. My impulse was always to talk to Ruth, before my brain would register a second later that that was no longer an option. And in the moment that followed, I would feel the loss of our friendship all over again.

18

Well, I would just have to talk to Schuyler and Lisa ASAP. Because, out of nowhere, Nate and I suddenly had issues. There was the song thing, and the possibly significant ex thing, and, most pressing of all, what I might have inadvertently suggested we do on prom night.

I had reached my English classroom and was—I checked my watch—fourteen minutes late. I sighed and pulled open the door.

CHAPTER 2

 mad_mac Hates being late for class. And getting detention because of it.

 KitKat → mad_mac WHAT ABOUT THE PROM COMMITTEE MEETING?!

 mad_mac → KitKat I'll be there! I might just be, um, fourteen minutes late.

 Shy Time Not understanding why we're still getting this much homework. It's MAY, after all!

 Shy Time Even though my phone keeps telling me it's November 1967.

Shy Time I hate my phone.

 La Lisse → mad_mac, Shy Time Madison et Shy, nous avons allez aux café après l'ecole? Oui? Non? Dites-moi, sil te plait.

 Shy Time → mad_mac, La Lisse Yes! I mean, OUI!

 mad_mac → La Lisse, Shy Time I'll be there! Very much need to talk to you two. Might be late—I have detention ☹ and a prom committee meeting, and at some point I have to deal with the DJ. I swear, I'm about to replace him with an iPod.

 DJ Tanner → mad_mac Okay, that was way harsh, Mad.

After the last bell of the day rang, I headed for detention, holding the dreaded yellow slip of paper in my hand. My English teacher, Mr. Underwood, true to form, had given me detention for as many minutes as I'd been late for his class. Which seemed excessive to me, considering that nobody was learning anything of importance in that class anyway.

After we'd gone through a semester of Agatha Christie mysteries and Sherlock Holmes classics, Mr. Underwood had switched course abruptly and we'd started reading Sir Ian Fleming's James Bond novels. Most of us in class—while we had sympathy for Mr. Underwood, his bad toupee, and the mental breakdown that had left him able to teach us only his favorite books—felt fairly certain that as a result of this year, we were all going to do very poorly on the English portion of the SAT IIs. And while I'd enjoyed the mysteries, I was finding the Bond novels a little hard to get through. I found it difficult to believe that during the Cold War, the fate of the free world always rested on some British guy in a tux. And really, why the tux? It seemed improbable that so many espionage missions needed to be conducted in formal wear.

I passed my old locker, which class couple Jimmy Arnett and Liz Franklin were currently making out against. I was beyond thankful that after the hacking mess—in which Jimmy and Liz had been particularly targeted—they were back together and going strong again. They were even riding in our limo on Saturday, with the condition that they might be sent to opposite sides of the car if their PDAs became too egregious.

Liz gave me a quick wave, then returned to kissing Jimmy. I waved back, even though she was clearly now focused on other things. My old locker had become Jimmy and Liz's favorite makeout spot, now that I was no longer using it. I had learned from Connor Atkins—Schuyler's boyfriend, the school's "Internet Liaison," and the one student Dr. Trent seemed to like—that after Dell had been expelled, there had been talk about changing all the locker combinations, since Dell had kept a copy of the locker-combination database. But it had been ruled too expensive, so only the students who'd been the victim of thefts had their lockers reassigned. Including me.

And my new locker was located in the school's equivalent of Siberia, which took at least five minutes to get to and from, making me even later than usual to my classes.

I made it to the basement and stood outside the classroom always used for detention. I really didn't want to go in, but I also didn't want to find out what would happen if you were late to a detention you got for being late to class. I took out my phone, updated my status, and headed inside.

 mad_mac Has been unavoidably detained. In detention.

"Here," I said as I handed my yellow slip to the teacher manning the desk.

"MacDonald," she said, glancing at it and raising her eyebrows. "We've certainly been seeing a lot of you lately."

I wondered how she'd managed to catch this, but never seemed to pay any attention to the arson kid, who at that moment looked much more gleeful than I felt comfortable with.

"Well," I said, "it's just that my new locker is really far away, and—"

"Just take a seat anywhere," she interrupted, signing my slip and nodding toward the desks. "You know the drill by now, I'm sure."

Feeling unfairly maligned, a victim of the school's poor layout, I scanned the classroom and saw Glen Turtell sitting in his usual spot, with an empty desk to his right. I smiled and headed over. Turtell and I had known each other since elementary school. He was a permanent fixture both in detention and outside Dr. Trent's office, as he was usually the first one called in after a theft or an altercation. While I'd always known that Turtell would have my back if I ever needed him, we'd never really hung out. But that had changed a few months ago. During the hacking fallout, we'd become closer friends, and he'd provided valuable information that had led me to figuring out Dell's role. And we had been inadvertently hanging out a lot more recently, as Turtell was dating Kittson, and Kittson continued to monopolize all my free time.

"Hey, Glen," I said, and Turtell glanced up from the textbook he'd been reading.

"Sup, Mad?" he asked.

"How's it going?" I asked, sliding into the seat next to him.

Turtell shook his head. "Not good. The Man's trying to keep me down."

This often seemed to be what landed Turtell in detention. "What happened this time?"

He closed his book and glared down at the cover, which featured a picture of Alexander Hamilton. "It's Dr. Trent." I nodded. This was most often the man Turtell was referring to. "I just posted some of my own opinions on my Q feed, and just like that, he shuts me down. Disables my account for the rest of the day. Can he even do that? I mean, what is this, the gazpacho?"

That gave me pause for a moment. "You mean the

gestapo?" I asked, and Turtell nodded. "Oh. Well, what did you say?"

"Nothing! Just that we need a regime change in this school. I mean, why does the *assistant* headmaster have this much power, anyway? And how can they spy on us like this?"

I smiled at him. "Glen, don't be ridiculous." As Status Q had started getting more popular, Dr. Trent had required that all Putnam High students using it follow the school's lame profile and allow the school account to follow theirs, as he had for Friendverse. He'd also insisted that students activate the GPS feature, to dissuade people from cutting class. But all that had seemed to do was allow people to meet up when they *did* cut class, so I had assumed that—as usual—the administration wasn't paying any attention. "Dr. Trent isn't *spying* on us."

Turtell shook his head. "He is. I swear. He's shut my account down at least three times. What about freedom of speech?"

"He's probably just watching yours now, because you keep saying inflammatory things. But there's no way he's watching everyone. The school's too big, and everyone updates about a million times a day." Turtell didn't look convinced. "How's it going with Kittson?" I asked, trying to change the subject.

Turtell got the slightly dopey look on his face that he always got whenever anyone mentioned his girlfriend. "She's amazing." He sighed. Kittson and Turtell were a bit of an odd match, but from everything that I could see, they seemed to be working out.

"Good," I said, smiling at him and sneaking a glance at the clock to see how much time was left. "I'm glad everything's going well."

"There's just one thing," Turtell said, his expression clouding. Clearly, I had spoken too soon. "You know she wants to win prom queen," he said.

"I'm aware," I assured him. I didn't think it was possible to live in the same zip code as Kittson and not be aware of that.

"And you know she's going to win," Turtell continued. I nodded. It was pretty much a foregone conclusion that Kittson would be crowned prom queen. Everyone also seemed to think that Justin, the ex Kittson and I shared, was a shoo-in for prom king. "Yeah," Turtell said, shaking his head. "That's the problem."

I looked at Turtell for a moment, trying to understand, wondering if this was another gazpacho thing. "I'm not following," I said finally.

Turtell turned more fully toward me. "The prom king and queen have a dance together," he said. "After the queen is crowned. I've looked into it. It's tradition."

"I know," I said, trying to stifle a small sigh. This had been the subject of one of my ongoing fights with DJ Tanner, who seemed convinced that "Arrgh! Love Is Dead!" would be a great song to mark this moment.

"I . . . I don't want Kittson to dance with anyone else," Turtell mumbled, now speaking, apparently, directly to Alexander Hamilton. "I mean, I'm supposed to stand there and watch some other guy dance with my girlfriend?"

"Well," I said. I couldn't think of any way around it. "Yes?"

Turtell shook his head again. "Yeah. Not going to happen."

"What do you mean?" I asked. "You want Kittson to win, don't you?"

"Of course I do!" Turtell looked offended that I would even have implied otherwise. "I just don't want her to dance with anyone else. That's all."

I felt like we were speaking in riddles. "But if she wins prom queen—"

"Which she will," Turtell said reverently.

"Yes. So if that happens, she's going to have to dance with whoever wins prom king."

"Not necessarily," Turtell said, opening his book with a small smile.

This didn't sound good. "Glen," I said carefully. I had the feeling that I needed to get in front of this before it got worse. Kind of like when Schuyler announced she wanted to go blond. "You're not going to do anything, right? I mean—"

"MacDonald!" the teacher at the front said, waving my yellow detention slip.

"Don't worry, Mad," Turtell said. "It's all good."

"What?" I asked, growing more concerned. "What's all good?"

"MacDonald!" the teacher yelled again, and I looked over at her. "Unless you'd like to stay a little longer . . ." she said.

"I'm coming," I said, standing and swinging my bag

over my shoulder. I looked down at Turtell. "We'll talk about this more," I said. "Right, Glen?"

"Sure," Turtell said, still focused on his book and not looking at me. "See you, Mad."

I headed to the front of the classroom and retrieved my signed slip from the teacher. I really didn't understand what Turtell was getting at. How did he expect Kittson to win prom queen but not dance with the prom king?

I added this question to my ever-growing mental list of things to deal with and walked to the classroom that had been assigned to us for prom committee meetings. It was, of course, located at the opposite end of the school, and as I hurried over there, I wondered if Putnam High had been laid out in this idiotic way just to give the students some extra cardio. As I got to the classroom, I glanced at my phone to check the time and realized I'd missed almost half the prom meeting. Through the door's narrow window, I could see Kittson holding forth.

"Madison!" someone called. I turned to look down the hallway and saw a skinny kid in a gray hoodie. Tanner Matthews, sophomore, aspiring DJ, and the number one reason this prom might be an epic disaster, was running toward me.

"Hey, Mad!" he yelled at full volume as he approached. I mimed taking something out of my ears, as I'd had to do every time I'd had a conversation with him. Tanner looked at me quizzically for a moment, then pushed back his hood and pulled out his earphones. Tanner was short, even for a sophomore, with long emo bangs he was always pushing out of his eyes. He wouldn't have been my choice for DJ, but he had been willing to do it for free, which became a necessity after Kittson spent our music budget on the highest level of personalized gift bags, which contained things like flash drives and pens that lit up.

"Hi, Tanner," I said. I glanced toward the door to see Kittson frowning at me and pointing at her wrist.

"I thought I might catch you here," he said, reaching behind his back and taking out a pair of drumsticks, one of which he twirled between his fingers. "We need to talk about the prom music."

"We do," I agreed. But Tanner didn't expand on this, just started drumming on the classroom door, causing Kittson to glare in my direction again. "Listen," I said, trying to move things along, "I need to get a sense of what kind of music you're going to be playing. The prom is this Saturday, after all."

"I know," he said, building his drumroll to a crescendo. "And I'm working on a playlist now. I can play it for you if you want. But I kinda need some guidance here, Mad."

"Just play . . . you know . . ." I said. I started to make a hand gesture, but then stopped, as hand gestures seemed to be getting me into trouble today. "Prom music."

"Yeah," Tanner said, now twirling the stick in his other hand. "You've said that. But I don't know exactly what that means."

The trouble was that I didn't, either. I'd never been to a prom, and neither had Tanner. And I didn't think the prom movies I'd watched were a good indication of reality, as everyone always seemed to be doing synchronized dances in them. "Just . . ." I started, wishing that Kittson hadn't bought illumination pens and we'd hired a real DJ. A real DJ would not be asking me these questions. "Just songs people want to dance to. And then slow songs, so people can slow dance. And . . . um . . . mix up the two."

Tanner's eyes lit up. "Songs like this one?" he asked. He handed me one of his earbuds, and knowing from previous near-deaf experiences that Tanner kept his music at full volume, I held it slightly away from my ear.

Tanner scrolled through his black iPod and selected a song. The sound of screeching tires reverberated, followed by a guy yelling, "Love is dead! Love is dead! Love is dead! *Dance!*"

I lowered the earbud and looked at him. "What is this?"

"Murderous Marionettes," Tanner said, looking pleased with himself. "Is that the kind of song you meant?"

I handed the earbud back to him, my ears still ringing slightly. "No."

Tanner's face fell. "But it said 'dance.' It said it right in the song!"

"Right," I said. "I heard that. And good . . . initiative." I looked toward the door again, very aware that with every minute that passed, Kittson was getting madder. "Look, I'll try to make you a list of songs so you can get a general feel for what we want. Okay?"

"Sure," Tanner said. "That would be good." He scrolled through his iPod. "Want to hear the playlist I pulled together anyway? Because maybe some of it *is* what you want."

I looked at the iPod doubtfully. "Does it have more of those Evil Puppets songs?"

"Murderous Marionettes," Tanner corrected. "And yes!"

"Um," I said, edging toward the door, "why don't you go ahead and save that playlist—just in case—and I'll try to come up with a list for you in the meantime?"

"Kewl," Tanner said, finishing up with a rim shot and twirling his sticks once more before shoving them into his backpack. "Catch you on the flip side, Mad." He headed down the hallway, and I pulled open the door in time to hear Kittson say, "That's all for today. See you at tomorrow's meeting. And please be on time, because Dr. Trent is going to be attending!"

I stepped aside as four of the other prom committee members filed out, all typing on their phones and handheld devices. They appeared competent and responsible, but I knew it was all a facade. Most of the members of the prom committee were résumé kids. They were there to put the committee on their college applications and really didn't care about it at all. So they were notoriously flaky, which was why Kittson and I were basically pulling the whole prom together ourselves.

Kittson was still standing at the front of the room, straightening up a pile of papers, her long blond hair hanging stick-straight down her back. I felt myself smiling, wondering what time she'd had to get up in the morning to achieve that look. The fact that Kittson and I had become friends was a source of constant amazement to me. It wasn't like we were incredibly close, but we were friends, no question. A few months earlier, I never would have thought it was possible. But then, a few months earlier, I could never have imagined her dating Turtell, either.

"Sorry," I said as she put her notebook into her designer purse. "I was talking to our esteemed DJ."

Kittson looked over at me. "And?" she asked.

"Well . . ." I stalled. "He's making . . . progress. He had a sample mix to play for me." I thought it was better that Kittson not know exactly what was on the mix.

"Oh, good," she said with a sigh of relief.

"How was the meeting?" I asked.

She shrugged. "Who knows if anyone was even paying attention?" she said. "But we went over procedures for the new voting system, and then talked about delivery of the Hayes crown."

I was suddenly very glad I'd missed the meeting. I'd been hearing about the Hayes crown since freshman year. It seemed like someone was always droning on about how it was one of the school's most treasured heirlooms and had been used to crown every prom queen since the fifties. And it must have actually been pretty valuable, since the year before, there had been a motion to get it appraised so that we could build a new gymnasium. But the school board had revolted, talking about "keeping tradition alive in our heart and on our head." At any rate, the crown was one of those things people seemed to go crazy about for absolutely no discernible reason. Every spring, anticipating various schools' senior prank days, Dr. Trent removed the crown from where it normally sat, inside the main trophy case, and locked it in his office.

I was also happy to have missed yet another discussion about the voting system. Dr. Trent had put a new system in place that would let students vote for the prom king and queen using a text-messaged code sent to their cell phones the night of the prom. It was supposed to ensure more immediate, accurate results and prevent smear campaigns.

"Oh, good," I said quickly, so she wouldn't fill me in. "So I'm all caught up, then."

"Dr. Trent is presenting the committee with the Hayes crown *tomorrow*," Kittson said gravely as she zipped up her bag. "So if you could avoid detention, that would be great."

"It's not like I *try* to get detention—" I started as my phone chimed, letting me know I had a new Q message. As subtly as I could, I pulled it out of my pocket and snuck a glance at it.

La Lisse ➜ mad_mac Mad, où es-tu? Are you coming?

Shy Time ➜ mad_mac Hey, Mad, are you still meeting us for coffee? I got you your ush, JIC.

"You're absolutely right," I told Kittson, wanting to wrap this up as quickly as possible. I clicked on Lisa's update to see her location and saw that she was already at Stubbs. My friends were waiting, and I hadn't seen them all day. "I promise I'll be at the meeting tomorrow."

"Good," Kittson said. She shook her head and slung her bag over her shoulder. "These people. They act like this is supposed to be *fun,* or something."

I pressed my lips together to stop myself from smiling and followed Kittson out of the classroom.

CHAPTER 3

Song: Coffee's For Closers/Fall Out Boy
Quote: "She generally gave herself very good advice,
(though she very seldom followed it)."—Lewis Carroll

Fifteen minutes later, I pulled Judy, née Jetta-son, my green Jetta, into a parking space in front of Stubbs Coffee, the place that had been our regular hangout for the past few years. Through the plate-glass window, I could see my friends sitting in their regular seats—Schuyler curled in the corner of the couch and Lisa sitting next to her. As I pulled open the door, I saw that they'd left my spot—the armchair—open for me.

"Alors!" Lisa said when she saw me. "Mad, where have you been? We were about to leave." I glanced at Schuyler, who shook her head and mouthed, *No we weren't.*

I smiled and studied my two remaining best friends. Lisa was petite, only about 5' 1", but she made up for it with both her big hair and personality. She had been on a French kick for a while now, constantly inserting Gallic phrases into her conversation. I'd gotten used to it, and so was always surprised when someone who didn't know Lisa met her for the first time and invariably assumed she was an exchange student. Schuyler towered over Lisa—she was 5' 10" —but didn't have the same forceful personality. Shy was, well, shy around people who weren't her close friends. But the two of them were BFF, and had been since Schuyler had come to Putnam High from Choate three years earlier.

"Hey," I said, dropping my bag and settling into my chair. "Sorry I'm late."

"Prom stuff?" Schuyler asked sympathetically, handing me a plastic cup.

"Thank you," I said gratefully. I took a sip and immediately felt better about life. Schuyler had gotten me that month's usual—an iced latte with caramel and an extra shot of espresso. "Prom stuff," I confirmed. "There's a very good chance that the DJ might ruin the prom, guys. Just a heads-up."

"If you need help, just ask," Schuyler said. "Tennis is over for the season, and Connor's super busy Internet Liaising, so I have some free time."

"I just might take you up on that," I said, thinking about all the extra prom duties Kittson had been dumping on me. I leaned back in the armchair and closed my eyes, letting the much-needed caffeine kick in. When I opened them again, I made sure to avert my gaze from the wooden chair next to me—the chair that had always been Ruth's.

"*D'accord*," Lisa said. "I have something to discuss.

36

But I wanted to wait until you got here, Mad."

"OMG, me too!" I said, glad that I could finally get their take on the Nate sitch. "I also have something to discuss, I mean."

"Well, *je suis la premiere*. I'm going first. Schuyler?" Lisa looked at her. "You want to get on the agenda?"

"After me," I added quickly.

"Oh . . . no," Schuyler said. She moved her long red ponytail to one side, leaned back against the couch, and smiled happily. "I'm good." Things certainly appeared to be good with Schuyler. She was utterly smitten with Connor, and from what I could tell, it was mutual. Lately, Schuyler seemed to walk around in a state of half-focused bliss and the somewhat anxious expression she had occasionally worn was totally gone. She hadn't chewed her hair in months.

"Bon," Lisa said. "So." She made a big production of stirring some brown sugar cubes into her café au lait, and I realized that she was stalling. But it wasn't exactly surprising. To say Lisa didn't like to talk about her feelings was something of an understatement. "It's Dave," she said finally. I glanced at Schuyler, who shrugged. Apparently, this was news to her as well.

Dave Gold and Lisa had been going out all year, and as a result, Dave had become one of my really good friends. I was a little surprised to hear that there was an issue with them, since they had always seemed really solid—not embarrassingly over-the-top mushy like Jimmy and Liz, but rather, just pretty consistently crazy about each other.

"What is it?" Schuyler asked, leaning forward.

"Well," Lisa said before taking a small sip of her drink. "Apparently, Dave is upset with the . . . pace . . . at which our relationship is progressing." She looked at Schuyler and me. *"Nous comprenons?"*

I nodded, then saw Schuyler's mystified expression. "Sex," I clarified, and Shy's face turned the same color as her hair. "Right?" I asked Lisa, who nodded. Last I'd heard about this, Dave had been wanting things to move more quickly between them, but Lisa had wanted to wait until Bastille Day—she liked the symbolism of it, for reasons I'd never wanted explained to me.

"But what about Bastille Day?" Schuyler asked.

Lisa shook her head. "It seems David feels that July is too long to continue to wait." I bit my lip. Whenever Lisa full-named Dave, you knew she was upset.

"Have you guys talked about this?" I asked. I was half-hoping that Lisa might just have made a verbal gaffe much like mine, and we could figure out how to handle our situations together.

"Non," Lisa said. "Not exactly. But he's been dropping a lot of hints lately. And every movie we've watched in the last few months has been a losing-your-virginity-on-prom-night movie. I mean, it's pretty obvious."

"Wow," Schuyler said. "So you think he's planning on prom night?"

"He might be," Lisa said huffily. "But I'm not. I mean, we had an agreement."

"Do you . . ." I said slowly. I wasn't exactly sure how to talk to her about this. I thought I'd have two more

38

months to figure it out. "I mean, do you *want* to sleep with him?"

Lisa looked from me to Schuyler, and took a breath as though she was about to say something. But then she just fluffed her curls, a gesture I realized she'd stolen from Marion Cotillard. *"Bof,"* she said. "That's not the issue. The issue is that we had an understanding, and he's trying to get around it in this underhanded way. And I just . . ." Lisa paused, and seemed to be having some sort of internal debate, but then just shook her head. "Never mind," she said. "I don't want to talk about it anymore. Forget I said anything." I opened my mouth to say something, but Lisa shook her head again. *"C'est fini,"* she said firmly.

"Mad?" Schuyler asked after a small pause, turning to me. "What did you want to talk about?"

I sighed and stared down at my ice cubes. "I think I accidentally asked Nate to sleep with me on prom night."

Lisa's mouth dropped open. *"Oh, mon Dieu,"* she murmured.

Schuyler frowned. "How do you *accidentally* ask someone that?" Lisa shot her a look. "I really want to know!" she said quickly. "I mean, so I don't walk around doing it by mistake."

"It was just a misunderstanding," I said. "We were making out during lunch, and then the bell rang. . . ." I told them what had happened, and about my unfortunate hand gesture. "But all I meant by it was that we could *keep making out* on prom night. I just didn't want to say it out loud!"

"So you implied that you wanted to sleep with him instead?" Lisa asked, raising an eyebrow. "*Tres intelligent*, Mad."

"It was a mistake!" I said desperately. "I just don't know what to do now."

"Do you," Lisa said, adopting the same tone that I had just used a moment ago with her, "I mean, do you *want* to sleep with him?" I glared at her, but she just shrugged one shoulder. "It's a valid question," she said.

I knew it was, but it was one I hadn't planned on addressing for a while. Like Lisa and Schuyler, I had never slept with anyone. I'd just always assumed that I would know when the time came along. That it would just feel right. And things with Nate had been progressing in a nice way, but at a pace that wouldn't put us there for a while. I guess I'd thought that maybe we'd get there in a few months, maybe. Not in *five days*. "I just . . ." I said, shaking the ice in my plastic cup, realizing that I was also stalling. "I just don't know what *he* thinks happened. I mean, maybe he didn't take it that way at all. Maybe this is all for nothing. Right?"

"Maybe!" Schuyler said encouragingly.

"Maybe not," Lisa said. "How did he react after you propositioned him?"

"It was a *hand gesture*," I said impatiently. "But . . . well . . ." I thought about how stunned Nate had looked, and how awkward our goodbye had been. "He seemed kind of freaked out," I said slowly. "Oh, God, this is bad."

"Just talk to him," Schuyler said. "I mean, relationships are about communication."

"But Nate and I communicate all the time!" I protested. I never felt out of touch with him; if we weren't texting, we were following each other's Q updates or iChatting or talking on the phone.

"Isn't it the best? Connor and I talk about everything," Schuyler said, getting the dreamy expression that she was perpetually wearing these days. "In fact, I'm going to update my status so he'll know that I miss him."

Lisa rolled her eyes at me, but I shook my head, refusing to go along with mocking Schuyler. I was truly happy for her. Connor was her first real boyfriend, and Lisa had been just as bad—if not worse—when she'd started going out with Dave.

Schuyler pulled out her new iPhone and stared down at it for a long moment before tapping the screen tentatively. Her father had bought it for her a month before, hoping that having a new top-of-the-line phone would stop her from throwing it out the car window, as Schuyler had been wont to do with her phones whenever she was talking while driving and thought she'd been spotted by the police. The iPhone—or ShyPhone, as Lisa and I had taken to calling it—had come with pages of apps preinstalled, and as a result, Schuyler had almost no idea how to do simple things, like place a call.

"So," Lisa said, turning to me. We both knew that Schuyler might be a while. "What are you going to do about Nate?"

"Talk to him, I guess," I said. I glanced at Schuyler, who was now holding her phone up to her ear and shaking it. "I just wish I didn't have to."

41

"I know what you mean," Lisa said, giving me a small smile. "*Donc,* what do you think we should do? Make a list? Pro and con?" As soon as she had finished saying this, her smile faded, as though she'd just realized what she'd said. We both looked over at the wooden chair that sat empty.

Making a list had been Ruth's solution to any problem. Whenever we were talking through something, she'd be writing down the pros and cons, and when we were done, she'd hand over a piece of paper covered with her neat, curly handwriting, and somehow the problem no longer seemed so unmanageable.

"Well," Lisa said quietly, looking from the chair to me and back again. I just nodded. There wasn't a whole lot to say about it. But I forgot sometimes that Lisa and Schuyler had lost a friend as well.

"Okay!" Schuyler said triumphantly. "I unlocked it. Oh." Her face fell as her phone beeped with a text. "I didn't realize it was so late. I have to get going."

"Already?" Lisa asked, pulling out her own phone and checking the time.

"Yeah," Schuyler said, unfolding herself from the couch. "Peyton just got back from boarding school, and my stepmother wants us all to have dinner together."

I tried to suppress a shudder. Peyton was Schuyler's stepsister. I'd met her only once, as she seemed to spend most of her time in the Alp-y parts of Europe in boarding schools that she was always having to leave for reasons that Schuyler never fully understood. But once had been enough for me. Peyton made Lisa look calm and placid.

My own phone vibrated, and I looked down and saw that I had a text from my mother.

From: Mom
Date: 5/20, 5:35 P.M.
Hi hon! I'm running late & on my way to get your brother. Can you pick something up for dinner? Thank you! Love, Mom

I shook my head as I read it. My mother insisted on signing her texts, even though I'd told her repeatedly that it wasn't necessary. "I better go, too," I said, standing. "I have to bring home dinner."

"D'accord," Lisa said a little huffily.

"What are you going to do about Dave?" Schuyler asked as we threw away our cups and headed out the front door, which was embossed with the Stubbs logo—a grizzled-looking sailor smoking a pipe and holding a mug of coffee, a whale's tail arching behind him.

"Nothing at the moment," Lisa said. "But I'm done watching the *American Pie* movies, I can tell you that much."

"Well, you know you can always call me if you want to talk," I said.

"Me too!" Schuyler said. Then she glanced at her phone doubtfully. "But, um, if you need to talk right away, maybe call my landline."

"I'm fine," Lisa said, waving our words away. "*Tres* fine." She unlocked her convertible Bug with her clicker.

43

"But thank you," she added more quietly. Schuyler gave Lisa a hug, then climbed into her SUV. Lisa got into her car, and both of them pulled out of the parking lot, Lisa waving goodbye to me through her open roof.

I stood alone by my car for a moment, feeling the loss of Ruth once more. Whenever the four of us had hung out, she and I would usually stay a little longer than the others and talk, just the two of us. I sighed, wondering why it was taking me so long to come to terms with the fact that things had changed between us and would never be the same again.

Feeling like some egg rolls might make me feel better, I headed to my car, planning to stop by The Good Person of Szechuan, my favorite Chinese restaurant. But just as I unlocked my door, my phone rang. DEMON SPAWN, the caller ID read. I answered it, wondering why my brother was bothering me.

"Travis?" I asked.

"Hey," he said. "Go pick up pizza for dinner."

"Um, excuse me?" I asked.

"Trav, honey, say please," I heard my mother say—presumably from the driver's seat.

"Please," he muttered.

"I'm picking up Chinese," I said, getting into my car and slamming the door.

"I already placed the order for pizza," he said. "Go get pizza."

"Travis," I said warningly. "That's really not a nice way to ask me, is it?" I made my tone as loaded as I could, and from his worried intake of breath, I could tell that my message had gotten through.

"Sorry, Madison," Travis said, his voice now polite and solicitous. "But would you mind picking up pizza? We'd really appreciate it."

"Not at all," I said. "See you at home."

"Very impressive, honey!" I heard my mother say to Travis before I hung up. I normally had almost no influence over my younger brother, who was thirteen and had, it seemed, been placed on this earth to make my life miserable. But he'd recently started going out—or whatever the current eighth-grade terminology for it was—with Olivia Pearson, Kittson's younger sister. Travis knew I was friends with Kittson, and seemed to live in fear that unless he stayed in my good graces, I would tell Kittson—who would then tell her sister—all my embarrassing stories about him.

And it had recently become *very important* to Travis that everything keep going well with Olivia, since they were going—as a couple—to Heidi Goldwater's bat mitzvah on Saturday. I was well aware of this, and getting all the mileage I could out of it. The only downside was that the bat mitzvah was also being held at the Hyatt. But I had investigated, and our respective ballrooms were at opposite ends of the hotel, so chances were we wouldn't see each other. And even if we did, we'd come to a mutual agreement to pretend we'd never met.

Giving up my dream of egg rolls, I started the car and steered it toward Putnam Pizza.

CHAPTER 4

Song: All The Boys/The Plus Ones
Quote: "As soon go kindle fire with snow, as seek to quench the fire of love with words."—Shakespeare

"Madison MacDonald!" a voice called as soon as I stepped into the restaurant. I saw Dave Gold standing in the back, near the ovens. "Fancy seeing you here."

"Hey, Dave," I said, heading over to him. It was a little strange to see him so soon after hearing Lisa talk about their issues, and I tried to keep my face from revealing anything. I knew from long experience with Jimmy and Liz that it was sometimes tricky to be friends with both halves of a couple; I'd just never before had this problem with Lisa and Dave.

Putnam Pizza was deserted except for Little Tony—the owner's son and Dave's boss when Big Tony wasn't around—who was sprawled in one of the booths, typing furiously on his phone. He glanced up, disinterested, as I passed, then went right back to typing.

"Since when do you work weeknights?" I asked Dave, pulling up one of the stools by the counter. On the other side of it were the pizza ovens, cash register, and prep area.

Dave took off his black-rimmed glasses and polished them on the bottom of his T-shirt, which had the *Mona Lisa* on it. *She Was Framed,* read the type underneath. "We're swamped this week," Dave said. "Big Tony asked for a favor."

I looked around the empty restaurant. "Yeah, I can see that," I said. "Really busy."

"Catering," Dave clarified. "We have about a million events this weekend. Everyone else is cooking in the kitchens across town, and someone has to mind the store." He turned, pulled down the huge metal oven door, and looked inside. "You're here to pick up your order?"

"You got it," I said. "The Demon Spawn called it in?"

"Just a few minutes ago," he said, closing the oven. "It'll be ready in about ten." He leaned his elbows on the counter and raised his eyebrows at me. "So what's the haps?"

I looked at him and realized that I had a great opportunity to get a male perspective on things. "Dave, you and Lisa have a song, right?"

He nodded. "Of course," he said. "'*Quelqu'un m'a dit.*' Carla Bruni."

"It's in French?" I asked with a smile.

"Naturally," Dave said. "But it's also a really great song. Why? You and Nate still don't have one?"

This was the problem with being friends with a couple. There were no secrets. I sighed. "Well, I tried to talk to him about it today, and he said that he thinks it's not

47

a good idea. But I just want to be able to dance with my boyfriend, to our song, at the prom."

"You want me to talk to him?" Dave asked. "I've been meaning to correct some of his misguided opinions on modern cinema, anyway."

"That's okay," I said. "But thanks for the offer." When Nate had started to hang out with my friends, I had been thrilled when he and Dave hit it off. They had become friends, even though you might not have realized it to be around them, as their friendship seemed to consist of the two of them constantly insulting each other.

"You sure?" Dave asked.

"Yes," I said. "But that's not even the biggest thing we're dealing with right now. I think Nate thinks that I proposed we sleep together on prom night." Dave's eyebrows shot up, and his face turned red. "It was an accident," I said quickly. "But I'm not sure how to handle things now."

"Whoa. What happened?" a voice behind me asked.

I spun around and saw Brian McMahon sitting up and looking over the back of the booth that had been camouflaging him. "Brian!" I said, hearing how strangled my voice sounded. I hoped against hope that maybe he had become temporarily deaf in the last five seconds and hadn't heard any of the details of what I'd just said. Brian was a friend of mine, and one of my Marine Bio lab partners, but we didn't exactly share our deep feelings. Under normal circumstances, I never would have told him what I'd just told Dave. This was for many reasons, the primary one being that Brian was actually good friends with Nate — they'd met at summer camp when they were kids. "When . . . um . . . did you get here?" I turned and glared at Dave, feeling that he should have warned me that there was someone there besides Little Tony, who was still utterly absorbed in his phone.

"About an hour ago," Dave said drily. "He's picking up an order."

"I'm paying for it!" Brian said. "I just have to count my money first." I took a step closer to his booth and saw that the table was covered with change that looked like mostly pennies. "Grounding," Brian said by way of explanation. Brian was always coming off one of his father's groundings, or throwing a party that would get him grounded again, but this last grounding had been epic. It had been six weeks and counting, because he'd thrown a party while he was still technically grounded for throwing his last one. I hadn't seen Brian outside of school in ages. He'd told me that the staff at Karl's Keg Kompany had sent him a get-well card, figuring that some grave illness must be the reason he hadn't required their services in so long.

"What does the change have to do with it?" I asked.

"Well," he said, "I'm allowed out of the house for three things: school, Young Investors Club meetings, and to pick up dinner. So I try to extend each one as long as possible."

"What about the prom?" I asked. "Are you going to be able to go to that?" When Brian had last filled me in, while we'd pretended to do a Marine Bio lab, he'd been lobbying his father hard for permission, but hadn't yet gotten an answer.

Brian smiled. "I'm going," he said. "As of last night, I officially have permission."

"That's great!" I said. "Who are you going with?"

"Well," Brian said, looking down at his pile of coinage, "that's still . . . um . . ."

"Tell her about the website," Dave prompted. Brian glared at him.

"What website?" I asked, looking from one to the other.

Brian sighed. "It's called Save the Last Dance," he muttered. "It's this site for people looking for last-minute prom dates. Mostly, it matches you with people from other schools." He looked up at me, then added defensively, "When you're grounded, you spend a lot of time on the internet."

"There's nothing wrong with that," I said quickly. "Seriously."

"Right," Dave added unconvincingly, a moment later.

"Well," Brian said, frowning at Dave, "I'll have you know, the quality of girls looking for prom dates went way up after the Stanwich prom was canceled. It's people who want to go to a prom, not just people who can't get dates."

"Like you," Dave pointed out helpfully.

"I've been *grounded*," Brian said testily.

"This probably isn't the best idea, then, is it?" I asked, gesturing to his pile o' change. "I mean, isn't your dad going to get suspicious that you're out having fun?"

Brian handed me his phone. "I just updated my

status," he said. "My dad can see my location." I looked down at his Q feed.

 Grounded_Brian Picking up pizza! Still!

"But how does your father know it's you sending it?" Dave asked. "I mean, *I* could have just sent that from your phone, and you could be off doing whatever."

Brian's eyes lit up. "Now *there's* an idea!" he said.

"No, no," I said quickly. "That wasn't a suggestion—"

"But what happened with Nate?" Brian asked, turning back to me.

"Seriously," Dave said.

"Yeah," Little Tony called from the corner of the room. As we all turned to look at him, he blushed and focused on his phone again.

"Nothing," I said as quietly as possible. "Forget I said anything at all."

"Um, that's not going to happen," Dave said. "Spill it, MacDonald."

"No," I said, not wanting to discuss it in front of Brian. Or, for that matter, Little Tony.

"Want me to ask Nate what happened?" Brian asked, taking back his phone. "I could send him a text right now—"

"No!" I said. Brian waved his phone threateningly at me, and I sighed. "Fine," I said. "I'll tell you guys. Just don't text Nate." I moved closer to the counter, and Brian leaned farther over the booth. It seemed that I was going to get *two* male perspectives on the situation. "Okay, fine. I think I *accidentally* said something that implied that I wanted to sleep with Nate on prom night. But all I really meant was that we could keep making out on prom night. But I don't know what Nate thinks I meant. And I don't know what to do now." I looked from Brian to Dave, both of whom were silent. "Guys?" I asked.

"Man," Brian said, eyes slightly glazed, "I really need to find a girlfriend."

"Well," Dave said, leaning forward, "you should probably clear it up with him. Because if you implied something, that's probably what he heard."

"Yeah," Brian said. "Right now, he probably thinks that you meant what you said. Because that's probably what he's *hoping* you meant. He is a guy."

"This is true," Dave agreed.

I realized that I might have been better off not having the male perspective. "You think?" I asked, my stomach dropping.

"Wait, Mad," Dave said, looking surprised. "Are you considering this?"

"I . . . don't know," I stammered.

"Well, that's just great," Dave fumed, and I looked at him, wondering why he was suddenly so upset.

"Dave?" I asked. "What's wrong?"

"What's wrong," Dave said, "is that you've been dating Nate for, what, six weeks? Maybe? And you're thinking about *sleeping* with him?"

"Nice," Little Tony called appreciatively from the corner of the room. I couldn't help wishing that Dave would turn down the volume a bit.

"Well," I said in a low voice, "not exactly—"

"And at my house, too, right?" Dave asked.

"Well . . ." I stalled. Dave was throwing the after-party, mostly because Brian's was no longer an option, Dave's parents were gone for the week, and his house had a pool. I was planning on going, and bringing Nate, but the issue of what we would be doing there hadn't really occurred to me until now. "Kind of."

"Meanwhile," Dave continued, looking more and more incensed, "I've been dating Lisa for a *year* now and she's barely even talking about it, because she wants to wait until Bastille Day."

"Well, when's Bastille Day?" Brian asked reasonably. "Like, next week?"

"July fourteenth," Little Tony called from his corner. We all looked at him, and he waved his phone in the air. "Wikipedia, fools."

"Anyway," I said, turning back to Dave and trying to pretend that there wasn't someone listening in on the conversation, "this has nothing to do with you and Lisa. So you don't need to get all upset about it."

"Upset?" Dave asked, yanking down the oven door with such force that it bounced halfway up again. "I'm not upset. Who's upset?" He pulled the pizza from the oven with the long wooden spatula-thing, slid it into a waiting box, and slammed the lid shut. "Eighteen dollars," he said to me, and I handed him a twenty.

"Keep the change," I said. "Seriously, Dave, this has nothing to do with you guys. It's just a misunderstanding with Nate."

"Well, if it is just a misunderstanding, you should probably clear it up," Brian said. He swept the change into his cupped palms, walked over to the register, and dropped it in front of Dave, who sighed. "Because by now, Nate probably just thinks it's normal or something."

Not understanding, I looked at Brian, who was taking his pizza box from Dave. "What do you mean?" I asked.

"Nothing," Brian said. "Just that I heard last year's prom night was when he slept with Melissa for the first time."

CHAPTER 5

Song: Mutiny, I Promise You/The New Pornographers
Quote: "He blinked, like some knight of King Arthur's court, who, galloping to perform a deed of derring-do, has had the misfortune to collide with a tree."
—P. G. Wodehouse

The world seemed to tilt on its axis, and I grabbed on to the counter for support. "Wait," I said, staring at Brian, "what?"

"What?" Brian repeated, looking at me. Maybe my face was showing something of what I was feeling—that is, total shock—because he suddenly began to look very nervous. "Wait, you didn't know that?" he asked.

I shook my head. "No," I said, not sure I trusted myself to say other words. Not entirely sure that I remembered any. I was in a state of complete shock. Nate had slept with somebody? He wasn't a virgin, like me? I'd just assumed that he was. But it hit me that I'd been assuming a lot of things about him. Because he'd never told me he hadn't slept with anyone. And we hadn't talked about it. It was beginning to occur to me that while we'd been talking a lot, maybe we hadn't been talking about the right things. But I would have thought that something like this *might* have come up, just in the course of conversation.

"Well, it might have just been a rumor," Brian said, speaking quickly. I glanced at the corner of the restaurant and saw that Little Tony was just watching us, his phone trilling occasionally, but seemingly forgotten, because clearly we were much more interesting. "I mean, I didn't hear it from Nate. And I didn't hear it from Melissa. I've never even met her. So who knows? Not me. Hey, is that the time?" Brian looked up at the *PIZZA TIME!* clock, where a knife and fork circled the toppings that stood in for numbers. "I'd better get going. See you in class, Mad."

Brian hustled out, and I watched him go, utterly stunned. Maybe Nate *had* always assumed we were going to sleep together on prom night, since apparently that was his habit. . . .

"Mad," Dave said quietly, pulling me out of my thoughts. He reached into the drink case, pulled out a Diet Coke, and handed it to me. "Here." I popped the top and gulped it gratefully. It did seem to help me focus a bit. "Just talk to Nate," Dave said. "Who knows what the situation is? Brian isn't exactly known for his great grasp of facts."

That was true; I'd seen Brian's last Marine Bio quiz. "I know," I said. "I just . . ." I wasn't sure how to finish the sentence. I hadn't known how to talk to Nate about my earlier gaffe. And now I was supposed to ask him questions about his past relationship?

"Seriously," Dave said. "Just talk to him."

"Right," I said, trying to smile at him. I glanced up at the clock and realized I should get going as well—the knife was almost on the mushroom. "Thanks, Dave. I'll see you tomorrow." I used all my acting skills to make it seem like I had it together, and not betray the fact that my thoughts were spinning and in utter disarray. I walked across the restaurant with my head held high, nodding politely at Little Tony, who was gawking at me.

"Uh, Mad?" Dave called just as I pulled the door open. "You forgot your pizza."

****

"What took so long?" Travis said as I entered the kitchen fifteen minutes later. He yanked the pizza box out of my hands and set it on the counter. "I'm starving."

"Hi, hon," my mother said, smiling at me as she set the kitchen table. She was still wearing her work clothes—a dark blue skirt-suit and the pearls she almost never took off. "Did you hit traffic?" I nodded mutely, figuring that was easier than telling her what had transpired at Putnam Pizza. "Sorry about that. Go get your father, would you? He's finishing up a column."

"Sure," I said, heading out of the kitchen. My father was the head sportswriter for our local paper, the *Putnam Post,* and worked most days out of his home office. My mother was the CFO of Pilgrim Bank and lately had seemed really stressed out because of some deal with some British people that had taken her to London for a week.

"Thanks, hon," my mother said. "The table's set, so—*Travis!*" This last word was very sharp, and directed at my brother, who had taken a slice out of the pizza box and was poised to take a bite, standing at the counter. Lately he was eating everything in sight. And he'd grown about three inches in the past two months, which meant that he was almost my height, something I was not very happy about. However, he didn't seem to understand how to organize these new inches into coordinated movement, which meant he was falling over a lot, something that I *was* happy about.

I headed to my father's study, a wood-paneled room covered in sports paraphernalia. His ancient Cubs hat was on, and he was typing furiously, hunched over his laptop. The hat was a sign that he was not to be disturbed, but I knew from experience that food was the exception to this rule. "Hey, Daddy," I said from the doorway.

My father spun his chair around to face me. "Hey, kid," he said. "Food?"

"Pizza," I confirmed. My father stood, stretching out his back, and we headed toward the kitchen.

"I heard a rumor from the office today," he said to me as we walked, "that a certain production is going to have its review in tomorrow's paper."

I turned to look at him as I pulled open the kitchen door. "Really?" I asked, trying to gauge from his expression if it was going to be good or bad. "Um, anything else about it?"

My father shook his head and we all took our seats around the table—Travis and I sitting as far away from each other as possible, something that had been mandated years ago during a wave of foot-stomping. "Just that it's going to run tomorrow. But I'm sure it's going to be a rave."

I hoped so. *Great Dane: The Musical Tragedy of Hamlet,* our spring musical, had closed the past weekend. It was an original adaptation of the Shakespearean tragedy, set in Denmark, Kansas, in 1929. I had played Felia, the female lead, a doomed farm girl who eventually goes mad and ends up drowning in the cow pond.

We'd had good audiences, and the shows had gone fairly well. But there had been a couple of technical glitches during our last show, and at one point, Mark Rothmann's English accent—which hadn't been particularly strong to begin with—took a tour of the British Isles and then lingered in South Africa for a bit before remaining in Australia for the rest of the play. All the theater kids had been waiting for the review to come out, and I had my fingers crossed that the reviewer had ignored these problems.

I grabbed a slice of pizza, thrilled to see that Dave had been able to get me pineapple slices on my fourth. As we ate, my father droned on about the article he was writing. It was about sports betting websites, and it seemed like he'd been working on it—and talking about it—forever. I knew far more about guaranteed return rates than I'd ever wanted to.

"The thing about it," my father said, "is that it's easy to tell if these websites are legit. Unless there's a certain, very high level of player, nobody's going to make any money. And those that promise to make you a lot of easy money are the ones to watch out for."

My father took a bite of pizza, and my mother, maybe seeing the opportunity to change the subject from the over/under, jumped in. "So, we have news," she said quickly. "Your father and I have been invited to a conference this weekend. It's for founders of charities that have been performing above expectations. And, happily, Comfort Food fits into that category this year."

"That's great," I said. "Congrats, Mom." Comfort Food was a charity that my mother had founded several years earlier. It really did a lot of good, bringing meals to the mentally ill. My mother didn't speak to my father for a week when he suggested she call it Soup to Nuts.

"Yeah," Travis said, his mouth full. "Nice job, Mom."

"Thank you," my mother said. She turned to me with the thoughtful expression that, from long experience, I had come to dread. "You know, Madison," she said, "you really need to think about doing more charity work."

This was a new one. "Mom," I said, "I'm pretty busy as it is. I'm trying to organize the prom at the moment."

"Which is why," my mother said, and I could tell from her tone that she wasn't going to give this up easily, "you should be thinking about those less fortunate than yourself. How many people would love to go to a prom like yours? But they can't afford tickets, or prom dresses. . . ."

I knew that it was best not to argue, unless I wanted to talk about it for hours. "Right, Mom," I said, grabbing a slice of pineapple that I had seen Travis eyeing. "I'll think about it."

"Good," she said, smiling at me. "Because you really need to give back, you know." She took a sip of water. "Now, the only issue with this conference is the location," she continued. "It's being held in South Carolina." She looked at my father expectantly. Clearly, they'd rehearsed this.

My father jumped in. "We thought about calling someone to stay with you. But we decided that you are old enough to be left on your own for a weekend." He looked from Travis to me. "What do you two think?"

I tried very, very hard to keep my expression from revealing my utter glee. "I think so," I said seriously. "Travis?" I asked, looking across the table, as though I cared what my brother thought.

Travis nodded gravely, and I saw that, for once, we were on the same page about how to handle this. "I think we're ready for that responsibility," he said.

"Good," my mother said. "I'm glad to hear it. We're leaving Saturday morning, and will be back Sunday night—and, of course, will be checking in frequently."

"Absolutely." I shot my mother my most trustworthy smile.

"Wait," Travis said, and I frowned at him, trying mentally to stop him from saying anything that might derail this plan. "How am I supposed to get to the bat mitzvah?"

"Well," my mother said, pausing and glancing at

my father before continuing—never a good sign—"we thought that maybe Travis could ride in your limo, Madison."

"What?" I looked up at my mother to see if she was joking. She didn't appear to be.

"Sweet," Travis said. "Olivia, too?"

"Wait a second," I said as I watched Travis take out his phone and start texting. "You want my little brother to come in my prom limo?"

"If it's a problem," my father said, "we can have someone come stay with you two and they could drive Travis."

I could feel myself battling internally. I did *not* want Travis riding along to the prom with all my friends. But I also really, really didn't want a babysitter. "Fine," I finally said. "He can come in the limo. But only if he promises not to embarrass me."

Travis rolled his eyes. "I'm going to be with my girl-friend," he said. "You better not embarrass *me*."

"Kids, please," my mother said placatingly. "I'm glad that's settled. Now, who wants dessert?"

My phone vibrated with a text, and I looked down at it.

INBOX   1 of 55
From: Nate
Date: 5/20, 7:35 P.M.
Gelato?

It seemed I hadn't wrecked things irreparably between us with my stupid innuendo and hand gestures. And now I would have a chance to talk to him about what Brian had told me. I wasn't sure how I was going to find the courage to do that, but maybe I'd come up with a plan on the drive over. "Dessert!" I said eagerly. "Great idea. I'll go pick some up." And then, without waiting for a reply—or, um, permission—I leapt out of my chair and headed for the door.

CHAPTER 6

Song: Us/Regina Spektor
Quote: "Just a boy in a Chevy truck." — Taylor Swift

I pulled into the parking lot of Gofer Ice Cream and killed the engine. Gofer was located next to Putnam Pizza and a hair salon that never appeared to have any customers. For years, Gofer had just been the place I'd stopped at for ice cream. But over the past few months, it had become something much more significant, and all because of Nate. I now thought of Gofer as *our* place, as much as the rock wall in Stanwich that we'd gone to on our first date (though Nate and I had a running argument about whether that had counted as our first date, or if our official first date had been when we'd seen *Clue* at the New Canaan Drive-In). We'd had our first real conversation outside of Gofer, and our first kiss, and every time I saw the little patio—even though it was just a few chairs, a bench, and a railing—I still got a little thrill.

I had made it there in record time, but as I got out of my car, I saw that Nate's red pickup truck was already in the parking lot. I also saw Dave's BMW and a huge, somewhat rickety-looking white van with PUTNAM PIZZA printed on the side, so it seemed Dave and Little Tony were still working. I didn't really want to deal with either of them, so I walked around the long way to avoid passing the pizza place's window. As I headed up the stairs to the patio, Nate stepped out of Gofer, holding a waffle cone in each hand.

"Hi there," he said, smiling at me.

"Hi," I said, feeling the flutter I still got in my stomach whenever I saw him. I took advantage of the fact that his hands were full to step between his arms and kiss him, resting my hands on either side of his face. He must have taken a bite of his ice cream already, because he tasted like mint chocolate chip. "I thought it was my treat this time," I said after a moment, taking my cone from him. I took a small bite and realized he'd gotten me my usual, hazelnut gelato.

"Well, I was here first," Nate said, leaning down and kissing me again. We lingered there for a moment, and I felt my earlier fears subside a bit. This was *Nate*. Whatever problems we had, we would be able to figure them out together.

We broke apart only when it became clear that we were blocking the doorway and preventing Gofer's customers from exiting. We crossed to the bench, and Nate stretched his arm over my shoulders. I leaned against him, resting my head back and taking a bite of my gelato.

"So how was the rest of your day?" I asked.

"Oh, you know," he said, tilting his mint chocolate chip toward me so that I could take a bite. "The ush." I smiled, knowing that Nate was making fun of my predilection for TLAs. He filled me in on the meeting with his headmaster. Apparently if any of the "people of interest"—now including Nate—had any other infractions, there would be serious consequences. Nate wouldn't graduate, and his Yale acceptance would be in jeopardy. For the first time since the prank stuff had begun, Nate looked a little worried. But he didn't seem to want to talk about it, as he changed the subject quickly, asking me about my day.

After we'd caught up, we just sat there together, finishing our ice cream. As the bug zapper flared to life and cast its fluorescent light over the darkening patio, I pulled my feet up onto the bench, so that my back was resting against Nate's side, his arm enfolding me. Nate ran his hand over my hair, and I felt him kiss the top of my head. "Listen," he said. "I wanted to talk to you about what you said earlier."

I felt my pulse quicken and could feel relief flood through me. The fact that Nate was bringing this up meant that I wouldn't have to find a way to do so myself. "Yes?" I asked, and held my breath.

"I've been thinking about it," Nate said, twining his fingers through mine.

"Yeah?" I asked, hearing my voice sound a little strangled. This was the moment I would find out what he thought had happened earlier. I realized that I didn't know what I wanted his answer to be.

"And I think," Nate said, "that we might be able to have a song together after all."

The relieved feeling came to a screeching halt.

Instead, the low-grade anxiety that had been plaguing me throughout the day returned and increased, now officially becoming mid-grade. "Oh," I murmured, trying not to sound disappointed.

"I mean, if we can both agree on a song, that is," he said. "Because it should be a mutual decision, don't you think?"

"Absolutely," I said. A few hours earlier, this would have made me really happy. But that was pre-gaffe. Pre–Brian bombshell.

"Good," Nate said. "Because I think you're right. . . . It would be nice to dance to it at the prom. Even if we do have to bribe the DJ."

Nate kissed the top of my head again, and it was so nice and peaceful that I really didn't want to wreck the moment. And I had a feeling that's exactly what would happen if I started interrogating him about his ex-girlfriend and his amount of sexual experience. "Oh, I think Tanner's probably pretty cheap," I said, trying to keep my voice light. I could feel Nate's laughter against my back, and I closed my eyes, just savoring the moment.

The moment was interrupted a second later when my phone vibrated with a text.

From: Mom
Date: 5/20, 9:35 P.M.
Hi hon. Time to tell Nate goodbye. And please remember to bring back ice cream this time. Love, Mom

I turned to Nate. "I think the jig is up," I said. "My mother appears to be onto us."

"We've been made, huh?" Nate asked. He removed his arm from my shoulders and we stood up. "That time you were here for two hours and went back empty-handed probably didn't help."

"Probably not," I admitted. We kissed goodbye, much more briefly than I would have liked, but I knew I had to get home soon, or my mother would just keep texting me.

Nate headed to his truck, waving goodbye as he pulled out of the parking lot. I waved back, glad that things were still good between us, but totally confused about how to bring up the other stuff. I gave up trying to figure it out for the moment and headed into Gofer to pick up my mother's sorbet.

****

When I returned home, we ate dessert, and I endured my father's lame jokes about how slow Gofer's service had gotten recently. After the table was cleared, my parents descended on it with their laptops, and I headed up to my room to check my Q feed and finish *Dr. No*.

I had just fired up my computer when there was a knock on my door. Figuring it was my mother coming to lecture me some more about charity work, I sighed and opened it. Travis was standing on the other side.

"What?" I asked, wishing I could still look down at him and hating that he was getting close to my eye level. It might be enough to make me start wearing heels.

"Oh, I was just wondering," Travis said, smiling pleasantly—always a bad sign—as he leaned casually against the doorframe. "How was detention this afternoon?"

I stared at Travis, too stunned to come up with a lie. "How did you know about that?"

His smile grew wider. "So it's true?" he asked. "Interesting. Did you happen to tell Mom or Dad, perchance?"

I scowled at him. "Not yet. But how did you know about that?"

Travis gave me a condescending look. "You put it in your status, Madison. It's pretty much public knowledge."

I blinked at him. "Wait," I said. "You're on Status Q? And you follow my updates?"

Travis was using the patronizing tone that made me want to smack him with something heavy. "It would appear so, wouldn't it?"

I crossed my arms. "Why didn't I know that?"

"Um, you have, like, a million followers," Travis said.

"That's not true," I snapped. Unlike the regular Friendverse, you could set your updates so that anyone could follow them, not just the people you were friends with, and my Q—like most of my friends'—was set up that way.

"Do you know everyone who follows you?" he asked.

"Well . . . no," I admitted. I probably only knew about half. But it wasn't like I was gossiping about other people anymore; I'd learned my lesson about that. But there was nothing wrong with giving out information about myself. Except, apparently, if my brother was checking my updates. "But I think I would have noticed your name."

"Well, maybe it's not my name," Travis said, still smirking. "Not everyone is who they say they are online, Madison."

"Well, that's just creepy," I said. "Stop following me."

"I just want to know if you're going to tell Mom and Dad, or if you want me to," Travis said. I suddenly had a feeling that he was making me pay for forcing him to ask me nicely to get dinner.

"Well," I said, adopting a similarly pleasant conversational tone, "I guess that depends on whether you want me to e-mail Kittson the picture I took in the Galápagos of you picking your nose. Or should I just put it up on my Friendverse? Because I'm sure Olivia would love to see it."

Travis stared at me, eyes narrowed, apparently trying to figure out if I was bluffing. "Fine," he conceded after a moment. "Forget it. Just don't do anything with the picture."

"Don't tell Mom and Dad anything," I replied, "and I won't."

Travis pushed himself off the doorframe and headed down the hall, only stumbling over his feet once as he headed back to his own room.

I rolled my eyes and shut my door. I pulled out *Dr. No* and was all set to start reading, but what Travis had said was bothering me a little. I put aside Mr. Bond, gently opened my computer, logged in to Status Q, and looked at my list of followers. Three hundred. That did seem like kind of a lot. Since I only followed the updates of my real friends, theirs were the only updates I saw. The other people who followed me didn't affect what I saw on my feed, so I almost never thought about them.

But as I looked at the list, I realized that there were a lot of names I didn't recognize. I didn't see one that seemed like it might be Travis's, but knowing him, he'd probably chosen some incredibly obscure name. I didn't know why all these people wanted to follow me, since most of what I posted would only make sense to my friends. But some people just liked to be following a lot of other people. Like those Friendverse members who had millions of friends, the majority of whom they'd never actually spoken to.

I thought about going through the list and deleting some of the people I didn't know, but I hesitated, my hand over the keyboard. I kind of liked having a lot of followers. Your social status had a lot to do with how many followers you had. Not that I really cared about that. But still.

I decided I'd simply stop sending updates about being in detention until I could figure out Travis's screen name and block him. Then I pulled up my iChat, preparing for my nightly conversation with Schuyler and Lisa—I needed to tell them what Brian had said. And then I would get back to the world of tuxedo-wearing spies.

You know, eventually.

CHAPTER 7

Song: Ungodly Hour/The Fray
Quote: "Nearly all men can stand adversity, but if you want to test a man's character, give him power."
—Abraham Lincoln

KitKat → mad_mac Madison, it's 7:04. Where are you?!

mad_mac → KitKat Um, at home. Half asleep. Getting ready for school. The ush. Why?

KitKat → mad_mac Why are you at HOME? You need to meet me at the Putnam Hyatt NOW. I got here at 6:45. We have to look at the ballroom before school.

mad_mac → KitKat Wait, what? Are you kidding?

KitKat → mad_mac I don't joke about this stuff, Madison. This is serious. This is the PROM. Get here ASAP!

mad_mac (grumbles)

 KitKat → mad_mac And why do you not know about this? Haven't you been reading my blog?

 mad_mac → KitKat Um, sure. All the time. FINE. Leaving now.

 KitKat → mad_mac And that doesn't sound like a positive promitude to me!

 mad_mac → KitKat It's 7 am, Kittson. This is the best you're going to get.

 KitKat → mad_mac Just get here. Speed if you must.

Yawning, I turned into the entrance of the Putnam Hyatt. I knew that I would have driven better—and would have been altogether more coherent—if I'd been able to stop at Stubbs for a latte. But I had a feeling that Kittson would not understand this, and the sight of me with a cup might be enough to send her over the edge that she was always so close to these days.

I stared up at the hotel as I drove through the gated entrance. The Putnam Hyatt was huge, easily the nicest hotel in town, and I'd been there a few times over the years—weddings, fancy school events, and lots of weekends in seventh grade for bar and bat mitzvahs. I pulled into the half-filled parking lot, updated my status, and got out of my car.

 mad_mac At the Putnam Hyatt on official prom business. Would be willing to pay a ridiculous amount of money for a Stubbs latte right now.

I crossed the parking lot and walked up to the hotel's main entrance, a series of doors, each one staffed by a sleepy-looking doorman wearing a heavily braided red uniform. As I approached the door nearest me, it was flung open by the closest doorman, who appeared to be stifling a yawn.

"Um, thanks," I said as I stepped inside and the door swung shut behind me. I headed across the lobby, which was very grand, with mirrors and gilt, a huge fireplace on each end, flower arrangements as tall as I was, and lots of uncomfortable-looking armchairs placed about. It was absolutely quiet, and my flip-flops seemed to make a ton of noise as they slapped against the thick carpet.

I continued to the side wing of the hotel, where the ballrooms were. We were booked in the Rosebud Ballroom, on the ground floor. There was another ballroom directly above it, but that one was nicer and had been outside the prom budget. There was a third ballroom all the way across the hotel—through the lobby and down a hallway. The hallway was so long there were benches scattered along it, most likely in case you needed to stop and have a rest halfway through. It was in this ballroom, thankfully, that Travis's friend's bat mitz-vah reception was going to be held.

There was a small sitting area outside our ballroom with more uncomfortable armchairs and bathrooms to each side. Two large wooden doors led to the ballroom. I yanked one open and stepped inside, letting my eyes adjust to the darkness. The ballroom had hardwood floors, high ceilings with moldings, a stage along one side, where the queen would be crowned, and an area with speakers and electronic equipment, where Tanner would be DJing.

Kittson was standing in the center of the ballroom, her back to the doors. She was staring at the stage with such intensity that I couldn't help thinking that she'd stopped doing whatever prom business she'd dragged me there for and was now imagining her own corona-tion. Sure enough, as I watched, she raised her right arm and turned her cupped palm to the left and then to the right—the perfect gracious prom queen wave.

"Hey," I called, my voice echoing in the empty ball-room. I wanted to stop her before she started making a speech or something.

Kittson dropped her arm and whirled around. "Madison!" she said, stalking toward me. "Finally."

"Sorry," I said, crossing to meet her in the middle of the ballroom, under a huge crystal chandelier. As had been my habit ever since I'd seen *Phantom of the Opera,* I moved a couple of steps to the right so that I wouldn't be directly underneath it, just in case a singing masked maniac decided to set it loose. "I would have been here at seven," I said, giving myself a great deal of credit, "but I didn't know I was supposed to be."

Kittson shook her head impatiently. "It's on my prom blog," she said. "Aren't you reading it?"

"Mmm," I said noncommittally. I glanced at Kittson's blog from time to time, but couldn't bring myself to read the thing. Lately, she seemed to be doing an interactive poll where she modeled her prom dress choices and asked people to vote on which dress she should wear.

"Well, you should," she said. "I have a lot of pertinent information on it. And it's very popular, you know." She smoothed her hair. "I had over a hundred comments on my *Updo/Updon't* post."

"Seriously?" I asked, stunned that there were that many bored people at our school.

"Yes," she said, a little smugly. "Apparently, my journey to the crown is being very closely watched." She looked around the ballroom and sighed. "Which will be worthless unless we can get things organized."

"Well," I said, glancing down at my phone to check the time. It took a great deal of restraint, but I stopped myself from also checking my status feed. "We have an hour before school. What do we need to do?"

Kittson handed me a clipboard. "We have to inspect the ballroom," she said, "and note any problems, so that after the prom, when the Hyatt people inspect it for damage, we won't be charged if something was broken before."

"All right," I said, taking out a pen and getting to work. I had thought that Kittson would be busy with her own list, but she just watched me check off boxes, her own clipboard hanging by her side. "Can I help you?" I asked after a few minutes.

"Yes, actually," Kittson said, as though this hadn't been a rhetorical question. "It's about Glen."

I focused on the list again, feeling that I had been put in the middle of far too many friends' relationships recently.

"He's being kind of stubborn," Kittson went on, "about this whole prom royalty thing. I mean, I know he wants me to win queen. He's told me so. But he also seems to have this vendetta against whoever is going to be king. He keeps saying he'll beat up whoever dances with me." Kittson had been frowning, but as I watched, it changed to a slightly dreamy expression. "He's just so . . . protective of me."

"Really," I said, trying to keep my expression as neutral as possible so that she wouldn't guess I'd had almost the same conversation with Turtell. The beating-people-up thing was new information, though.

"Yes," she said, the dreamy expression fading. "And now all these guys are saying that they don't want to be prom king. I think they're afraid that Glen's going to beat them up. You know, because he keeps telling them he's going to."

"I think you should talk to Glen," I said. "Relationships are about communication." I paused, wondering why that sounded so familiar, before I realized it was what Schuyler had said to me the day before. "Just tell Glen that he has nothing to worry about. And tell him to stop threatening to beat up our potential prom kings."

"I didn't think you'd mind," she said slyly. "I mean, since it's probably going to be Justin."

I put my clipboard down and looked at her. Although we didn't talk about it much, Kittson and I had a shared history with Justin. She'd dated him after I had, but had broken up with him after only a few weeks and then immediately started dating Turtell. But the me-and-Justin thing felt like ancient history. Justin paled in comparison to Nate. It seemed like we'd dated in another lifetime. I couldn't even remember the last time I'd thought about him. "I don't want Glen to beat up Justin," I said. "I don't want Glen to beat up anyone."

"Oh," Kittson said, looking disappointed. She'd probably been hoping that there was still some drama to be mined from the situation. "I just thought you might still be mad at him."

"Not at all," I said. "I mean, compared to Nate, Justin's just . . ."

"I know," Kittson said. "Same with Glen, that is." She took a lip gloss out of her bag and applied it skillfully. Watching her, I suddenly felt bad for Justin. After all, both his ex-girlfriends were in relationships with other people, and both were happy to not be dating him anymore. As far as I knew, Justin hadn't dated anyone since Kittson had dumped him. Which, it now struck me, was a little strange. Guys like Justin were rarely unattached. After Ruth, pretending to be me, had dumped him on Friendverse, he'd been single less than forty-eight hours before Kittson asked him out.

"Back to business," Kittson said briskly, capping her lip gloss and frowning at me, as though I was the one who'd gotten us off track. "Where are we with the gift bags?"

"Hello?" a voice called out from the ballroom entrance. I turned and saw a girl standing in the doorway, but I couldn't see her face, as she was silhouetted by the light outside.

Kittson looked over as well, and I could feel her stiffen beside me. She stood up and crossed toward the girl. Not wanting to miss anything—and happy to take a break from the inspection form—I followed.

The girl was on the short side, even though she was wearing a serious pair of stiletto heels. She looked about our age, but was dressed older, in a pencil skirt and gauzy shirt that, I could tell just by looking at it, had probably been incredibly expensive. She had dark brown hair pulled back in a ponytail, with blunt bangs, and she was carrying a thick black binder.

"I thought I heard your voice," the girl said as Kittson approached. She gave Kittson a tight smile, and her eyes flicked to me before returning to Kittson. "Doing some last-minute preparations?"

"Not at all," Kittson said, and her voice was cold to the point of being frosty. I looked at her, a little surprised. I'd never heard her use such a serious tone before. Not even when I'd suggested that our theme be *Just Prom It*. "We're all prepared for Saturday, and have been for weeks. Overprepared, really."

Following Kittson's lead, I nodded, wondering why she was blatantly lying to this girl I'd never seen before.

"I don't believe we've met," the girl said, looking at me again and raising her eyebrows at Kittson.

"What am I thinking?" Kittson asked with a bright and—I knew her well enough by now to realize— incredibly fake smile. "Madison, this is Isabel Ryan. Isabel, this is Madison MacDonald, one of my assistants on our committee."

"Hi," I said, deciding to let the "assistant" thing go. Lately, I'd been thinking that the less credit I received for the prom, the better off I might be.

"Isabel is head of the prom committee at Hartfield High," Kittson continued, her tone still falsely cheerful.

"Madison MacDonald?" Isabel asked, looking at me with new interest. "Really?"

"Um, yeah," I said. "Nice to meet you."

"You too," Isabel said, still looking at me closely. "Your reputation precedes you."

"It does?" I asked. I had never even heard of this girl, so I had no idea how she might have heard of me. A moment later, it hit me that it might have been the hacking. Had people as far away as Hartfield been aware of it?

"Yes," she said, still staring at me. Then her expression became less intense, and she smiled. "You're in all the plays at Putnam, right?"

"Oh," I said, feeling relief flood through me. "Yes, I am."

"Shame about the review this morning," she said, tucking a lock of hair behind her ear.

"Wait," I said. I tried not to be distracted by the fact that I could now see her enormous diamond studs that

80

looked—as far as I could tell—real. "What did it say?"

"So, what are you doing here, Isabel?" Kittson asked. "Not that it isn't *lovely* to see you again."

Isabel took a piece of paper out of her binder. "The hotel's inspection sheet. They're such sticklers, aren't they?"

"What do you mean?" Kittson asked, looking down at Isabel's paper—exactly the same as mine—and back up at her again.

"Oh, didn't you know?" Isabel asked. Even though I'd just met this girl, I could tell she was taking delight in this conversation. "We're holding our prom here this Saturday."

Kittson was gaping at Isabel and didn't appear to have the faculty of speech at the moment, so I stepped in. "I thought that your prom was going to be held in your school's gym," I said, and Kittson nodded mutely. I remembered all too well Kittson's stakeout of the Hyatt. She had been concerned about Stanwich or Hartfield taking the Rosebud, so she had made it her—and, by extension, my—business to know where the other local proms were being held. Before Stanwich's had been canceled, it was going to be at the Stanwich Yacht Club. And Hartfield's had always been at the school.

"It was," Isabel said. "But you might have heard about the little stunt that Stanwich High pulled on Senior Prank Day."

"No," I said quickly. "I've heard nothing at all."

"Well," Isabel said, shooting me an odd look, "our school was broken into and our mascot costume was stolen. And our headmistress thought that due to the security breach, we'd be better off at a public venue, where other precious Hartfield items wouldn't be on display for those who wished to do them harm. So we settled on the Lily Ballroom."

"The one directly above this?" Kittson asked, apparently recovering the power of speech. "This Saturday?"

"Yes," Isabel said. "Which is why I've got to get this form filled out. You're *so* lucky to have an assistant."

"Wait a second," I said, feeling that it was time to clear this up. "I'm not actually—"

"You can't be holding your prom at the same time as ours," Kittson said, ignoring me entirely.

"But I am," Isabel said with a smile. "I guess we'll really get a chance to compare the two side by side, won't we?"

"But . . ." Kittson said, wrinkling her nose slightly, which she did when she was thinking hard. "But—"

"Anyway," Isabel interrupted, "just wanted to say hello. It was lovely to meet you, Madison. Finally. And Kittson, do come up and see the Lily if you'd like. It's just stunning." She looked around the Rosebud with a small smile. "Not that yours isn't, of course. TTYL!" She gave us a little wave, then headed out of the ballroom.

Kittson blinked at the doorway for a moment, then turned to me, her face stricken. "This is a disaster," she said.

"Why?" I asked, hoping to defuse a possible Kittson meltdown as quickly as possible. "I mean, so their prom is above ours, on the same night. It's not like we're going to get in each other's way. Much. Hopefully."

"Isabel Ryan," Kittson said, practically spitting the name out, "has been making my life miserable this whole year. I haven't wanted to burden you with it," she said magnanimously. "But she's determined to have a better prom than us. She's constantly commenting on my blog. And now she's in the better ballroom. She probably stole that mascot costume herself, just to get this to happen."

"No, she didn't," I said automatically. Kittson raised an eyebrow at me. "Not that I know anything about it," I added. "Because I don't."

"What are we going to do?" she asked, a little desperately. "She's been out to get me ever since I made fun of her theme."

"What's her theme?" I asked. Ours was *A Night to Remember,* and it seemed to me that people who came up with themes that referenced books about the *Titanic* really shouldn't throw stones.

"*Take My Breath Away,*" Kittson said, rolling her eyes. I had to admit, that was pretty bad. And even more morbid than ours, which I hadn't thought was possible. "She's never let me forget it. And she's going to try to sabotage our prom, I bet you anything."

"No, she's not," I said as calmly as I could. I steered Kittson toward one of the chairs that were lining the side of the ballroom, and she sat down. "Listen, Kittson, Isabel wants to have a great prom. So do you. That's all. There's no sabotage going on. It's all going to be fine. Okay?"

"Okay," Kittson said, taking a deep breath. "You're right. Thanks, Mad."

"Sure," I said. I glanced down at my phone again. "We'd better get this finished. We don't have much time before school starts."

"You're right," Kittson said, springing into action. "We've been wasting all this time talking. . . ."

We finished the inspection in fifteen minutes and probably could have done it in less if Kittson hadn't kept making asides about how much nicer the Lily Ballroom was. Duties finished, I gave the Rosebud a last look and followed Kittson to the area just outside the ballroom, nearly running into someone as I did so. It took me a moment to realize that the person I'd almost crashed into was Schuyler.

"Shy?" I asked. I was glad to see her but had no idea what she was doing there. I glanced down and saw that she was carrying an iced Stubbs drink in each hand.

"Morning," Schuyler said. She handed me one of the drinks, and it was all I could do not to hug her. "Here. For you."

"But how did you know?" I asked gratefully, taking a sip.

"Um, you put it on your Q," Schuyler said. "You said you were here, and that you wanted a latte."

"You are the best friend ever," I said, smiling at her. "Thank you so much."

"Hi," Schuyler mumbled to Kittson. Schuyler was still a little intimidated by Kittson, even though I'd told her repeatedly that there was no need to be.

"Wow," Kittson said, looking at my drink. "You certainly do have good friends, Mad." She sounded maybe a little wistful.

Schuyler flushed. "I—I would have gotten you one," she stammered. "But I didn't know what you drink. Or, um, that you were here."

"No worries," Kittson said.

"Plus," Schuyler continued, lowering her voice slightly, "I thought Madison might need a little something this morning."

"Why?" Kittson asked.

"Yes, why?" I asked, totally perplexed.

"Oh," Schuyler said, looking surprised. "Because of the *Dane* review. I thought you would have read it by now."

"No," I said, fumbling in my bag for my phone. Between this and what Isabel had said, I was getting a very bad feeling about it.

"So, this is where the prom is going to be?" Schuyler asked. I glanced up from the depths of my bag—which my phone had somehow vanished into—and saw Schuyler peeking inside the ballroom.

"Yes," Kittson said. "And it's all going to go perfectly." She seemed to be saying this for her own benefit as much as for Schuyler's.

"Oh," Schuyler said. "Well, good!" She turned back to us, and I could see her face was glowing. "I'm just so excited!" Kittson asked her about her dress, and Schuyler started describing it, shyness apparently forgotten in the face of important prom dress details.

I finally excavated my phone and looked up to see

Schuyler and Kittson, still deep in conversation, headed for the lobby. "Wait," I said, trying to catch up with them and access the *Putnam Post* website at the same time. By the time I reached them, they were standing in front of the lobby doors, Schuyler excitedly describing how Connor's cummerbund matched her dress. "Guys," I said. "Thanks for waiting."

"Oh, sorry," Schuyler said, eyes shining. "I was just getting Kittson's opinion on my dress. I can't believe that the prom is in just a few days! I'm so excited! Aren't you excited, Mad?"

"Um . . ." I stalled. I didn't have the heart to tell her that the DJ might play terrible music and that all the potential prom kings might be suffering concussions. I hadn't seen Schuyler this happy in a long time. "Sure. Of course I am."

"Oh, Kittson," someone called. I turned and saw Isabel heading toward us. "I had one last question for you—" Isabel stopped short, and her mouth dropped open. "Schuyler?" she asked, sounding stunned.

I turned, surprised, to see that Schuyler had gone pale and her hands, clutching her Stubbs cup, were shaking slightly. "Isabel?" she asked faintly, almost like she was afraid of the answer.

"You two know each other?" Kittson asked, looking from one to the other.

"Oh, we go way back," Isabel said, her voice cold. She was staring hard at Schuyler, who looked like she was about to pass out. "Isn't that right, Schuyler?"

"We, um," Schuyler said in a voice so faint I had to lean closer to hear her, "went to boarding school together."

"Choate," Isabel said, and I watched Schuyler flinch at the word. Because of whatever had happened to her at Choate—and for three years, Schuyler had refused to tell us—we were forbidden to speak the school's name in her presence. Occasionally, under the influence, Schuyler would mumble something about "The Evil Place." But that was the most we'd ever been able to get out of her. "What are you doing here?" Isabel asked.

Schuyler glanced at Isabel but then immediately looked at the floor. "I was just, um, bringing Madison a coffee," she said, mostly to the carpet.

"So you go to Putnam?" Isabel asked, eyebrows raised. Schuyler nodded, still not looking up.

"And it looks like you've managed to make some friends," Isabel said, glancing at Kittson and me. "Isn't that nice!" She smoothed her bangs, and her eyes dropped to my Stubbs cup, which had *Schuyler* scrawled on it in black marker. "I think the best thing about having close friends is *telling* them everything. No secrets between friends, am I right?"

I looked from Schuyler to Isabel, trying to figure out what was going on. I suddenly felt like I was watching a foreign movie without subtitles. "Um, sure," I said after a moment, breaking the uncomfortable silence.

"So, we should be heading to school," Kittson said, making a big show of checking her watch. "What did you want to ask me, Isabel?"

"You know," Isabel said, still looking at Schuyler, "I seem to have totally forgotten. I'll e-mail you if it comes to me, though."

"Please do," Kittson said with another falsely bright smile. "I'll look forward to that. See you around, Isabel."

"Not if I see you first!" Isabel called back, which seemed a very strange response to me. Then she stalked off in the direction she had come from, and Kittson headed out of the lobby. I looked at Schuyler, who appeared shell-shocked.

"Shy?" I asked, touching her shoulder. "You okay?" Schuyler blinked at me as though she wasn't quite sure who I was, then nodded quickly.

"Fine," she said. "I just wasn't expecting to see her, that's all." She walked toward the lobby doors, and I followed.

"So, what was that about?" I asked.

"What was what about?" Schuyler asked as we walked to the parking lot, Kittson a few feet ahead of us and already talking on her cell phone.

"The whole thing with you and Isabel," I said. "What was going on there?"

"Nothing," Schuyler said quickly. "I just knew her from Choate. That's all."

"Shy," I said, "come on."

"It's nothing," Schuyler said, beeping open her SUV.

Kittson, standing next to her pink Mini Cooper, lowered her phone and turned to me. "Madison," she said, "do *not* forget that we have a prom meeting after school today. Okay? Dr. Trent is presenting us—"

"With the Hayes crown," I finished for her. "I know."
She nodded, got into her car, and pulled out of the parking lot. "Seriously," I said, turning back to Schuyler, "I was there. That wasn't nothing. That was *weird*."

"Really, Mad," Schuyler said in a slightly strained voice. "It's nothing to worry yourself about. She just never liked me, that's all. We never really got along. And then she got expelled and then I left, and I hadn't seen her since."

"She got expelled?" I asked, shocked. "What for? And why did you leave, again?" I threw the last one in there hoping that she'd forget that she'd refused to answer that very question for the past three years.

"I can't talk about it," Schuyler mumbled, looking at the ground. "Just forget it, okay? I have to get to school. See you there, Mad." And before I had a chance to say anything else, Schuyler climbed into her SUV, stuck a lock of hair in her mouth, and drove away.

Gingersnap Oh my god, has anyone seen the *Putnam Post*? They just reviewed *Dane*. It's not pretty. . . .

the8rgrrl → mad_mac Wow, Mads, did you see this? www.putnampost.com/greatdane_travestyatputnamhigh They called your performance "acceptably adequate." Ouch!

mad_mac Currently not happy with people who review plays. And write bad reviews of them.

Gingersnap → mad_mac Well, at least you got off better than Mark Rothmann. I mean, *wow*.

the8rgrrl → mad_mac How are you holding up, Mads?

 mad_mac → the8rgrrl I'm fine. I'm acceptably adequate. But can someone please make sure Mark Rothmann doesn't see this?

 Roth Mann Reading the *Dane* review in the *Putnam Post.* Trying not to weep.

 Roth Mann Not succeeding.

 Gingersnap → Roth Mann I don't think that drama critics should be allowed to write reviews if they are going to be filled with such, um, libel. Libel's a crime, right? Can we sue?

 the8rgrrl → Gingersnap, mad_mac, Roth Mann Well, we can all discuss it today when we strike the set. Maybe we can get them to print a retraction.

 the8rgrrl → mad_mac Are you coming to the strike, Mads? I know you've had a lot of other more important commitments lately.

 mad_mac → the8rgrrl I'll be there, Sarah. Might be a few minutes late, but I'll be there.

 the8rgrrl → mad_mac Totally understandable! Do you have detention again?

mad_mac ➔ the8rgrrl Um, no.

 the8rgrrl ➔ mad_mac Great! See you later, then!

 mad_mac Beginning to rethink the kind of stuff I share in my updates . . .

 Dave Gold ➔ mad_mac Then maybe you shouldn't update about it? Just a suggestion . . . ;)

 mad_mac ➔ Dave Gold Good point.

CHAPTER 8

Song: To The Workers Of The Rock River Valley
Region, I Have An Idea Concerning Your
Predicament . . ./Sufjan Stevens
Quote: "You will do foolish things, but do them with
enthusiasm."—Colette

"And so, after the Putnam High School prom of 1953, when her granddaughter Mariel was crowned with it, Mrs. Ida Hayes most generously entrusted to the school the Hayes crown, so that it could be used in every subsequent coronation. It is therefore one of the school's most valuable possessions. . . ."

Dr. Trent, standing at the front of the classroom, droned on about the Hayes crown, as he had been doing for the past—I snuck a glance at the clock—forty-five minutes.

The classroom was filled with the entire prom committee. All the résumé kids were in attendance for once, drawn by the presence of the assistant headmaster. Kittson, sitting in the front row, was holding the crown with both hands and seemed enraptured by it. I was just trying not to fall asleep and wondering how quickly I would be able to get out of there. I wasn't particularly interested in hearing about the crown's venerated history. And seeing the crown up close and in person, I didn't think it was even that special-looking — it was small, and looked kind of dingy.

"And so!" Dr. Trent boomed, shaking me out of my reverie. "With the full power of the office of assistant headmaster, I am entrusting this crown to the junior prom committee for its safekeeping and transport to the Putnam Hyatt." Dr. Trent took the crown back from Kittson — who seemed to go through some sort of internal struggle before surrendering it — and placed it inside a large dark blue jewelry case. He then closed the case and handed it back to Kittson as the résumé kids burst into applause.

The meeting broke up after that, with most of the résumé kids drifting off, no doubt to the next activity they were pretending to participate in. I noticed Kittson talking to Dr. Trent at the front of the classroom, frantically motioning for me to join her. I grabbed my bag and headed up there.

"I've no doubt you can handle this responsibility," Dr. Trent was saying to Kittson, who was clutching the jewelry box. "The planning of this prom thus far has been exemplary. . . ." I bit my lip hard to keep from laughing as Dr. Trent looked over his glasses at me. "Oh. Madison," he said. He frowned at me. "I see you've managed to avoid detention this afternoon."

"Oh," I said, completely thrown. I hadn't known that

the assistant headmaster kept tabs on who was in detention every day. But maybe he got a list or something. I was half tempted to tell him that my detentions were all his fault, since he'd made me move lockers. "Yes," I finally said, not sure how else to respond.

"Good," he said, still frowning at me. "Because it doesn't reflect well at all on our class officers when they are constantly receiving disciplinary action."

I opened my mouth to protest, or try to defend myself, but Dr. Trent had turned to Kittson and was going over crown details with her.

I stared at him, still a little stunned. I'd known that in the wake of the hacking thing, I hadn't exactly been Dr. Trent's favorite student, but once that had been cleared up, I'd assumed that things would be fine again. But maybe he was just stressed about the crown, which he was being super paranoid about.

Dr. Trent finished telling Kittson exactly how to bring the crown to the hotel, said goodbye to her, nodded at me, and left the classroom.

"Was that weird?" I asked when the door shut behind him and Kittson and I were alone in the classroom.

"What?" Kittson asked, stroking the box reverently.

"Dr. Trent," I said. "It's like he suddenly hates me or something."

"Well, of course he does," Kittson said matter-of-factly. "You made him expel one of his prized students."

"You mean Dell?"

"Who else? He'll get over it," she said breezily, as if

having the assistant headmaster turn against you was nothing to be worried about. Then she opened the box and peeked inside. "Oh my God," she breathed. "Isn't it beautiful?"

"Very nice," I lied. "Want to try it on?"

Kittson snapped the lid shut and stared at me, looking horrified. "Are you kidding me?" she asked. "That's *incredibly* bad luck."

"Okay," I said with a shrug. Just as there were all kinds of theater superstitions, I guess it only made sense that there were prom queen superstitions as well. "So I should get going—"

"Here," Kittson said, thrusting the box at me.

"Wait. What?" I asked. I took a step back from it. "I don't want to try it on."

"No," Kittson said, rolling her eyes. "Though God knows it wouldn't be bad luck for *you*. I need you to bring it to the hotel."

"Seriously?" I saw Kittson take a breath, and I continued before I would have to receive her "there is nothing funny about the prom" lecture one more time. "Fine. Seriously. But we just heard Dr. Trent's speech about how he considers this no less important than the Hope diamond. And also, apparently he hates me now. I think he's going to want you to bring it to the hotel."

"Well, of course he does," Kittson said. "But I don't have time this afternoon. I have to talk to the gift bag people, and then go to the florist, and then get my highlights refreshed. I don't have time to bring it to the hotel. I just don't have the time. Okay? *Okay?*" Kittson's voice was getting progressively higher and more hysterical, and I decided not to argue with her.

"Okay," I said in what I hoped was a soothing tone. "Just calm down. I'll take it over." I took the box from her, even though making another trip to the Hyatt had not been in my plans for that afternoon.

"The concierge will be waiting for it," she said, already looking calmer. "And then he'll lock it in the safe, where it's going to stay until right before the crowning. So all you need to do is drop it off. Think you can do that?"

"Yes," I said, trying very hard not to roll my eyes. "I think I can handle that." I dropped the jewelry box into my bag, causing Kittson to flinch a little.

"And how's the music coming?" Kittson asked as we headed to the door and snapped the lights off.

"Fine," I lied, remembering that I'd promised Tanner a playlist.

"Good," Kittson said as she shouldered her bag. "The last thing we need is something *else* to worry about on prom night."

I was about to reply that some of us had lots of other things to worry about on prom night—like our little brothers riding in our limos and accidental propositions we might have made to our boyfriends—but Kittson was already heading down the corridor, waving backward at me as she went.

I took out my phone and updated my status.

mad_mac I am currently in possession of . . . THE HAYES CROWN! About to deliver it to a top secret, undisclosed location. Details given to those with Top Level clearance only.

Almost immediately after I had finished sending this, my phone chimed with a new update.

 Gingersnap ➜ mad_mac Mad, I guess that means you're not making it to the strike? ☹ No worries. But let's catch up ASAP!!

I looked at Ginger's message, torn. I had been a Thespian—part of Putnam High School's theater group—since my freshman year, but didn't tend to hang out a ton with the other theater kids, most of whom traveled in a *Glee*-quoting, Sondheim-belting pack. And since prom stuff had taken over my life, I'd been spending even less time with them, and I had a feeling that it was causing some of the theater kids to feel hurt.

I also had a suspicion that a certain former understudy of mine was stoking these feelings, and I knew that the best way to defuse the situation would be to make an appearance at the strike. I glanced into my bag at the crown, then made a decision. I could just drop the crown off after the strike. It wasn't like anything was going to happen to it. And it wasn't like the hotel was going to close. After checking quickly that Kittson was really gone, I reversed direction and headed down to the theater wing. I was actually happy to have the chance to talk to the other theater kids about the review. It had been pretty terrible and hadn't gotten any less stinging the six times I'd read it over the course of the day.

I reached the greenroom and found it deserted except for Mark Rothmann, who was sitting slumped against the back wall, staring at the floor. "Hey, Mark," I said. "How's it going?"

Mark didn't even look up; he simply shrugged. Clearly, it was not going well. But given the review, that was to be expected.

"Are you going to the strike?" I asked, gesturing toward the blackbox.

"What's the point?" Mark asked bitterly, sitting up a little and looking at me. "I'd probably just mar a mildly competent production with my preposterous attempt at an accent and tone-deaf affectation." I took the fact that Mark was reciting whole passages from the review to be a bad sign.

"It's just a stupid review," I said. "I mean, they called me 'acceptably adequate.'"

"But that's a good thing!" Mark said. "That's a positive thing. They didn't call you 'a blight on the entire production, and perhaps on the institution of theater itself.'"

"Well, no," I admitted. I'd actually been kind of hurt by the "acceptably adequate" thing, but it didn't seem like Mark was going to appreciate that right then. "But maybe striking the set will make you feel better," I said. "I mean, you'll get to break things."

Mark just shook his head. "Go on without me," he said, slumping over again. "I'll be okay."

It didn't seem like it, but it also didn't seem like

Mark wanted company at the moment. I headed out of the greenroom, walked through the lightlock, and made my way onstage. The stage was in a state of disaster, as the main set—Ham's home, Elsie Nora Farm—was currently being dismantled. I walked carefully around my fellow Thespians, most of whom were wielding hammers with entirely too much vigor and entirely too little expertise. After watching the destruction for a few moments, I decided I liked my appendages too much to be there. I carefully backed out of the blackbox, left through the lightlock, and headed into the costume shop.

The first thing I saw was a huge pile of costumes. But a moment later, half buried beneath them, I spotted Ginger Davis, a tape measure looped around her neck. Ginger was my closest theater friend, the only one of the Thespians who was—ironically—above all the drama. She was super sweet, even though she did have a tendency to get drunk on nonalcoholic beer at every cast party. She did the costumes and makeup for every show and was incredibly talented. In fact, the costumes in *Dane* had been practically the only thing that the reviewer had liked.

"Hey, Ginger," I said, and she looked up as I approached.

"Mad!" she said with a smile. "Oh, good, you're here. Sarah had been asking where you were. . . ."

I allowed myself a small eye roll at that. Since freshman year, Sarah Donner and I had found ourselves competing for roles. She usually ended up understudying me, as she had on *Dane*. Our relationship had never been great,

99

and she had even been one of the people I'd suspected of hacking my Friendverse. But she hadn't been involved, and we'd actually had a talk about it that had made working together a little easier. But that didn't mean she still didn't seize every opportunity to make me look irresponsible.

"I'm here," I said, dropping my bag in the corner and heading over to the pile of clothes. "How's the costume strike going?"

Ginger looked around, then sighed. "Slowly? But I'm making progress. I think."

"Mads, you're here," someone behind me said. I turned and saw Sarah Donner striding up, clutching a clipboard. "I wasn't sure you were going to make it."

"I'm here," I said again, doing a quick check of her outfit. I was pleased to see it was a normal T-shirt and jeans. Until recently, Sarah had been far too attached to what she'd called her "rehearsal clothes"—overalls and a bandanna that were incredibly unflattering. Ginger and I had staged an intervention a few weeks earlier and Sarah hadn't worn the overalls since. Ginger had given her a makeover, and without the bandanna, Sarah was really surprisingly pretty.

"So," Ginger said, looking up from a long flowered gown, "did you guys hear who doesn't have a prom date?"

"Oh, you heard about Brian?" I blurted.

"No," Ginger said, looking at me. "What?"

"Nothing," I said, frustrated with myself for accidentally breaking my no-gossip rule. Sarah was looking at me, clearly interested in hearing more, but I pressed my lips together and shook my head firmly. "Forget it. Who doesn't have a prom date?"

"Well, Mark doesn't," Sarah said. "Is that who you meant?"

"Mark doesn't have a date?" I asked, surprised. I suddenly felt very out of the loop and wondered if when I'd stopped gossiping, people had stopped returning the favor.

"No, he's going solo," Sarah said. Then she sighed. "Me too."

"Seriously?" I asked. I wished we'd gotten her to ditch the bandanna a few weeks earlier.

Sarah shrugged, trying for nonchalant, but as always with her acting, she overdid it. She turned to Ginger, clearly intent on changing the subject. "You and Josh are going together, right?"

"Yes," Ginger said, blushing slightly. Josh Burch had played Ham in the production, and he and Ginger had been an item since the tech rehearsal. I liked Josh, but I didn't know how Ginger was putting up with him, because he wasn't exactly the sharpest tack in the toolbox. Or wherever it is that you keep tacks. But Josh and Ginger seemed to be working out, and I was happy for her.

"And Madison, you're going with Nathaniel?" Sarah asked, sounding a little disgruntled.

"Nate," I corrected. "And it's actually Jonathan." Sarah had decided that Nate must be a nickname for Nathaniel. And that she was going to call him that, even though he'd never asked her to. And the fact that it wasn't actually his name. "But yes."

Sarah sighed dramatically. "Well, tell me who *doesn't* have a prom date," she said, turning to Ginger. "It might make me feel better."

Ginger looked around the costume shop, and I smiled at her paranoia. "Ginger, I think we're alone in here," I said.

"You never know who's listening," she said gravely.

"Just us, I'm pretty sure," I said, but I moved a step closer to her. "Spill." Just because *I* wasn't gossiping anymore didn't mean that I couldn't reap the benefits of those who were.

"Justin Williamson," Ginger said, a bit of wonder in her voice. "Can you believe it?"

"Not really," I murmured, stunned. While I'd known that Justin hadn't gone out with anyone post-Kittson, I had assumed he would have a prom date. Guys like Justin didn't go to the prom stag.

"Mad, is it true that you have the Hayes crown?" Ginger asked, clearly done with talking about Justin. "Like, with you?"

I paused, wondering how she'd known that, before I remembered my Status Q update and smiled at Ginger's incredulous expression. "I do."

"Could I see it?" she asked. "Just for a minute? To examine the construction?"

I considered it. It wasn't like it could hurt the crown at all to be taken out of the box. And I couldn't think of anyone who would treat it more carefully than Ginger. "Why not?" I said. I walked over to my bag, pulled out the jewelry box, held it out to Ginger and Sarah, and opened it.

The crown was resting on a bed of dark blue velvet, patchy in spots, that matched the case. It was surprisingly small and made of white gold, with four teardrop crystals standing up from it. Or they might have been diamonds, I realized with a sinking feeling, remembering how everyone went on and on about the crown's value. The crystals—or (hopefully not) diamonds—were nevertheless very sparkly, and they caught the costume shop's light and sent rainbows onto the walls.

"OMG," Ginger breathed. "It's so . . . beautiful."

"You think?" I asked, staring down at it.

"You don't?" Sarah asked, leaning closer to it. "It's stunning."

"I like the one that you had me wear in *Romeo and Juliet* better," I said to Ginger.

"But that was rhinestone," Ginger said, eyes still on the crown. "This is real."

I stared at it, beginning to worry that she was right, and suddenly feeling nervous about having to transport something that had real diamonds in it. If this was as important as Dr. Trent was making it out to be, I couldn't help wishing that he'd hired an armored car or something.

"Mad, would you try it on for me?" Ginger asked excitedly. I looked at her and saw what I recognized as designing frenzy in her eyes. She got like this whenever she was sketching for the next production. When it hit, she became almost impossible to say no to. It was how I ended up modeling potato sacks, to see if she could make one of Felia's costumes out of them. She couldn't. And for the record, potato sacks are not comfortable.

"I don't know . . ." I said, fearing the Wrath of Kittson if she found out.

"Please?" Ginger asked, hands clasped. "Please please? Just so I can get some pictures of it? For my files? Please please please?"

I looked down at the crown. It would probably be easier to try it on than to listen to Ginger beg me for an hour. And it wasn't like I was ever going to be prom queen, so this would probably be my only chance to wear it. "Fine," I said, reaching for the crown.

"Wait!" Ginger said, looking around the pile of costumes she was mired in. She dug through the clothes, tossing shirts and dresses over her shoulder, making even more of a mess. "Aha!" She pulled out a beautiful taffeta dress and held it up.

"That's gorgeous," I said, taking it from her. It really was. It was pale pink and cut fifties-style—strapless with a tea-length skirt that stood out slightly, thanks to the crinolines underneath. It looked like something a young Audrey Hepburn might have worn. I suddenly liked my own prom dress—a modern column-style peach sheath currently on hold for me across town at Caitlin's Closet—a little bit less.

"Put it on!" Ginger said, clapping her hands. "It doesn't make any sense to see the tiara with what you're wearing, Mad."

I didn't need convincing. I'd wanted to put on the dress since Ginger had held it up. I handed the jewelry box to Sarah and headed to the small curtained area at the back of the costume shop. I changed quickly and looked at myself in the mirror. Unbelievably, the dress fit. Not able to resist, I did a little twirl, just to see the skirt flare out gently.

"Mad?" Ginger called, and I tore my eyes away from the mirror and pulled aside the curtain. Ginger smiled when she saw me. "I knew it would fit," she said. "Crown?" she said to Sarah, who shook her head and held on to it.

"I don't know," Sarah said. "I think it might be bad luck or something."

"It's not bad luck," Ginger said quickly. You had to admire her. Normal Ginger, who was deeply gullible, would have absolutely believed this. But when she was on a costume-related mission, she was relentless.

"I think it's only bad luck if you're in the running for prom queen," I said. "Which I am not."

"I just don't know," Sarah said. "I mean, what if there's a curse or something?"

"There isn't a curse," Ginger said dismissively.

"How do you know?" Sarah asked. "I mean, maybe it's not supposed to be worn by anyone until the prom queen, when she's crowned. There *might* be a curse."

I glanced down at the crown, which looked small and sparkly and totally innocent. I shook my head. "There isn't a curse," I said with a little more certainty than I felt. I picked it up off the velvet base. It was heavier than I'd thought it would be, and I admired it for a moment before placing it on my head and pressing the small combs into my hair to secure it.

"Oh, that's perfect," Ginger said. She struggled to her feet and pulled her phone out of the pocket of her jeans as Sarah watched, frowning, arms folded.

"I don't like this," Sarah said. "Just so that's out there."

"We heard you," I said. I wasn't sure if this was actually about the crown, or if she was just upset that Ginger had asked me, and not her, to try it on. "I promise it'll be fine."

"Okay, just a couple?" Ginger asked, flipping her phone open. "Smile, Mad. . . ."

I looked pointedly away from Sarah and smiled, trying to do my best fifties-prom-queen expression, as the camera phone clicked.

****

Two hours later, I headed out to the junior parking lot. After she'd finished taking pictures, Ginger had become all business and had put Sarah and me to work taking the costumes to the vault. The costume vault was off the blackbox, and Ginger was the only student who had keys to it. It was a huge room where all the costumes from all the past shows were stored, in the hopes that they could be used for future productions. It was like being in a candy store, and I would have been content to wander around it for hours, but after we were done, Ginger hustled us out of there and locked up.

I was completely wiped out, and the thought of going to the Hyatt now and dealing with the hotel's concierge was incredibly unappealing. From the depths of my bag, I could hear the sound of the French Kicks—Lisa's ring. I dug my phone out of my bag and answered. "Ah, *bonjour.*"

"Mad," Lisa said, and I could hear her sighing. "The French *never* answer the phone that way."

"Oh," I said. "What do they say?"

"*Allô*," Lisa said firmly. "And nothing else."

"Got it," I said. "I'll remember that the next time I'm in France. And answering a phone. What's up?"

"*Rien*," Lisa said. "Just wanted to catch up."

"Me too," I said, suddenly remembering the incident at the hotel that morning. "Have you talked to Schuyler much today?"

"*Non*," Lisa said. "Which is kind of weird, since we had the same lunch, and I never saw her. Why?"

"Well, this thing happened at the Hyatt this morning that was really strange. . . ."

"What?" Lisa asked eagerly. "*Dis-moi.*"

I had made it to my car, and pulled the phone away from my ear to check the time. If I hung up with Lisa now, I could still make it to the hotel before I had to be home for dinner.

Or . . . I could just bring the crown tomorrow. I wanted to talk to Lisa, not just to try to figure out what had been going on with Schuyler but because I'd become aware that friendships—even best friendships—could end. And between Lisa's call and Schuyler's coming with coffee, I was feeling really lucky in the friend department these days.

"Mad?" Lisa asked. "Are you busy or something?"

"Nope," I said. "Totally free." I unlocked Judy and got behind the wheel. "Meet you at Stubbs in fifteen?"

"*À tout à l'heure!*" Lisa said, and hung up.

I smiled, started the car, and headed out of the parking lot.

CHAPTER 9

Song: I Saw It On Your Keyboard/Hellogoodbye
Quote: "If at first you don't succeed, try, try again.
Then quit. There's no point in being a damn fool
about it."—W. C. Fields

"So then," Nate said to me from my computer screen, "I said, 'You can threaten to take away my parking permit, that's fine, but I still have no information to give you.' And then I did my best Nicholson and told him that sometimes, pal, it's just better not to know."

"You didn't," I said, smiling. I was sitting on my bed, laptop on my lap, and I leaned back against my headboard. "Really?"

Nate was smiling, too, looking a little embarrassed. "I did," he said. "But it's okay. I don't think the headmaster is much of a *Chinatown* fan."

Nate and I hadn't been able to get together at lunch, or after school, or after dinner, so we had resorted to late-night iChatting.

"I can't believe they're getting this upset over the prank," I said, taking a sip of my CFDDP—that is, Caffeine-Free Diet Dr Pepper. I didn't touch the hard stuff after eleven.

"I know," Nate said, his smile fading. "I have the feeling that I'm on pretty thin ice these days."

"But you'll be fine," I said as confidently as I could, especially since I didn't like how worried he was looking. "Right?"

"Right," Nate said, giving me a small smile. "Here's hoping. How was your day?"

"Oh," I said lightly. I wasn't about to burden him with Kittson's demands or the Schuyler weirdness or the possibility that I might have tried on a cursed tiara. "It was fine. But I have a favor to ask you," I said, suddenly remembering the fairly dire music situation.

"Yes," Nate said immediately.

I smiled at him, feeling it take over my face. "I haven't even asked yet," I said.

"What, like I'm going to say no to you?" he said. "I don't see that happening."

"Anyway," I said, trying to stop smiling so wide. I could see myself in the small window that showed my side of the conversation in the upper left-hand corner of the screen, and it was a little ridiculous. "Here's the thing—"

"Yes," Nate said again, cutting me off.

"Stop it," I said, laughing. "Okay. So. The DJ—"

"Ah, the estimable DJ Tanner," he said, his smile widening. "What now?"

"Well, he's asking me for prom playlists so that he can get an idea of what to play. He's never been to a prom. He's just a sophomore." I wasn't entirely sure that Tanner would have gone to a prom even if he had been a senior, but I left that out for the moment.

"That's a quality DJ you've got there," Nate deadpanned.

"Well, he's what we could afford," I said. "Kittson spent the music budget on flash drives."

"What?" Nate asked, looking perplexed.

"Oh, you'll see on Saturday," I promised. "So anyway, since you've been to a prom . . ." I took a deep breath, trying to push past the thought of what he might have done after his prom with a girl named Melissa. "I wondered if you could make me a playlist of prom music? Just to give Tanner something to go off of?"

"Sure," Nate said easily. "I'll do it tonight and e-mail it to you."

"Thank you," I said, smiling at my boyfriend, feeling incredibly lucky. Though it would have been preferable to be with him in person—when there could have been kissing— I liked seeing him in his room, a tiny bit rumpled. I felt like Nate sometimes had his guard up, and it was nice to get a glimpse of him totally relaxed, in his own environment. "So, um," I said, trying to begin to broach the questions that had been haunting me. "About your prom last year. Was it . . . fun? Um, memorable?"

"Sure," Nate said with a shrug. "It was fine."

"You went with Melissa, right?" I asked. I was using

all my acting ability to try to say her name with as little weight as possible.

"Mad, you okay?" Nate said, leaning forward, looking concerned. So much for my acting skills. I hoped this didn't mean that the reviewer was onto something with the "adequate" comment.

"Fine!" I said brightly. "I was just trying to um . . . find out about your prom. We haven't really talked about it."

"We can if you want to, I guess," Nate said, leaning back in his computer chair.

"Okay," I said, trying to marshal my thoughts and decide how best to approach this. "So . . ."

Just then, my iChat dinged. I looked away from Nate and saw that I had an invitation from Kittson. Normally, I would have ignored this, but I was happy to have a moment to figure out what I wanted to say. "Can you hang on a sec?" I asked. "It's Kittson."

"Sure," Nate said. "I'll be here."

I minimized Nate and accepted Kittson's chat. "Hey," I said. But there was nobody looking back at me. I was staring at an empty—and very pink—bedroom. "Kittson?" I called.

"Here," she said, coming into view.

In the upper left-hand corner, I could see my jaw drop. Kittson's hair was up in a towel, and she was wearing a light blue mask that covered her entire face, except her eyes and lips. "Wow," I said, not sure what else to say. "You look really . . ."

"It's my pre-prom beauty regimen," Kittson said, as

111

though this should have been obvious. "I started doing this *months* ago. Anyway. How'd it go with the tiara?"

"Oh, fine," I said, looking down at my keyboard. It had gone fine, after all. The task just hadn't been completed. But, technically, she hadn't asked about that.

"Good," she said. "And the music?"

"I'm working on it," I said, glad to be able to tell the truth. "But actually, I'm chatting with Nate right now, so I don't have much time—"

"I'll wait," Kittson said.

"No," I said, "that wasn't what I meant. . . ." I wasn't about to rush to finish up a conversation with my boyfriend so that I could keep talking prom matters with Kittson. But she had disappeared from view again, and I sighed and clicked on the Nate conversation.

"Hey there," he said as I returned. "Everything okay?"

"Oh, the usual craziness," I said.

"You mean the ush craze?" he asked, teasing me.

"Right," I said, smiling at him. "Exactly." I took a deep breath and tried to start again. "So. Last year, your prom. Well, actually, after your prom. Your prom night . . ."

"Oh, that's right," Nate said. "You wanted to . . . Wait." He stopped. "Did you say my prom *night*?"

"Did I?" I asked, trying to stall. "Um . . . I don't know if that's what I meant. . . ."

"Then what did you mean?" Nate asked, looking genuinely confused.

I saw that while I'd been talking to Kittson, Nate had

changed location. He wasn't at his desk anymore. He seemed to be on his bed now; I could see a pillow in a blue case to his right. My heart began to beat a little bit faster. I was seeing Nate's *bed*. He was looking at me while he sat on his bed. I was practically in his bed with him. For some reason, this was all I could focus on. And it was making it harder for me to gather my thoughts. Or speak clearly. "Well," I said, wondering why I suddenly felt so warm, "I just . . . of the . . ."

Suddenly, Nate looked away from me for a moment. "Mad, can you hold that, uh, thought?" he asked. "I've got another chat."

"Sure," I said, glad that I could have a chance to collect myself. I was about to go back to the Kittson conversation when my iChat dinged again and I saw I had an invitation from Lisa.

"Hey," I said, accepting, as Lisa appeared on-screen. She was wearing her glasses, which she only did when there was no chance of being seen by anyone who wasn't Schuyler, Ruth, or me. Though it occurred to me that the Ruth part was probably no longer true.

"Alors," Lisa said, looking worried. *"OMD.* So I just spoke to Schuyler. . . ."

Nate's chat flashed again, and I looked down at it. "Lise, can you hold on a moment? I'm chatting with Nate."

"D'accord," Lisa said, waving one hand in the air. *"Je t'attends. . . ."*

"Be right back," I said. I clicked on Nate, who seemed a little more stressed than when I'd left him. "Hi," I said.

"Sorry about that," he said. "Melissa's having a bit of a meltdown. I'm trying to talk her off the ledge. Can you hang on a minute longer?"

I felt my stomach drop. *Melissa* was who he'd been talking to? "Oh, sure," I said as breezily as I could.

"Thanks," he said, and disappeared again.

I stared at the screen, shocked, as my chat dinged again, and I clicked it to go back to Lisa. "OMG," I said. "You'll never—"

"Where have you been?" I looked at the screen and saw that I'd accidentally pulled up the chat with Kittson—who I'd forgotten about completely. "I've been *waiting* here—"

"Oh. Sorry," I said. "I was just . . . give me one second." I clicked on Lisa's chat. "Sorry," I said. "That was Kittson, and she's being a—"

"I can imagine," Lisa said.

"Being a *what*?" Kittson snapped, and I saw that I'd accidentally brought up both chats. She folded her arms, and I saw that she was now wearing some sort of weird plastic mitts on her hands.

"Being an effective leader, as always," I said as quickly as possible. I turned to Lisa. "I'll be back in one second."

"Non!" I heard Lisa cry as I minimized her chat.

"What?" I said, going back to Kittson. But she wasn't saying anything. She was just staring offscreen, sullenly. "Kittson?" I asked. She continued to sulk, refusing to make eye contact with me. "Look," I said, a little more gently, "I'm sorry I forgot about you. . . ."

"Whatever," she said, looking a bit hurt. "I kind of wanted to talk to you about Glen, but never mind. You seem busy."

"Let's talk tomorrow," I said hurriedly, seeing that my other two chats were now flashing and I had an invitation for a new chat—this one from Schuyler. "At the prom meeting?"

"Fine," she said. "And please try to be on time for once!"

Before I could defend myself, she disappeared from view, and I accepted Schuyler's chat. "Hey, Shy," I said. "Can you hold on one second?" Schuyler, staring down at her keyboard, just nodded, and I minimized her chat.

I clicked back to Lisa. "Hey," I said. "So Shy just chatted me. But I'm chatting with Nate, and he's chatting with Melissa!"

Lisa leaned forward. "*Sex* Melissa?" she asked.

"We don't know for sure," I said. "Please don't call her that."

"But ex Melissa, right?" Lisa said, and I nodded. "*Zut alors*. Why is he chatting with his ex?"

"I don't know," I said, feeling incredibly stressed as I looked at the chats flashing at the bottom of my screen. I was beginning to realize that I wasn't really capable of this level of multitasking. "I mean, they're friends."

"*Bof*," Lisa said. "He doesn't need friends who are girls, who are single."

"We don't know she's single," I said, a little desperately. "Maybe she's in a very committed relationship."

"If she was, then she'd be talking to her boyfriend,

not her ex," she said knowingly. "Do you bring your problems to Justin?" I shook my head mutely, and Lisa nodded. "*Et voila.* Trust *moi.* I'll find out if she's single. I'm going to Friendverse Stalk her."

"Okay, I'll see what Nate says." I was hoping he would say Melissa's problems all revolved around her very long-term boyfriend. "But I should get back to him. And then see what's up with Shy. . . ."

"I don't know about Schuyler," Lisa said. She shook her head, looking worried again. "She was being *trop* weird with me. The way she was acting, it was kind of a . . ." She shrugged. "*Je ne sais quoi.* Just call me when you're off with her."

"Will do," I said. Then I closed Lisa's chat and brought up Nate's. "Hi," I said, feeling out of breath, even though all I'd been doing was talking and clicking.

"One more second?" he asked, looking apologetic.

"Sure," I said, "me too."

"BRB," he said, giving me a faint smile before disappearing again.

"Hey, Shy," I said when I'd brought up Schuyler's chat. She looked up at me from her keyboard, and I leaned closer to the screen. Schuyler looked terrible. Her face was red and blotchy, and her eyes were red, too, making it look like the color on my computer monitor was just a little bit off. "Are you okay?"

"I'm fine," Schuyler said, obviously lying. Her voice sounded strangled. "I just . . . well . . . wanted to tell you that you're a really good friend, Mad. You've been a great friend to me, and I appreciate it."

116

"Oh. Well, sure," I said, getting more worried by the second. "But what's going on with you?" I asked, racking my brain for what could be wrong. "Is it Connor?"

Schuyler let out a sob and looked away. "No," she said, her voice shaking. "Connor's wonderful. And so trusting, and honest . . ."

She was beginning to scare me now. "Shy, I'm worried about you," I said. "Lisa is, too. Maybe I should come over or something."

"No, no, I'm fine," she said. "I just wanted to say . . . thanks. And that I'm sorry. Look, I'll see you in school tomorrow. . . ."

"Shy, come on," I said. "Let's talk about this."

"There's nothing to talk about," Schuyler said, her voice still sounding choked. "I was just . . . I just wanted to tell you that your friendship . . . it's meant a lot to me. See you tomorrow."

Schuyler disappeared, leaving me staring at the screen. I was with Lisa—that had been *trop* weird. I thought about heading over to Shy's house, or at least seeing if I could get my parents' permission to head over there. But the last time I'd dropped by Schuyler's, the security guard who patrolled her private road had pulled me over for twenty minutes of questioning, and that had been in the middle of the afternoon.

I took a restorative sip of my CFDDP and clicked on Nate, who gave me a slightly weary smile. "Hi there," I said.

"Hey," he said. "So sorry about that."

"Is everything okay?" I asked. "Was Melissa having . . . um . . . boyfriend problems?"

"No," Nate said, then looked thoughtful. "You know, it's funny. She's not dating anyone, and hasn't dated anyone since we broke up. I don't get it. She's such a great girl."

I felt my stomach drop again, and took a deep breath. "Oh," I said, trying to sound as neutral as possible.

"Yeah," Nate said. "She's just kind of upset about the prom being canceled. I think she was looking forward to it."

"There's this website," I suggested. "Brian's been using it. It's called Save the Last Dance. It pairs up people who are looking for prom dates."

"I'll suggest it," Nate said, smiling, and I could see him writing the website name down. I was secretly hoping that Melissa would meet someone at a prom in Darien, or somewhere, and start dating that guy, and stop taking her problems to my boyfriend.

Nate looked up at me and I decided to try once more to find out what had happened with them. "You guys . . . I mean, you must have had a lot of fun last year," I said.

"Yeah," Nate said, without a great deal of enthusiasm. He looked away, as if picturing something else. I hoped that it wasn't Melissa, naked. "It was okay. Not . . . exactly what I'd been expecting."

I blinked at him, trying to figure out what that had meant. I was happy that he didn't seem to have had the best time at the prom with Melissa, but I didn't know how to ask him how—or if—sex had fit into the picture. "Oh," I said finally.

"Yeah," he said. He focused back on me and smiled. "But I'm really looking forward to Saturday."

Was that because he thought we were going to be having sex? I really, really needed to know but had no idea how to ask him. And if I was going to be honest, I was afraid of what his answer might be. "Me too," I said. It was the truth, despite the recent drama. After all, there was still going to be a prom. Nate in a tux. And we would slow dance, even if we didn't have a song. Yet. "So," I said. I took a breath. I hadn't known how to bring up this next topic without feeling like I was implying something, but I figured that I should just tell him. "You know, the after-party is at Dave's. And I was planning on staying over. Especially since . . . I just found out that my parents are going to be out of town all weekend."

"Oh, yeah?" Nate asked. "Are they having someone stay with you guys?"

"Nope," I said. "They're leaving us alone."

"Oh," Nate said.

"Yeah," I said. I looked at Nate, and he looked back at me, neither of us saying anything. It felt like suddenly we were on the edge of a precipice, and the slightest movement might send us over the edge. "So . . . I just wanted to tell you that."

"Right," Nate said. He looked at me intently, and without meaning to, I found that my eyes kept drifting back to his bed. "Well, I'm glad you did."

We looked at each other for a moment longer. Something seemed to be happening, even though I wasn't sure what it was.

Then he smiled, breaking our eye contact. "I'd better get cracking on your mix, my Mad," he said. "Otherwise, we're all going to be dancing to death metal on Saturday."

"Thank you," I said, smiling back at him, feeling that my heart was suddenly so full of something that it scared me a little.

"My pleasure," he said. "Talk to you tomorrow?"

"Definitely," I said. "Night."

"Good night," he said. He smiled at me again, then signed off, leaving me staring at my computer screen, trying to figure out what had just happened.

CHAPTER 10

Song: When I Fall/Barenaked Ladies
Quote:"Trust everybody, but cut the cards."—Finley
Peter Dunne

From: Schuyler
Date: 5/22, 12:35 P.M.
Hey, Mad. So I was just wondering. Do you still have
the crown? You probably brought it to the hotel already,
right?

To: Schuyler
Date: 5/22, 12:36 P.M.
Um, not yet. It's safe and sound in my car at the
moment—I no longer trust my locker ☺ Dropping it off
after school, want to come with?

From: Schuyler

Date: 5/22, 12:37 P.M.
Maybe. Are you going to gym today?

To: Schuyler
Date: 5/22, 12:37 P.M.
Unfortch. Are you?

To: Schuyler
Date: 5/22, 12:37 P.M.
Shy??

"And then she didn't respond to your text?" Lisa asked, eyes wide. We shoved our clothes and bags into the gym locker she, Schuyler, and I shared. Gym lockers were very hard to come by, given out in the beginning of the year through a lottery system. Lisa and Schuyler had each gotten one, but Schuyler could no longer remember where hers was, and at any rate, wanted to avoid it at all costs, since she was pretty sure she'd left a sandwich in there. And I had shared one with Ruth, until recently. So now the three of us squeezed our stuff into Lisa's. It was a little crowded, but it worked out. I slammed the door and leaned all my weight against it until I heard the lock catch. Then Lisa and I headed out of the locker room and toward the back gym.

"No response," I confirmed, shaking my head. "And why would she ask if I was going to gym? I'm always in gym these days." That, sadly, was the truth. I hadn't missed a single class since I found out that I'd dropped a letter grade in the tennis portion of the semester, probably due to the fact that I'd spent most of the time talking to my friends and no time at all playing tennis.

"Something's going on," Lisa said. "But we'll find out what. We'll have plenty of time to talk. We're playing badminton today, for *l'amour de Dieu*."

We walked through the empty, echoing gym and I could see most of our class waiting outside by the volleyball court, which meant that Lisa and I were a tad bit late. Which normally I wouldn't care about, but I wasn't about to have to repeat junior year because I failed *gym*. We hustled outside and tried to blend in with the class and look as though we'd been there from the beginning. Thankfully, Mrs. Bellus was talking to Coach Petersen, who taught boys' PE at the same time. I looked around for Schuyler, figuring that she'd just gotten changed more quickly than we had. But, thinking about it, I couldn't remember seeing any of her things in our locker. If she didn't hurry, she was going to be seriously late for class. Though, due to the fact that she actually could play tennis well, her grade was not at all in danger.

"All right," Mrs. Bellus called. "You girls will have a choice today. You can continue with the badminton practice that we began last week. Or you can do the climbing course with Coach Petersen's class."

I looked over at the rock climbing wall, where various boys were already harnessed in and rappelling up and down at what seemed to me to be highly unsafe speeds. I turned to Lisa. "Badminton?"

"Um, *oui*," she said firmly, and we took a step closer to each other. The class started breaking up, with most of the girls heading toward the badminton nets and only a couple walking over to the rock wall. Lisa looked around. "Okay, *where* is Schuyler?"

"No, no, no," Mrs. Bellus said, striding up with her clipboard, pointing at me and Lisa. "I'm splitting you two up. MacDonald, go do the ropes."

"But . . . um . . ." I tried to think quickly of some excuse that would get me out of rock climbing. Failing to come up with anything, I sighed and gave a small wave to Lisa.

"Good," Mrs. Bellus said as I started to walk away. "Go spot Miller."

My feet slowed as she said this. I looked ahead and saw Ruth standing by the wall. I glanced around to see if there was anyone else I could partner with—or at least get to join us and help this be less awkward. But everyone else was paired up. And I really didn't think I could protest again, unless I wanted to go to summer school for gym, which was just about the most humiliating thing that I could imagine.

I walked over to my former BFF, slowing my steps even more. Ruth was standing alone, hands in the pockets of her gym shorts, her white T-shirt ironed and neatly tucked in. Her dark blond hair was back in a perfect, bump-free ponytail. She wasn't wearing her glasses, and I wondered if she'd gotten contacts. There would have been a time, not that long ago, when I would have known. She gave me a small smile as I got closer.

124

I smiled back, trying to think rationally. I knew, logically, that Ruth and I weren't really friends anymore, and certainly not BFF. But there was nine years of habit that made it hard to remember this. My first instinct was always to run up to her and start talking. My first thought of her was always as my best friend.

"Hi," she said as I reached the spot by the wall where she was standing. There were three people climbing it—two boys and one of the girls from our class. There were also three people on the ground beneath them. I think they were meant to be spotting, but at the moment, all of them were texting. "You're doing the ropes?" she asked, sounding surprised.

"Not by choice," I said. "I was coerced into it."

"Ah," Ruth said. "Well, all the harnesses are being used right now, but as soon as one is free, we can take a turn."

"Great," I said, trying to sound as though this was a good thing. Silence fell and I looked down at the ground and bit my lip, hating this, hating how things had changed.

"So," I said after a moment. "Are you going to the prom?"

"I am," she said, nodding. "No date, though. Flying solo. And you—I think I heard you're going with Jonathan? I mean, Nate?"

"Yes," I said. "You got it." Silence fell again and I tried to think of something else to say. "Hey," I said, remembering, "you know what I found the other day? That picture of us dressed up as prom queens for Halloween. Remember that?"

Ruth smiled. "I do," she said. "I love that picture."

"We got a lot of candy that year," I said.

"And everyone thought we were princesses and we had to tell them we were *prom queens.* . . ."

"That's right," I laughed, remembering how the whole idea of the prom had seemed impossibly glamorous at the age of nine.

"So I guess you're going with Lisa and Dave and Schuyler and everyone?" Ruth asked, her smile beginning to fade.

"Yeah," I said. "We're all, um, sharing a limo."

"Got it," Ruth said. She looked up at the climbers. "Well, that sounds fun. I hope you all have a good time."

"Thanks," I said. "And you, too."

Ruth let out a short laugh, still looking at the rock wall. "Yeah," she said softly. "Sure."

"Next!" Coach Petersen yelled. "Next to climb!"

"You can go ahead," Ruth said. "I don't mind."

"It's really okay," I protested. Then I looked over and saw Mrs. Bellus watching me. I sighed and headed to the wall. The climber on the left jumped the last few feet to the ground, and the guy meant to be spotting him looked up disinterestedly before going back to his phone. The climber took off his helmet and turned around, and I saw to my surprise that it was Justin.

"Hey, Mad," he said, looking surprised to see me as well. I glanced over at Ruth, who hadn't moved from her spot and was studying the ground with great interest.

"Hey," I said. I should have remembered, of course, that Justin was in this PE class. Before we'd started going out, there had been a monthlong period when I'd used PE to simply admire his triceps from afar. Come to think of it, the D that Mrs. Bellus had threatened me with was actually starting to seem kind of generous.

"So how's it going?" he asked. "Haven't talked to you in a while."

"I know," I said with a nod, as though this had been bothering me as well. But since Justin and I hadn't spoken that much even when we'd been going out, I actually hadn't noticed the difference.

"It seems like everything's going well for you, right?" he asked. I nodded, a little unsure what he meant. "Good," he said. "That's great for you." After a moment of silence, he handed me the helmet and snapped himself out of the harness.

"Thanks," I said, taking the gear. As usual, it appeared that he'd put a little too much gel in his blond hair. Justin always looked like one of the Abercrombie guys who, for inexplicable reasons, were always running around shirtless with long pants on. But while I could see how the rest of the world—especially those who shopped at Abercrombie—might see him as cute, it was no longer a kind of cute that appealed to me at all. And now, looking at him up close, I could see that he seemed . . . dimmer, somehow. Not stupider—just a little less engaged or something. "Justin," I said, trying to catch his eye. "Is everything okay? I mean—"

"See you, Mad," he said as he walked away toward the main gym.

"Bye," I called after him. I watched him go, his shoulders rounded a little. I couldn't shake the feeling that there was something going on with him.

"Ready?" Coach Petersen boomed at me. Maybe it was partial deafness from too many years of blowing his whistle, but Coach Petersen was always several decibels louder than he needed to be. His pencil was poised over his own clipboard, and I took a moment to wonder what it was with gym teachers and this particular office supply item.

I hooked myself into the harness and buckled the straps. "Ready," I said.

Ruth stepped forward and picked up the belaying rope. "Ready," she said. I looked at her face, trying to read what she'd thought about the interaction that Justin and I had just had—but her expression seemed carefully blank.

"Okay," Coach Petersen practically shouted. "Now, the thing about climbing is that you're not doing it alone. You have to trust your equipment, but most of all, you have to trust your partner." He looked from Ruth to me. "You two trust each other?" he asked.

There was a very long silence. I looked at Ruth and saw that she was focused down on the rope, looping it over her wrist again and again.

"Ladies?" Coach Petersen asked again. "That wasn't a question for my health. When people don't trust each other, someone gets hurt."

I wasn't quite able to speak for a second. When that moment passed, I took a deep breath and looked up at him. "Got it," I said, as brightly as I was able. "We'll be careful."

"Good," Coach Petersen bellowed. "Up you go, then."

I glanced back at Ruth, who had just reached up to adjust her glasses—the way she always had done when she was thinking—only to drop her hand down when she must have realized they were no longer there.

"Okay," I said, and Ruth nodded. I looked up at the wall, which appeared very high from the ground. There were fake rocks and ledges planted all up and down its surface, to use as foot- and handholds. Toward the bottom, they were spaced pretty close together, in intuitive spots. As you got up higher, though, they became fewer and farther apart, which seemed to me exactly the opposite of how it should go.

I stepped up onto the first foothold and soon was halfway up the wall, finding my rhythm, moving hand over foot fairly easily. But as I got almost to the top, I made the mistake of looking down. All of a sudden, I saw just how high I really was. The world seemed to spin and wobble. I clutched more tightly to the fake rock I was holding, closed my eyes, and waited for the vertigo to pass.

"Maddie?" I heard Ruth call from below me. "You okay?"

I nodded, still not opening my eyes. "Fine," I called down to her. "I just need a second."

"Okay," she called up to me, sounding worried. "Well, I'm right here, in case . . . in case you need me."

"Thanks," I called back, hoping that I wouldn't have

to test that. Because as I'd learned, there was a distinct possibility that she wasn't going to be there when I needed her most. I took a breath and opened my eyes. The world was no longer swirling around. "I'm okay," I called down. I looked and saw that I'd climbed higher than I'd realized; I was close enough to the top of the wall that I could see over it. I moved up one handhold—the one I'd been gripping had gotten slippery—and looked out over the top of the wall. I could see the whole back side of the school from up there, and had a lovely view of the junior parking lot.

As I prepared to climb down, a movement in the parking lot caught my eye. It was a girl, hustling back from a row of cars, her long red hair streaming behind her. Was that Schuyler? What was she doing in the parking lot when she was supposed to be in gym class? I squinted and leaned forward to try to see more clearly, but as I did so, I lost my handhold. I grabbed for the next one I could, and hoisted myself back up, feeling my heart pound. But as I looked across the parking lot again, it was totally empty, as though no one had been there at all.

CHAPTER 11

Song: Bankruptcy/Call Me Kevin
Quote: "Truth makes many appeals, not the least of which is its power to shock."—Jules Renard

 KitKat Don't forget to buy your prom tickets! On sale in the student center!

 mad_mac → Shy Time Shy, where are you? Why were you AWOL from gym? R u ok?

 Dave Gold → mad_mac Hey, Mad, I want to talk to you about something.

 mad_mac → Dave Gold Sure. Shoot.

 Dave Gold → mad_mac No, um, I mean in private. I'll call you later?

mad_mac → Dave Gold Sure! Whenevs!

 La Lisse → mad_mac Um. WHAT?!?!

 mad_mac → La Lisse IDK!

 Jimmy+Liz → mad_mac Mad, what did you do? I heard over the loudspeaker that Dr. Trent wants to see you in his office! (this is liz)

 mad_mac → Jimmy+Liz NO IDEA. But I guess this means I'm going to be late to English. Jimmy, tell the Toupee?

 Jimmy+Liz → mad_mac Affirmative, MacDonald. (this is jimmy)

 Glen → mad_mac Speak truth to power, Mad! Damn the Man!

 Glen THIS ACCOUNT HAS BEEN TEMPORARILY DISABLED

"Dr. Trent will be with you in a moment," Stephanie, Dr. Trent's secretary, said to me from behind her desk.

"Great," I said, trying to find a comfortable position on the bench outside the office, wondering what on earth I was doing there. I'd been heading to English, the last class of the day, trying to speedwalk and skim my copy of *GoldenEye* at the same time, when an announcement had come over the loudspeaker that I was wanted in Dr. Trent's office. I had no idea why, and just hoped that he would write me a pass back to English. I wasn't about to get detention *again*, just because Dr. Trent wanted to talk to me about something.

I figured that it was just another prom thing—though why he wasn't talking to Kittson about it, I had no idea. I looked down at the bench, to see if Glen had tagged it recently—or carved any of the tiny bench portraits that had become his specialty—but it was free of any graffiti. I wondered if it had recently been replaced.

The door to Dr. Trent's office swung open, and he stepped out and frowned at me. "Miss MacDonald, go wait in my office," he said, his tone very sharp.

I blinked at him, surprised. He had never spoken to me like that—like I was actually in trouble for something. But the tone was familiar, and I realized after a moment that it was how he sounded when he spoke to Turtell.

I stood and picked up my bag. As I walked past her desk, Stephanie shot me a sympathetic smile, which made me start to get worried. Was I in trouble? Once inside Dr.

Trent's office, I took the seat across from his desk and, trying to calm myself down, looked at the collection of framed inspirational posters that covered the walls.

"Well. Madison." Dr. Trent walked into the room and closed the door behind him. He sat behind his desk, steepled his fingers, and looked over his glasses at me in silence.

I didn't say anything. I had learned from Turtell that this was one of Dr. Trent's techniques—he would remain silent to get you to start talking out of nervousness, which increased the chances that you'd accidentally say something to incriminate yourself. But I hadn't done anything wrong, as far as I knew, so I just sat there silently and looked back at him.

Dr. Trent sighed, pulled a file from his drawer, placed it on the desk, and drummed his fingers on it. I assumed it was mine, though I couldn't see my name. While it wasn't as large as Turtell's—which resembled the final *Harry Potter*—it seemed considerably thicker than it had been just a few months earlier. "Do you know what this is?" Dr. Trent asked.

"My file?" I asked, glad that he had broken the silence first.

"Indeed." He stopped drumming his fingers and rested his hand on it.

"Am I in trouble?" I blurted out, unable to stop myself. This whole thing had the feeling of an interrogation about it, and I could no longer believe that he'd called me out of class to tell me what a great job Kittson was doing organizing the prom.

He raised his eyebrows at me. "Why? Have you done something that would get you in trouble?"

"No," I said firmly. "I was just wondering why I'm here. I'm missing class, after all, so I figured it must have been pretty important."

"Yes," Dr. Trent said, spinning his chair around to face his computer. It was angled so that I couldn't see the monitor. "You're currently missing English with Mr. Underwood."

"That's right," I said, figuring that he was looking at my schedule.

"Or as you refer to him, the Toupee?" Dr. Trent turned back from his computer and raised his eyebrows at me again.

"Um," I said, thrown. "I'm not sure what you mean. . . ." Jimmy and I called Mr. Underwood that, but it was really just a private joke between us. I was starting to get a horrible suspicion. I leaned forward slightly, and as I did so, caught a glimpse of Dr. Trent's monitor. I saw just enough to see the background of my Q page, with all my updates, displayed on his computer. I sat back, shocked.

"Don't you?" Dr. Trent asked. "You know, Madison, that I have access to all the Putnam High students' Status Q pages." He put air quotes around *Status Q*, for some reason. "And I have to say, yours has given me pause recently."

"I didn't . . ." I said haltingly. I was still trying to process this. Dr. Trent was reading our updates? Seriously? Maybe that was how he'd found out I'd been

135

in detention. So Turtell had been *right.* "I mean, I know you have access, but I didn't think you checked them. I thought you might have more, um, pressing matters to attend to."

"I do," Dr. Trent said shortly. "And of course I don't check everyone's. Just those of the students who have . . . come to my attention."

"And that's me?" I asked, stunned.

"Of course," he said. "Especially after . . . the incidents of a few months ago."

"Oh," I said, relieved. Suddenly, this all made sense. "You mean you're making sure nobody hacks me again? I appreciate that, but you don't have to check my page. I'd let you know if anything happened."

"That is not my concern," Dr. Trent said, flipping open my file. "Miss MacDonald, several people have been . . . unhappy with the way the incidents of this spring were handled."

"Okay," I said slowly, not sure what that had to do with me. After all, he was the one who had handled them. But my relief was beginning to ebb.

"A student—an honor student, at that—was expelled because of your actions. Another exemplary student was suspended. . . ."

"Wait a minute," I said. "What do you mean *my* actions? Dell was the one who hacked me. And he was the one who had the locker-combination database, and was stealing from people. He admitted it!"

"He admitted it," Dr. Trent said tightly, "when you

were recording him without his knowledge or consent. And some would call that entrapment."

I blinked, not quite able to believe that this was happening. "But he still did it," I said. "He damaged a lot of things in my life. And in other people's . . ."

"Nevertheless," Dr. Trent said, "the manner in which you obtained this information was spurious at best, and does not take into account any personal agenda you might have had."

"What are you saying?" I asked, stunned. I didn't know what had changed in the past few months. Shouldn't this conversation have occurred before Dell was expelled and Ruth was suspended? A terrible thought hit me. "Is Dell—I mean, Frank—coming back to school?"

"No," Dr. Trent said, frowning at me. "We have a zero-tolerance policy here. Once a student has been expelled, they cannot be readmitted to Putnam High School. And the decision to expel him ultimately did not fall to me, but to the headmistress. But his parents have put in a petition to have his record expunged."

"You mean they're trying to get Dell's record cleared?" I asked, my disbelief turning to anger. "He'll just get *away* with it?"

"He was expelled, Madison," Dr. Trent said. "I'd say that's punishment enough, wouldn't you?"

I just stared across the desk at him. It seemed like the small justice I'd gotten was being taken away from me. But it also seemed like Dr. Trent was now blaming me for the fact that I got hacked and ended up losing my best friend in the process. The poster right behind Dr. Trent's head caught my eye. It read *Dedication: Keep trying until you just can't try anymore . . . then try a little harder!* and featured a weary-looking eagle. Dr. Trent really did have the worst, least inspiring inspirational posters ever.

"But to the point," Dr. Trent said, steepling his fingers again, "your updates have been troubling me of late."

"Oh?" I asked, struggling to keep my voice level. It did bother me that Dr. Trent had been reading my updates. But I couldn't think of anything I'd said in them— besides insulting Mr. Underwood—that he might have objected to.

"Yes," he said. "For example . . . it seems as though Miss Pearson gave you the Hayes crown. And then you sent out a status update—in a public forum—that it was in your possession."

Oh. That. "Yes," I said carefully, thinking about the crown, currently in the trunk of my car in the junior parking lot.

"And yet, when I contacted the Putnam Hyatt this morning, they had no record of it being dropped off yesterday, when it was expected."

"The thing is," I said, trying to stall in the midst of my rising panic, "as you know, I'm involved in many different activities, the better to have a well-rounded application, and yesterday was the strike of the *Dane* set. And part of my responsibility as a member of the Thespians is—"

"Madison," Dr. Trent interrupted me. "You're saying that you still have the Hayes crown?"

"Well," I said. I tried to think of any other option, but then gave up and decided to tell the truth. "Yes. But I can assure you that it is very, very safe."

Dr. Trent massaged his temples. "Part of the bequest of the crown has always involved letting the students take possession of it so they might learn to manage responsibility. I have never agreed with the philosophy, but there it is. But I am not happy that the responsibility has passed from the chairperson to you, and also not happy that you have shirked this responsibility."

"I didn't shirk it," I protested. "I just didn't have time. . . ."

"Take it to the Hyatt immediately after school," Dr. Trent said. "And I will hold you personally responsible if it is not delivered safe and sound. Should something happen to the crown, I will consider it destruction of school property, an offense that carries severe penalties. Do we understand each other?"

I looked across the desk at Dr. Trent, who was glaring at me. I suddenly got an inkling to why Turtell was always defacing Dr. Trent's bench. Something had clearly shifted. Whatever the reason, Dr. Trent no longer saw me as the responsible student I'd been—at least in his eyes—for the past three years. Somehow, I'd crossed over into the troublemaker category with Turtell, and I had a feeling there was no coming back from it.

Dr. Trent didn't like me.

I didn't like him, either, but that was beside the point.

He'd basically told me that if I did anything to give him the opportunity, he would punish me. It was a position I'd never been in before. And I didn't like it. "Yes," I said after a moment.

"Yes what?" Dr. Trent asked.

I stared at him, figuring that he couldn't be serious. There was a piece of me that kept expecting this to turn out to be a big joke. But his expression was stony. "Yes. We understand each other," I finally said.

"Good," Dr. Trent said, standing, crossing to the door, and opening it for me. "Stephanie will write you a late pass. Good afternoon, Miss MacDonald."

I picked up my bag and stepped through the door he was holding open. It closed immediately behind me, and I turned to Stephanie. "So, um," I said. I was feeling shaken by the whole interaction. It was a lot to process—the Dell bombshell, the information that Dr. Trent was reading my status updates, that he knew about the crown, and the fact that I'd suddenly become persona non grata to someone who could potentially do a lot to influence my future. "I guess I need a pass. . . ."

"Here, hon," Stephanie said, sliding one across her desk at me. She looked at Dr. Trent's closed door, and for a moment I thought she was going to say something, but then she just shook her head. "I signed you out for the whole period. Thought you might need a moment."

"Thank you," I murmured. I was incredibly glad that I wouldn't have to return to class and discuss James Bond's irresistible attraction to strangely named foreign women.

"Take care," she called after me as I left the office and headed up toward the student center. My thoughts were spinning, but the one thing that I couldn't stop turning over in my mind was the Dell situation. Because it seemed like he might not suffer any consequences for his actions, in the long run. And that I might actually get in trouble because he'd done his best to wreck my life.

As I reached the student center, I looked around for Schuyler—I knew she had an open this period. But she was nowhere to be seen. I checked the time on my phone and realized that I had twenty minutes before class ended. I decided to beat the rush out of the junior parking lot and just take the crown over to the Hyatt now. That way, I could get Dr. Trent off my back for one thing at least, and I could stop worrying about it.

I walked out to the junior parking lot and headed toward Judy. I had just reached in my bag for my keys when a movement ahead of me caught my eye. I looked up and saw Schuyler, walking very quickly across the parking lot, her expression determined. "Schuyler!" I called, glad to finally have the chance to see what was going on with her. But she didn't appear to hear me, because she just kept walking. I followed after her, walking more quickly to try and catch up. "Shy!" I called, a little louder this time. But Schuyler, with her mile-long legs, was making very good time and must have been out of earshot.

For some reason, she seemed to be heading out of the junior parking lot and toward the empty lacrosse field. I was totally confused by this, and had no idea why Schuyler would choose to spend an open there. Unless she and Connor were meeting for an al fresco makeout session. As this thought occurred to me, I slowed down a little bit—also, the speed-walking was giving me a stitch in my side—but kept following her.

Schuyler was now cutting directly across the field, where I could see that someone—definitely not Connor—was standing. I squinted, and saw that the person on the field was wearing high heels and a skirt—and it looked like she had blunt-cut bangs. As I got closer, the person came into focus. It was Isabel Ryan. She was standing in the center of the field, arms crossed, watching Schuyler with a smile on her face.

As I hustled to catch up, I saw Schuyler reach Isabel. The two of them were talking, though I wasn't close enough to hear what they were saying. But then Schuyler nodded, reached into her bag, and pulled something out. She held it for a moment, and I saw that it was a dark blue box. It looked like a jewelry box. A jewelry box that I recognized . . .

"Oh my God," I said aloud as I realized that it was the box with the Hayes crown in it. I had no idea how Schuyler had gotten it, but I knew that I had to get it back. Immediately. I broke into a run. "Shy!" I yelled.

Schuyler didn't seem to hear me. She opened the box and held it out to Isabel, who peered inside and nodded. And then as I watched, horrified, Isabel took the crown out of the box and held it up. "Schuyler!" I yelled, continuing to run toward her. *"NO!"*

Isabel held the crown with both hands and gave Schuyler a smile. Then she turned and walked off the field with the crown, toward a black SUV. "Schuyler!" I yelled again, out of breath. While I watched, not close enough to stop anyone, Isabel got into the passenger side of the SUV. It sped away, off school property, as her door was still closing. Realizing that I wasn't going to catch the car, I kept running toward Schuyler, who was sitting on the ground with the empty box.

As I reached her, I saw that she was sobbing, her face buried in her hands. "Oh my God, Schuyler," I gasped, looking from her to the dust the SUV had left in its wake, feeling like I was about to start crying myself. "What did you do?"

CHAPTER 12

Song: Tick, Tick, Boom/Lenin and McCarthy
Quote: "DON'T PANIC." — Douglas Adams

"I'm so . . . so . . . sorry," Schuyler sobbed ten minutes later. She had said very little else, but had finally stopped crying quite so hard and was now occasionally able to get words out. "I'm so sorry, Mad. . . . I just . . ." She shook her head and broke down into sobs again.

I was sitting next to Schuyler on the lacrosse field, one hand resting on the pulse in my throat, wondering if I was going into cardiac arrest, and if so, whether I would know when it happened. "Let me understand this," I said, feeling very much like I was on the verge of having my very first panic attack. "You gave the Hayes crown to Isabel Ryan. The *Hayes* crown. You just *gave* it to her."

"I had to," Schuyler said, taking a big, hiccupping breath. "You don't understand, Mad. . . ."

"No, I don't understand!" I yelled, and Schuyler's face crumpled and she started crying full force again. I made myself take a deep breath, both so I wouldn't keep

144

yelling at Schuyler, and to try and slow my pulse down a little. "Explain it to me," I said more quietly.

"She . . ." Schuyler hiccupped. "After we saw her at the Hyatt, she got in touch with me. She sent me a message on Friendverse yesterday, telling me that I had to get the Hayes crown and give it to her."

"Or *what*?" I asked, trying not to scream. "Why didn't you say no? Why would you do that?"

"Because she was going to tell everyone," Schuyler said, looking at me, her lower lip trembling furiously. Her voice dropped to a hoarse whisper. "She said that if I didn't get the crown to her, she was going to tell everyone what happened at Choate."

"And what was that?" I asked. I was still furious— and panicked—but there was a piece of me that was glad to get the answer to a three-year mystery.

Schuyler closed her eyes. "I *can't*. . . ." she said.

"Schuyler," I said, keeping my voice as calm as possible, "you have to tell me. It's time."

Schuyler took a shaky breath. "Okay," she said after a moment, in a small voice. She started ripping up the neatly mown grass in handfuls. "I never wanted to tell you guys," she murmured. "Because I knew as soon as I did, you wouldn't be my friends anymore. But . . . I guess that's going to happen now anyway." Schuyler wiped her hand across her face, which was blotchy and puffy, and now had a few blades of grass stuck to it. She was still crying, but not as hard now. Now the tears were just continually, steadily falling.

"It was the first semester of my freshman year, in

November. And Isabel was my roommate. And we weren't exactly getting along, but I knew we were both really having trouble with geometry. And you don't know what boarding school is like, Mad. People go crazy about their grades, and Isabel kept telling me that if she didn't get a good grade on the midterm, it would affect her entire transcript, and entire future. . . ." Schuyler took another hiccupy breath. "So I stole a copy of the answer key from my teacher, and I made a copy for me and I gave a copy to Isabel. I thought it might make things easier between us."

"You were going to cheat?" I asked, stunned, since this was so out of character for her.

Schuyler winced and nodded. "But I didn't," she said, a little desperately. "I swear. I couldn't—it just didn't seem right. And the day before the midterm, I went to my teacher and I told him that I had been planning on cheating."

"So if you confessed, what's the problem?" I asked.

"He wanted to know who else had a copy of the answers. He promised me that nobody would get in trouble. So I told him about Isabel." Schuyler sounded weary. "So I got detention for a month. And an F on the midterm. But Isabel was expelled." Schuyler closed her eyes, the tears still flowing.

"But you just made a mistake," I said. "You didn't think she'd get in trouble."

Schuyler shook her head. "But nobody believed that. *Nobody*. Isabel thought I'd done the whole thing to set her up. And as she was moving out, Isabel told me how this was going to affect her whole future—how she'd have to go to *public school*. How she'd never be able to get into a good college now. And she told me that she'd get me back for this, if it was the last thing she did."

"Oh, Shy," I murmured. I was still furious with her, but she looked so wretched, I also wanted to give her a hug.

"So the hazing started pretty much immediately after that," Schuyler said, her voice hollow. "It got so bad that by the time Christmas came along, I told my father I wasn't ever going back. And I guess he believed me, because he let me move home and go to Putnam." She looked miserable but somehow resigned to it. "I know you don't believe me," she said. "And I know you're not going to be my friend anymore."

"Schuyler," I said, staring at her. "Why didn't you tell us earlier?"

"Because," she said with a sigh, "because you would have stopped being my friend. When I came here and met you and Lisa . . . and Ruth . . . it was like a miracle or something. And I didn't want to do anything that would ruin it."

"I don't care," I said. "Seriously," I added as Schuyler started to shake her head. "You didn't do anything wrong. You just made a mistake. You were trying to do something right."

Schuyler blinked at me. "You mean you believe me? Really?" she asked, looking like she was afraid to trust this. "I mean, really?"

"Really," I said firmly. "I believe you. And also, I don't

care. And I'll bet you anything Lisa won't care, either."

"That's . . . that's amazing," Schuyler murmured. "I wish I'd known that, because I . . ." Some realization seemed to be dawning. "Because then I wouldn't have done this," she said slowly. A horrified expression came over her face. "OMG, what have I done?"

"You gave the Hayes crown to Isabel because she blackmailed you," I said. My heart was still doing funny things whenever I thought about what Schuyler had done. But maybe if I said it out loud enough, I might come to accept it as a reality.

"Isabel said she'd get back at me," Schuyler said with a short laugh. "And I guess she just did. Because now she's just gotten me to wreck my life here at Putnam. Because now I've ruined everything all over again. I mean, you guys are never going to be my friends after this."

I thought about it. Schuyler had stolen the Hayes crown and given it away. It was bad. It was very, very, very, very, *very* bad. But I didn't think the situation was going to get better by never speaking to her again. I couldn't lose another friend. And I didn't want to. Schuyler had done something incredibly stupid, but that didn't change the fact that she was one of my best friends and always would be. "Shy," I said. I took a breath. "Of course we're still friends after this."

Schuyler looked afraid to believe it. "We can't be," she said. "Not after . . . after what I did."

"Oh, I'm still mad about it," I assured her. "And, you know, possibly going into cardiac arrest." I wiggled the fingers of my left hand, making sure they weren't going numb. "But . . . I mean . . ." I took a breath, feeling on the verge of tears myself. At this rate, the two of us were going to get dehydrated. "I can't lose you, too," I said a little thickly.

Schuyler reached over and gave me a hug, and I hugged back. When we broke apart, a thought struck me. "How did you even get the crown?" I asked.

Schuyler, looking ashamed, reached into her bag and handed me my car keys. "Gym locker," she said. "I'm so sorry, Mad. I'm so, so, so, so sorry. I'm so, so—"

"I got it. It's okay. I mean, it's *not*," I said. "But you don't have to keep saying it." I stared down at the keys in my hand, trying to think.

"So, um," Schuyler said, wiping her eyes and looking at me. "What do we do now?"

CHAPTER 13

Song: Spinning/Jack's Mannequin
Quote: "Implacable fate sat waiting just over the horizon." — Tove Jansson

"This isn't going to work," Schuyler whispered to me as we entered the lobby of the Hyatt.

"Of course it is," I said, trying to sound much more confident than I actually felt. "Also, we don't have any other ideas."

"But what if they check inside?" Schuyler hissed as we walked across the plush carpeting.

"I don't know," I whispered back. "Maybe they won't."

"But what if they do?" she asked. She pulled me over to a huge white marble pillar, and we stood behind it. "Listen, Mad," she said, looking determined, "I think we should go back to my plan."

I rolled my eyes and shook my head. On the drive to the hotel, Schuyler had told me her plan for dealing with the aftermath of giving away the crown. She had clearly put a lot of thought into it. She was going to confess everything, take the blame on herself, leave town, and get her father to enroll her in the Swiss boarding school that her stepsister, Peyton, had just been kicked out of. It was pretty much the worst plan I had ever heard.

"Your plan involves you moving to Switzerland," I said. "We're not doing your plan. And anyway, it wouldn't help matters. Dr. Trent is going to hold me personally responsible if anything happens to the crown."

"You don't know that," Schuyler said.

"Yes, I do," I said. "He told me an hour ago. So this is our only plan for the moment." I took the jewelry box out of my bag, flipped open the lid, and we both peered inside. Sitting on the dark blue velvet was a plastic pearlescent pink Hello Kitty crown, which, at the top, featured a small picture of Hello Kitty wearing a tiara. We'd purchased it at Small Rascals—they'd had to change their name after they got sued—on the way to the hotel.

"But what's going to happen on prom night?" Schuyler asked. "I mean, this doesn't look anything like the Hayes crown."

"I know that," I said, closing the lid. "This is just a placeholder. Until we figure this all out. But Dr. Trent is going to know that something is wrong if I don't bring the crown this afternoon."

"Okay," Schuyler said. She took a deep breath and held out her hand. "This is all my fault, Mad. I'll do it."

I shook my head. While I appreciated the gesture, I knew I had to try to get the box into the concierge's possession without raising any suspicion. "Just come with me," I said, and Schuyler nodded, looking hugely relieved.

We stepped out from behind the pillar and crossed the lobby, Schuyler a step or two behind me. The lobby was more crowded than it had been when we'd been there in the early morning. There were people sitting in the uncomfortable armchairs, and a woman in a long skirt playing a harp in the corner. The desk was at the back of the lobby, and it seemed it had been designed to be intimidating. It was long and wooden and polished to a gleaming surface, with a fancy Putnam Hyatt crest behind it.

I took a breath and walked the last few feet to the desk, behind which a tall, thin man was standing, talking on the phone. There was a shorter woman at the other end of the desk, typing rapidly on a computer, checking in a harried-looking businessman. As I got closer, without looking at me, the tall man raised one finger in my direction, to indicate that I was to wait.

I let out a shaky breath, trying not to panic, and trying not to look like I was trying not to panic. I had hoped that I would be able to get the jewelry box to the concierge right away. With every second that passed, I was getting more and more nervous, and feeling more and more like we were never going to get away with this. Trying to calm my thoughts, I looked ahead of me and saw that behind the desk there was an inlaid door. It matched the wood of the wall behind the desk perfectly; I only noticed it because it was slightly ajar. There seemed to be a small room behind the door. I leaned to the side, trying to get a better view, when the thin man's volume increased, bringing my attention back to him.

"D'accord," he said in a flawless French accent. *"Très bien, Monsieur Fabien. À bientôt!"* He hung up and started typing rapidly on a computer. "May I remind you," he said in a clipped voice, addressing the woman at the other end of the counter. Now that he was speaking English, it was with a frosty British accent that put Mark's to shame. "I am not accustomed to dealing with the routine matters that you should be handling. I can't be the *only* person on staff who speaks French."

"But, um, you are," the woman said, sounding terrified. "Since you fired Dominique, that is."

"Then hire someone else," he said, still not looking up from his computer screen. "An intern. I don't care. Yes?"

This last statement was directed to me. Startled, I tried to get my bearings. "Oh. Hello," I stammered. "I'm looking for the concierge?"

"And found him," the man said with a tight smile. His voice was more pleasant now, but falsely so. It was somehow more frightening than when he had been yelling. He pointed to a gold name tag on his suit that I hadn't noticed before. *Mr. Patrick,* it read, *Head Concierge.*

"Oh," I said. "Oh, good. Well. Okay. So we . . ." Here I turned to indicate Schuyler as well. Despite having three inches on me, she had somehow managed to make herself smaller, and was hiding behind me.

"Hi," Schuyler said in a whisper, poking her head out and then disappearing again.

"We're from Putnam High School, and we're supposed to drop off our tiara with the concierge."

"Are you . . ." Mr. Patrick typed something into his computer and then looked up at me. "Madison MacDonald?" he asked.

I swallowed hard. "Yes."

"I've just heard from your headmaster," he said.

"Assistant," I said before I could stop myself.

Mr. Patrick looked at the computer again and then back up at me. "Yes," he said. "Quite. He wanted me to contact him as soon as the item was delivered. I understand it was supposed to be here yesterday."

"Yes," I said, feeling myself beginning to sweat. "But there was . . . an unexpected delay."

"Naturally," he said with another small, completely humorless smile. "Well then?" He reached out his hand for the jewelry box, and trying to look like there was nothing at all unusual about the contents, I handed it to him. Behind me, I heard Schuyler let out a small whimper that I hoped was covered by the harp. "So," Mr. Patrick said, resting his hand on top of the case, "I am going to take this item into the temporary possession of the Putnam Hyatt, where it will be secured in our house safe. At ten thirty P.M. this Saturday, I will return said contents back to the person who dropped them off—in this case, you. Does that sound acceptable?"

"Sure," I said, hoping he wouldn't notice that my hands had started shaking. I clasped them behind my back. "But, um, why ten thirty?"

"I have here that it was at the request of your headmaster," he said, looking at the screen.

"Assistant," Schuyler piped up from behind me.

"Yes," Mr. Patrick said. "That's right. It seemed that he was worried about security. Your crowning is scheduled to take place at ten thirty-five, so I am under instructions to release it no more than five minutes prior to that."

"Ah," I said, trying not to think about how Dr. Trent had managed to squelch any plan I might have been starting to come up with. Mr. Patrick started to open the lid, and I began speaking as quickly as I could, to distract him. "I see. Quite. Yes. And I understand that there's another prom happening here the same night? Um . . . Hartfield High's prom?"

"Yes," he said, lowering the lid. "You're correct. Though apparently, they do not have the same sort of treasure you do, as there has been no request from them to use our safe. If I may . . ." he said, beginning to lift the lid again. "I've heard *such* things about this crown. . . ." He raised the lid and I closed my eyes, just wanting the fallout to be over as quickly as possible.

"Mr. Patrick? Sorry to bother you again." I opened my eyes. It was the girl at the other end of the counter, cowering behind her computer. Mr. Patrick lowered the lid and turned to glare at her. "Mr. Fabian is on the phone again, and I can't seem to . . ."

"Fine," he snapped. He motioned her over. "Lock this in the safe. It is not to be removed until ten thirty on Saturday. Can you handle that?" She nodded, and he moved down to where she had been standing, picked up a phone, and began speaking in French again.

The woman picked up the jewelry box without opening it and walked through the door behind the desk. A moment later, she returned, empty-handed. "You should be all set," she said. "Was there anything else?"

"No, no," I said quickly, incredibly relieved. "Thank you so much for your help. We'll be going now." I turned, grabbed Schuyler's arm, and we hustled out of the lobby. I wasn't even paying attention to where we were going; I just knew that we needed to get out of there ASAP.

I pulled Schuyler out the first exit I saw, and we'd been walking for a few moments before I realized that I'd taken us down the World's Longest Corridor. We walked a few more feet; then we both collapsed onto the first of the resting benches.

"Oh my God," Schuyler said.

"I know," I agreed. We sat in silence, and I tried to think. All I'd been focusing on was getting a temporary tiara into the Hyatt so that Dr. Trent wouldn't be suspicious. But I had no idea what to do now. Somehow, I had to get the real tiara back from Isabel. And then get the real tiara into the safe. Which was locked.

"You know, I think Switzerland is supposed to be nice," Schuyler said after a moment. "They have chocolate there. And cuckoo clocks."

"You're not going to Switzerland," I said. "Let's just think a minute." I rested my head in my hands and tried, but my brain felt worn-out, like it had been through far too much today to be expected to come up with things like plans.

"I'm just saying, this is not the way to handle things!"

I heard a familiar-sounding voice say. I looked up and saw, to my surprise, Dave and Lisa coming down the Endless Hallway toward us. Schuyler looked over as well, then turned back to me, eyebrows raised. I shrugged. I had no idea what Dave and Lisa were doing there.

"And all I'm saying is that we need to be able to talk about this like . . . Oh. Hi." Dave, spotting Schuyler and me, stopped speaking midsentence. He and Lisa seemed equally surprised to see us. "What are you two doing here?"

"Did you ask her to meet you here?" Lisa asked Dave, looking furious.

"Who?" Schuyler asked, looking perplexed. "Me? Because no."

"Madison," Lisa said, practically spitting out my name.

I blinked at her. Too much of what had gone wrong today had been at least partially my fault. But my exhausted brain could not begin to fathom what I had done to Lisa. "Wait," I said. "What?"

"Oh, I just thought," Lisa said, "since you and David are having such big *conversations* these days . . ."

I looked at Dave, frowning. It occurred to me that Lisa was truly angry to a degree I'd never seen her before. Not only was she full-naming Dave, she hadn't yet spoken a word of French. "I don't understand," I finally said.

"Lisa," Dave said coldly, and suddenly I could see that he was just as angry with her as she was with him, "is apparently mad about the conversation we had at Putnam Pizza."

"What conversation?" Schuyler asked.

"Exactly," Lisa glowered.

"Wait, what conversation?" I asked, trying to think back. I'd talked with Dave at Putnam Pizza on . . . Monday. Monday felt like three years ago. "Oh," I said, remembering. I'd told him about the Nate misunderstanding. And then he'd gotten upset about him and Lisa. . . . It started to dawn on me that I probably should have mentioned that part of the conversation to Lisa. But it had been completely eclipsed in my mind by Brian's Melissa bombshell. "That."

"Yeah," Lisa said, glaring at me. "Ring a bell now?"

"Lisa, I'm really sorry—" I started.

"What conversation?" Schuyler interrupted.

Dave squinted at her. "Have you been crying?"

"The conversation," Lisa said to me, "that you failed to mention to me for *three days*. The one where you talked to Dave about how you're going to sleep with Nate on prom night—"

"You *are*?" Schuyler asked, turning to me, shocked.

"Wait a second," I said quickly. "I never said I was going to sleep with him—"

"And all I said," Dave interjected, matching Lisa's rising volume, "was that Madison has been going out with Nate for, like, a second —"

"Two months," I amended quickly.

"While we've been going out for a year. And that your insistence on waiting until Bastille Day is—"

"So what are you saying?" Lisa asked, her voice getting a little trembly. "That you're no longer willing to wait, just because *Madison* is going to sleep with someone right away?"

"Hold on a second," I said, feeling that things needed to be cleared up. "I never said that I—"

"But you're thinking about it, right?" Dave asked, turning to me. Lisa and Schuyler turned to me, too, and I suddenly felt very put on the spot.

"I . . . don't know," I stammered. I hadn't decided anything, but I hadn't ruled anything out yet, either. "But it's a completely different situation."

"Thank you!" Lisa said triumphantly, then looked confused that she'd just agreed with me.

"Right," Schuyler said. "I mean, Nate's not a virgin. We don't think."

"Well, how do you know that I am?" Dave asked, sounding a little flustered. Schuyler and I just looked at him. Did he truly not realize that Lisa told us everything? Also, he was currently wearing a T-shirt that pictured a robot fighting a bear.

"Anyway," I said, feeling that we ought to move on, "I don't see what this has to do with me."

"It has nothing to do with you," Dave said. "Except that I used you as an example, that's all, just to start a conversation."

"A conversation," Lisa said, sounding distinctly teary, "that you should have had with me first. Not with Madison." Lisa and Dave stared at each other for a moment; then Lisa sat down on the bench next to Schuyler, leaving Dave staring at the carpet, his hands in his pockets. It occurred to me that one of the problems with having a fight in a very long hall-way was that nobody could storm out in an efficient manner.

"So," Dave said after an excruciating pause. "What are you two doing here, again?"

"Well," Schuyler said, glancing at me. "Um . . ."

"We had to drop off the crown," I said quickly. Until we knew what we were going to do about the fact that we'd just replaced a priceless school artifact with a child's toy featuring Hello Kitty, it probably wasn't a good idea to be telling lots of people.

"Oh?" Lisa said, a slightly hard tone to her voice. "I'm surprised you were able to part with it."

I frowned at her. "What are you talking about?"

"The pictures of you wearing the crown," she said in an extra-patient manner that told me she was still mad at me. "Ginger posted them on her Q-pic."

"What?" I asked, stunned. Lisa shrugged and handed me her phone. I brought up Status Q, and there they were, posted last night—pictures of me smiling at the camera, unmistakably wearing the Hayes crown. "Oh, no," I murmured. As I stared down at Lisa's phone, my own rang, and I answered it without checking the caller. "Hello?"

"Madison!" Kittson yelled through the phone at me. I held it away from my ear. "Where are you? We have a prom meeting right now."

"Oh," I said. I had totally forgotten about it. "Whoops."

"Yes," she said. "And I don't know what's happening

160

with the crown, and Dr. Trent is asking me. It's at the hotel, right?"

"Yes," I lied. "I just dropped the box off." That part, at least, was true.

"Well, good," Kittson said, sounding hugely relieved. "Because I've been getting these weird messages from Isabel Ryan."

"What kind of messages from Isabel Ryan?" I asked, repeating her name for the benefit of Schuyler, who immediately looked terrified.

"Just stuff about how I'm going to freak out when I see their crowning, and how their crown is just going to blow my mind. Stuff like that. Who knows where they picked one up. . . ."

Our lacrosse field, actually. "Right," I said hollowly. "Who knows."

"So everything's okay on your end?" she asked.

"As well as can be expected," I said evasively. "Just make sure Tanner got those lists of songs I e-mailed to him, and I think we're fine."

"Don't forget, we need to stuff the gift bags!" Kittson said. "I hope you're not going to bail on *that,* too."

"I won't," I said. "Sorry for missing the meeting."

"Don't let it happen again," she said before hanging up. Goodbyes weren't really Kittson's strong suit.

"Sorry," I said to everyone—who had been clearly listening to the entire conversation—as I put my phone away.

"Why were you lying to Kittson?" Lisa asked, staring at me, her head tilted to one side.

"What?" I asked, shocked. More and more these days, I was beginning to doubt my acting ability. Maybe the reviewer had been onto something after all.

"To Kittson," Lisa said. "About the crown. I know you, Madison. . . ."

"So! Um," Schuyler interrupted loudly. "What are you two doing here? And all?"

"Oh," Dave said, looking a little thrown by the turns this conversation had taken. "I had to do some stuff for work. Putnam Pizza is catering the Hartfield prom and a bat mitzvah here this weekend, and I had to drop some stuff off."

I stared at Dave and thought about what Kittson had just said. I still had Lisa's phone in my hand, and I scrolled absently through our mutual friends on Status Q, thinking. Between Ginger and Turtell and Kittson . . . and Sarah . . . and Lisa and Dave . . . "Wait a second," I murmured. The plots of all the James Bond novels I'd had to read recently were suddenly bouncing around in my head. A plan, a very vague one, was beginning to take shape. "Dave, are you working on Saturday?"

"No," he said, looking taken aback. "Big Tony keeps asking me to, but it's prom night."

"But if you wanted to, you could?" I asked.

"I guess . . ." Dave said, looking flummoxed. "But it's *prom night.*"

"Right," I said, standing up. The idea was slowly coming together, but I needed to talk it out first with the one person who actually knew what was going on. "Well, Schuyler and I have to get going now."

Schuyler looked at me for a moment, confused, then jumped to her feet. "Right," she said, a little too loudly. "That's what we're doing now."

"Madison," Lisa said, frowning, "we're not done here."

"I know!" I said as I started heading down the hallway, Schuyler trotting behind me. "In fact, you guys, don't make any plans for tonight, okay? I might need you."

"Mon Dieu!" I heard Lisa grumble.

"What are we doing?" Schuyler whispered to me.

"We're getting coffee," I said as we headed for the exit. "And then we're making a plan."

CHAPTER 14

Song: A Simple Plan/Pedro the Lion
Quote: "What the caterpillar calls the end of the
world, the master calls a butterfly." —Richard Bach

"Okay," I said, looking across the Stubbs table at Schuyler,
who nodded encouragingly. She'd gotten us drinks while
I'd scribbled down my initial thoughts on a Stubbs napkin.

THINK BOND!
Dave/Lisa — Putnam Pizza   Sarah D?
Schuyler/Ginger — wardrobe   Brian/Mark
GLEN!
CREW OF 9

ACCESS   DISGUISE
INFORMATION   PREPARATION
MISDIRECTION . . . all to TAKE BACK THE CROWN!!!!!!

"I think," I said, studying the napkin doubtfully. "I
think that maybe I have a plan."

"Oh, good!" Schuyler said, looking relieved. I was about to tell her that there was a distinct possibility that we wouldn't be able to pull it off, and that we couldn't be too relieved just yet, when the ShyPhone rang. Schuyler pulled it out and stared at it for a long moment.

"You just slide the arrow over to answer it," I murmured after a minute of listening to the ringtone of "Lover Boy." And much as I loved that song, the other Stubbs patrons didn't really seem to share my opinion, as they were now glaring in our general direction. "There are little instructions right there on the screen. . . ."

"No, I got that," Schuyler said, still staring at the phone as Mika kept on singing. She looked up at me, stricken. "It's Connor."

"Oh," I said. Schuyler made no move to answer her phone, but instead just kept staring at it as it vibrated in her hand. "And you . . . don't want to talk to him?" She just looked back down at the phone, which was now silent. "Shy?" I asked.

She shook her head. "He's going to know something is wrong," she said. "As soon as I talk to him, he's going to know."

"You can tell him what's going on," I said. "I just didn't want to tell Lisa and Dave yet, until we figure out the plan." I looked down at my scrawl. "Such as it is."

Schuyler shook her head. "I can't tell him what I did back in Choate," she said sadly. "Are you kidding, Mad? You know how he is. He once *volunteered* to go to detention because he was ten minutes late to class. It's one of the things I like best about him—he has such a strong sense of right and wrong. . . ."

I nodded, as though I agreed. But actually, what Schuyler found appealing, I found pretty annoying. It was Connor's elevated sense of right and wrong that had put me through two recounts before he'd conceded that I had, in fact, beat him for class secretary. Twice. But it was also this conviction that had led to us getting a confession out of Dell. I had to admit that Connor's rigidity had been helpful with that.

"But I know that we would be over if he found out about any of this. He wouldn't be able to get past it. What I did at Choate, then giving away the crown, lying to Dr. Trent, misrepresenting items to hotel personnel . . ."

"Seriously?" I asked.

She nodded. "I know him. If he found out about this stuff, he'd never look at me the same way again. So I can't talk to him until I can find a way not to sound different so that he won't be able to tell that something is wrong."

"But, Shy," I said, thinking of a conversation we'd had in this very coffee shop only a few days before, "didn't you say that you guys tell each other everything? And that relationships are about communication?"

"I did say that," Schuyler said, a little sadly. "But that was then." She looked across the table at me and took a breath. "But anyway . . . the plan."

"Well," I said, looking down at the napkin again. "Let's not get ahead of ourselves. I think 'plan' might actually be too strong a word. Maybe we should just call it the *idea* for the moment."

"Great!" Schuyler said, leaning forward to peer at the napkin. "Is this it?" She looked up at me and frowned. "I don't understand."

"I know," I said. "Me neither, really. But I think that there might be a way to fix the crown situation."

"Really?" Schuyler asked, looking doubtful. "Because I don't think Isabel is going to give it back to us."

"I don't think she is, either," I said. "But when I talked to Kittson, she said that Isabel had been bragging about Hartfield High's new crown. I think she's planning on using the Hayes crown to crown their prom queen."

"And we're going to have to crown our queen with Hello Kitty," Schuyler said, turning pale. "OMG, this is bad."

"No, it's good," I said quickly. "Well, not *good*. But this means that we know where the crown is going to be. Isabel's not selling it on the black market or anything. And I think . . ." I rotated the napkin. "I think we might be able to take it back."

"Steal it?" Schuyler asked, eyes wide.

"Well . . ." I demurred. This had been a bit of a sticking point for me, too. "She took it from us, right? And it's *our* property. Even though you gave it to her voluntarily."

"So sorry about that," Schuyler murmured. "So, so, so, so, so, so . . ."

"I know," I said, cutting her off in the interest of time. "But even though you gave it to her, she coerced you into it. So I think we're justified in taking it back. We just have to do it before ten thirty on prom night, when they're going to open the safe."

"Can we do that?" Schuyler asked, looking at me seriously. "Really?"

"I think so," I said. "I mean, I hope so. But I think that maybe it's possible." I looked at Schuyler across the table, and I felt the first very tiny glimmer of hope that we might be able to get out of this after all.

Schuyler nodded. "Well, I'm in," she said. "I mean, of course I am. It's my fault, after all. And I'm so, so, so, so . . ."

"Shy," I said, trying to stop her before she got going.

"Right," Schuyler said, sitting up a little straighter. "What can I do?"

I pushed the list of names across the table at her. "Feel like organizing a get-together tonight?"

****

Four hours later, I looked around the group that had gathered in Brian McMahon's living room: Lisa, Dave, Schuyler, Brian, Mark, Sarah, Ginger, and Turtell. Schuyler had sent out the SOS text, and amazingly, everyone had come—though it might have been because they were curious about why they'd been asked. We'd settled on Brian's house; even though his father wasn't home, his housekeeper was under strict instructions not to let Brian leave the premises. But he was permitted to have people over if they were there in some academic-related capacity. It was where the Young Investors Club had been meeting ever since the beginning of this grounding—which, coincidentally, was when his father had forced Brian to join the group.

168

So we were there under the pretense that we were a study group. Though I'd been to Brian's house a lot, it had always been for a party, and the place looked different when it wasn't filled with overturned furniture, discarded red plastic cups, and tipsy people stumbling about.

Dave, working overtime at the restaurant, had been allowed to leave only if he was on a delivery. So we'd called in an order that Schuyler had insisted on paying for, and Dave had arrived within the promised thirty minutes with five pies. I had thought it was going to be too much food, but now there was barely any left. It seemed like Turtell had eaten almost an entire pie himself.

It was a bit of a motley crew, I realized as I looked at the group. I was friends with everyone there, but it now struck me that that didn't necessarily mean that they were all friends with each other. Mark and Sarah, sitting side by side on the couch in the living room, looked particularly out of place, and I realized they'd probably never been to one of Brian's parties before.

Feeling that I should get things going, I went to stand in front of the TV, where the three couches, forming a horseshoe shape, all faced. "Hi," I said. "Um, has everyone eaten?" The eight people sitting in front of me nodded, and I cleared my throat. "Good," I said, wondering how to begin this. "Okay. So."

"Question for you, Mad," Turtell said. He picked up the two remaining slices of pepperoni, layered one on top of the other, folded them lengthwise, and took a bite as Sarah stared in amazement. "What are we doing here? I mean, it's always cool to hang, and thanks for the grub,

169

but what's this about? My girlfriend wasn't too happy about me bailing on her tonight."

Everyone else turned to me, expectant, except for Sarah, who was still watching Turtell eat with a kind of horrified fascination. "Right," I said, realizing that I just had to bite the bullet. I looked over at Schuyler, who nodded encouragingly. Schuyler hadn't eaten anything except her hair, until Lisa had taken over and forcibly pulled it back into a bun. "So here's the thing," I said. "We're kind of in trouble. Schuyler and me. But especially me. I have a plan—well, an idea—for getting out of it, but it's kind of complicated. I asked you guys here because you all have unique abilities that we'll need in order to pull this off. But I totally understand if you don't want to do this. What I'm going to ask you to help with is pretty risky. And I basically have a guarantee from Dr. Trent that there will be severe punishments for everyone if he finds out about this. So I don't want anyone to feel like they have to do it." Mark raised his hand. "Um, yes, Mark?" I asked as I saw Brian smile behind his hand.

"What is it exactly that you're talking about?" he asked. "Or did you guys go through it before I got here?"

"No," I said. "I just wanted to give everyone a chance to walk away first. Before anyone knows anything that might get them into trouble."

"*Mon Dieu*, Mad," Lisa said. She was sitting at the opposite end of the couch from Dave. I knew, seeing this, that they hadn't worked things out. Usually, couches were the ultimate aphrodisiac for Lisa and Dave. "What is it?"

"I'm getting to it," I said. "Anyone want to leave, first?"

I looked around at my friends. Lisa appeared tempted, but remained sitting, drumming her fingers on the arm of the couch. Nobody moved from their seats. "Okay," I said before taking a deep breath. "Here goes. So this Saturday, on prom night, we need to get the Hayes crown back from Isabel Ryan, the Hartfield High prom chair."

Ginger let out a laugh, but then stopped when she realized that she was the only one. "Wait," she said, her smile fading. "Seriously, Mad?"

"I'm afraid so," I said.

"How did she get the Hayes crown?" Mark asked, frowning.

"Well," I stalled, not quite sure how to tackle that particular question.

"I gave it to her," Schuyler said from her corner of the couch.

"You *gave* it to her?" Lisa asked, jaw dropping.

"Not voluntarily," I jumped in. "She was black-mailed."

"With what?" Dave asked, looking skeptical.

"Seriously," Turtell said. "What's she got on you?"

"We probably shouldn't focus on that," I said quickly. "The problem is, she has the crown. And we need to get it back, or I'm going to be in serious trouble."

"But I told Mad that I was willing to take the blame," Schuyler piped up in a shaky voice. "I have a plan. I can move to Switzerland."

"OMG," Sarah murmured. She looked from me to Ginger. "I knew this would happen."

"You did?" I asked, stunned. If that was the case, I

171

would have appreciated a heads-up, or a text.

"Yes," she breathed. "It's the curse!"

"What curse?" Brian asked.

"The curse on the crown," she said. "I told you not to try it on, Mad."

"You tried it *on*?" Turtell asked, looking horrified. "The Hayes crown?" I couldn't help but admire Kittson's influence. A few months earlier, I would have bet money that Turtell hadn't even heard of the Hayes crown, and that if he had, he couldn't have cared less about it.

"Well, yes," I said. "But there isn't a curse."

"There might be," Sarah pointed out. "Look at what's happened since you tried it on."

"And if there is a curse," Mark chimed in, "do we even want it back? I mean, wouldn't it be better to leave the crown with this Isabel person so it can work its dark magic?"

"There isn't a curse!" I yelled.

"We have to get it back," Lisa said. "This is the *Hayes crown*."

"Also, Mad's totally screwed if we don't," Dave added. "Right?"

"Right," I said, hoping we could get the focus on that detail, which was particularly troubling to me.

"So we get it back," Dave said, as though this was a given.

"We're doing this?" Brian asked, glancing to either side of him. "Whatever it is?"

I looked at my friends. Most were nodding, even Lisa, though she didn't seem too happy about it. I looked over at Sarah, worried. Because of our history, she was the one person I really wasn't sure of. But even Sarah was nodding, and I was suddenly filled with relief and an overwhelming wave of affection for my friends. "You guys," I said, my voice catching a little in my throat. "Thank you so much. I really appreciate it."

"So what's the plan?" Mark asked. "You do have one, right?"

"Yes," I said. "Well, it's more like an idea. But I think it's going to work. Here's how it should go—" I was stopped by the doorbell chime. My first reaction was panic, since whenever I'd been at Brian's house before, and the doorbell had rung, it meant that the cops had arrived to break the party up, and everyone was either fleeing the premises or running to find a hiding spot within the house. Personally, I always went for the closet in the upstairs laundry room. But then I realized that there was nothing to get in trouble for now—unless you counted faking a study group.

"I got it," Brian said, hoisting himself up from the couch and heading for the door.

"So," I said, trying to get back to the plan, "I think I've figured out something that will play to everyone's strengths. And I can't tell you guys how much I appreciate it."

"Well." I turned around and, to my horror, saw Kittson standing in the doorway of the living room with a panicked-looking Brian. Her arms crossed, Kittson's gaze lingered on Turtell before locking in on me. "Just what is going on here?"

CHAPTER 15

"Is she going to be okay?" Schuyler asked me in a low voice.

"Um," I said as I glanced at the sofa. I wasn't exactly sure. Kittson was slumped forward, a hand over her eyes. Sitting next to her, Turtell stroked her hair and glared at me intermittently. We didn't have any smelling salts, but Ginger was hovering nearby with hot pepper flakes, just in case. It turned out that, understandably, Kittson had found Turtell's excuse of needing to go to the aquarium tonight somewhat suspect. It hadn't helped that he'd updated his status when he'd arrived.

 Glen Look! Whales!

174

His real location—Brian's house—had been embed-ded in his status, and she'd come to investigate. Once she'd gotten there, Turtell had spilled the beans imme-diately. As soon as Kittson had heard about the crown, she'd sunk onto the couch and hadn't moved or spoken since.

"Kittson?" I asked, taking a step closer to her couch. "Are you okay?"

She lifted her head and glared at me, and I under-stood immediately why there had been so many movies made about murderous prom queens. Because you did *not* want to cross them. "Am I *okay*?" she repeated, ris-ing slowly. "No, Madison, I am not okay. You had one job to do. One."

That actually wasn't true at all, but this didn't seem to be the time to correct her. I nodded. "I know."

"And not only did you not bring the crown to the hotel, you *gave it away*. You *gave it away* to the girl who has been trying to ruin our prom from the outset. Our prom has been wrecked. We no longer have our school's most precious heirloom. My sworn enemy has it instead. Because you *gave* it to her. So no, I am *not* okay!"

"Actually, that was me," Schuyler said, standing up. I looked at her, surprised, and saw that she was trembling, but she was facing Kittson head-on. "I gave Isabel the crown."

Kittson turned her glare on Schuyler. "And why did you do that, again?"

"Because she was blackmailed," Sarah piped up.

"We don't know why," Mark added.

"And what are all these people doing here?" Kittson asked, finally seeming to notice that there were eight others in the room, all watching the drama unfold. "Were you all getting together to laugh about how you managed to wreck the prom?" She turned back to me, shaking her head. "I should have known you would do something like this, Madison. Ever since you suggested *All About Prom* as a theme, I should have known you were trying to sabotage it."

"I asked people here because we need to get the crown back," I said.

"Oh, great idea," Kittson scoffed. "Like Isabel's ever going to give it back."

"Well," I said. This seemed as good a time as any to start going through my plan. Or idea. "I wasn't thinking that we were going to ask for it back. I was thinking that we were just going to take it."

Kittson became very still and looked across the room at me. "Steal it?" she asked.

"Steal it *back*," I clarified. I looked around the room—everyone had gone very quiet. "On prom night. Without getting caught by Dr. Trent, or Isabel, or any of the hotel staff. This is why I gave you guys a chance to get out before you heard any details," I said.

"I can't steal anything," Sarah said. "I'm going to be president of Thespians next year."

That was news to me, since we hadn't had elections yet. "You are?" I asked.

"Yes," she said. She glanced at me and Mark. "Well,

most likely. Anyway, I can't have something like that on my record."

Brian nodded. "Not that I don't want to help, Mad," he said. "Because I do. But seriously, I get caught doing one more thing and I'm going to military school. My dad showed me the brochures and everything."

"And I really need to get a scholarship if I want to go to RISD," Ginger said, setting down the pepper flakes and edging away from them as though she wanted to distance herself from the whole situation. "So . . ."

I nodded, swallowing hard. I should have known this would happen. It was very easy to agree to something before you knew what the risks were. It was much harder when it might actually cost something. "Right," I said quietly. I glanced at Schuyler, who looked stricken. "I understand."

"This is *complètement merde*," Lisa said, surprising me. We all turned to look at her. "What, everyone was on board until it seemed like there might actually be consequences? Mad is our friend. And she and Schuyler need our help. And this is what friends do. They help each other when they need it most. So if you walk away from this, it's basically admitting that you're not a good friend. So if you want to do that, *d'accord*. There's the door." She gestured dramatically.

"It's actually over there," Brian murmured, pointing in the opposite direction.

"Whatever," Lisa snapped. "The point is, I'm not leaving. But if you are, you should go. Now." I looked at

Lisa, incredibly touched, but she refused to meet my eye. She was clearly still mad about the Dave conversation. I figured I would deal with that when things had calmed down. Maybe in the next millennium.

Ginger twisted her hands together but remained seated. Sarah stood up, shouldered her bag, then glanced at me and sat back down again.

"So you're in?" I asked, not really able to believe it. "Really? Everyone?"

There was a collective silence; then Dave cleared his throat. "What's the plan, Mad?" he asked.

"Well," I said, pulling out my napkin, "here's how I thought we could get the crown back—"

"No," Kittson interrupted. She was sitting again, Glen's arm around her. She no longer looked furious. Instead, she looked oddly calm, which actually frightened me even more.

"No?" Schuyler repeated, looking at her. "But . . . um . . . don't you want the crown back?"

"I meant," Kittson said, "that it's not enough to get the crown. We'll get it back—we'd better—but we need to get *her* back for this. She can't be allowed to get away with it."

"Well, she won't," I said, wondering if I hadn't explained this clearly enough. "Because we're going to take the crown back from her."

"It's not enough," Kittson said. "She's trying to ruin our prom. I say we do the same to hers."

"Kittson," I said, a little desperately, "I think we need to just concentrate on one thing at a time."

"We get revenge on her or I'm going to Dr. Trent with all of this," she said in the same calm, terrifying tone.

"Kittson's right," Schuyler said in a small voice. I turned to her, shocked. "No, I mean it," she continued. "She shouldn't be allowed to get away with this. With any of the things that she's done. She should pay."

I could see that Kittson wasn't about to back down. "Fine," I said. I looked down at my napkin, at my vague idea, which now had to be rethought. "We'll get back at Isabel, too. I promise."

"Good," said Kittson and Schuyler simultaneously.

"All right," I said. I took a swig of Diet Coke to help clear my head. First, we needed to find out everything we could about Isabel. I turned to Brian. "Do you have your laptop?" I asked.

FRIENDVERSE... *for your galaxy of friends*

Isabel Ryan

is having a very good day ;)
Female
17 years old
Hartfield, CT
United States

Status: Single

Song: Take My Breath Away/Berlin

Quote: "I am extraordinarily patient, provided I get my own way in the end."—Margaret Thatcher

TOP 8:

Zach Baylor

iluvrobpatz!!!!

Beatrice

TEAMEDWARD!

HHS Honor Society

KitKat

ChoateAlums

Anonymous

Isabel Ryan's Blog

Prom Update! Just 3 days to go!! It'll "take your breath away"!

We've secured the Lily Ballroom for the prom! It's going to be great!

I h8 smug, self-congratulatory people.

Family. You can always count on them!

About Me
Currently putting the finishing touches on the prom!

Music:
Mahler, Chopin, Mozart, Stravinsky.

Movies:
The Unbearable Lightness of Being, *8½*, anything by Bergman.

Television:
Television? Please.

Books:
Proust. But only in the original French.

Idols:
Robert Pattinson, Jude Law, Orlando Bloom, Daniel Radcliffe!

Education: High school

Graduated: Next year

Isabel's Comments
Displaying 4 of 4

Zach Baylor
Um, hi, Isabel. So I guess we're all set for the prom. So did you want me to pick you up? Or should we just meet there?

Beatrice
Hey BFF! Just wanted to see how your day was ;) Call me latah, kay?

KitKat
Of course I don't mind that you're in the same hotel that we are! There's enough room for all of us, right? ☺

Anonymous
SO looking forward to Saturday. You have no idea. Wouldn't miss it for the world.

I looked up at Kittson from Brian's laptop. "You're on here," I said, surprised, as I passed it on. "You're in her Top 8."

"I know," Kittson said, patting her slice of pizza with a paper towel. Once we'd agreed to her revenge scheme, she'd lost her scary demeanor and had helped herself to dinner. "I'm sure she thought it would make her look good . . . you know, the prom chairs getting along."

"But you're not," Ginger clarified.

Kittson shook her head. "Well, especially not now. And you should see the kind of stuff she's posted on my blog."

"Totally harsh," Turtell agreed.

"I don't see how this helps," Mark said as he looked at the profile.

"It's incredibly helpful," Sarah said, looking at it with him. "You just have to know how to read it."

"And you do?" Mark asked.

"Sure," Sarah said. "You can see that she has a date to the prom, this Zach Baylor guy. But he's not her boyfriend and he doesn't seem that excited about it, so I'd say it's a date of convenience. Also, she's a cultural snob but has a major thing for British guys."

Kittson looked at Sarah with respect. "Nicely done," she said.

"Thanks," Sarah said, trying to appear nonchalant but clearly thrilled.

I had scribbled out a new plan on a Putnam Pizza napkin, thinking back to all the James Bonds I had read recently. It looked as though incorporating the revenge element might actually make the crown stealing easier. But it meant that we were going to have to be at the Hartfield prom as much as possible, and we needed someone on the inside. Someone who could be close to Isabel all night. . . . I looked up, getting an idea. "Mark, did you ever get a prom date?"

"No," he said with a kind of wounded dignity. "I've come to terms with going alone. There's nothing inherently wrong with it."

"Not at all," I said. I smiled, tapping my pen on the table. "Okay," I said as I looked down at my napkin. "Let's figure this out."

****

An hour later, I flopped back on the couch and stared at the whiteboard in front of me. When things had expanded way beyond my napkin, Brian had dragged out the board his father used to record his groundings on. Every inch of it was now covered with the Plan.

ACCESS: Mark—use STLD—Operation Prince William
                Sarah—Hartfield date—use STLD
                Dave—Catering!!
                Glen—Locks, entrances, lookout

WARDROBE: Ginger
FRENCH/SMALLNESS: Lisa
LOOKOUT: Brian
TECHNOLOGY: Kittson
COORDINATION: Schuyler—keeping track of Putnam prom, Madison—go between both proms
COMMUNICATION: USE STATUS Q!!

Thursday night: Operation Mata Hari—Sarah, Mad, Dave, pizza
Friday: Review of the plan

Saturday: PROM

Meet at Dave's — 7 p.m.

Enter hotel at 8 p.m. — 2 vehicles — limo, van

Embedded in Hartfield prom: Sarah, Mark, Mad
        (floating)

Dave — in Hartfield prom, with cart

*Find out location of crown. Get it AWAY from Isabel.
        Transport to secure location via Dave's
        cart.

10:25 — CROWN REPLACEMENT (Lisa, Mad,
        Schuyler) Put real crown in place of H.
        Kitty.

10:30 — Dr. Trent sees that Hayes crown is fine.
        (fingers Xed)

10:35 — Don't Cry For Me, Hartfield (Sarah)

10:40 — Putnam High queen crowned with Hayes
        crown (Kittson)

"Take my name down," Kittson said, pointing at the bottom of the whiteboard. "We don't know that I'm going to be the queen. And it's bad luck to put it there." I got up and wiped Kittson's name from the board.

"I think that bad luck's already happening," Sarah said.

"Which means we don't need to add to it any more, am I right?" Kittson asked. She swung her legs over Turtell's lap and kissed his cheek. "Are you okay with this, baby?" she asked.

"I just don't know," Brian said, shaking his head, causing Turtell to glare at him.

"I think Kittson was talking to Glen," I told him. "But what is it, Brian?"

"Well," Brian said, frowning at the board, "I understand how this will work—I think—*if* everything goes according to plan. But what if something goes wrong?"

"What could go wrong?" Dave asked.

"What *couldn't* go wrong?" Lisa muttered. I turned to look at her, surprised, since she had been the one to convince everyone to get on board. "*Je suis desolée,* but I'm with Brian. This is only going to work if there isn't a wild card."

I didn't really have a solution for this, except for all of us to start praying that that wouldn't happen. "Well, there won't be," I said as confidently as I could.

"Why are we using Status Q updates to communicate?" Dave asked, frowning. "I mean, wouldn't it be better—and less public—to text?"

I shook my head. Using the updates to communicate was integral to the plan. "We're not going to have time," I said. "There are ten of us, after all. I'll set up one Q account for all of us to follow so we can get alerts. It's going to be much faster to update your status once, so we can all see it, as opposed to texting nine people."

Mark raised his hand again.

"Seriously?" Turtell asked him. "This isn't homeroom, dude."

Mark turned crimson and sank a little lower in his seat. "Sorry, Turtell. I mean, Glen. Sir. I was just wondering why we're not worried about Isabel telling on us. If everything works out and all, and we get our crown back and use it to crown Kittson—or whoever," he added quickly, as Kittson frowned at him, "how do we know that she's not going to go to Dr. Trent and tell on us?"

"Because then she'd have to admit what she did," Schuyler said. She looked around at all of us. "Right? Because then to get us in trouble, she'd have to admit that she blackmailed me and took the crown."

"Well, then, why don't we just go to Dr. Trent now?" Ginger asked. She looked thrilled by this option. "And we'll tell him what Isabel did, and then she'll get in trouble, and we won't have to go through all this."

"We can't do that," Dave said. "Because as far as Dr. Trent knows, Mad just allowed the crown to be given away. And she could get suspended for that—"

"Or expelled," I interrupted with a sinking feeling.

"Right," Dave said after a small pause. "Or that. But if we get the crown back, no matter what Isabel says, we'll be okay."

There was a moment of silence during which we all looked at the board, at the Plan, at everything that had to happen—without something going wrong—for us to get away with this unscathed.

"Is this going to work, Mad?" Schuyler asked in a small voice.

I let out a breath I hadn't known I'd been holding. "I really hope so," I said.

The meeting broke up after that, when Brian's housekeeper came in and told us that his father was en route, and study group or not, we should probably be getting on our way. Sarah went looking for the bathroom,

Schuyler took several pictures of the whiteboard with the ShyPhone (after Kittson showed her how), and then we erased the evidence that we'd been there doing anything other than studying for a Marine Bio test.

We filed out the door, everyone—now technically "the crew," as we had dubbed the group—looking a little shell-shocked.

"Lisa," I said as she passed me. I just wanted us to talk and get the whole Dave thing cleared up.

But she just shook her head, barely slowing her pace. "I'm helping, Mad," she said. "But that doesn't mean I'm not still *absolument furieuse* with you." I watched, feeling helpless, as she and Dave walked away in opposite directions, clearly still not speaking. Lisa got into her Beetle, and Dave, armed with an excuse for why a routine pizza delivery had ended up taking him two hours, climbed into the white Putnam Pizza van.

Schuyler walked to her SUV but stood outside it, staring down at her phone. She might have been trying to answer it again, but I had a feeling that she wanted to talk to me.

"That was something, Mad," Brian said, standing in the doorway next to me. "Most interesting study group I've ever been to."

I felt my conscience give a little guilty twist. Besides me—and maybe Schuyler—Brian had the most at stake if this didn't work out. And I really didn't want to be responsible for his getting sent to military school. I had a feeling that he wouldn't do particularly well there. "Brian," I said, "if you don't want to do this, you don't have to. . . ."

"No," Brian said. "I'm in." He smiled at me. "It's just nice to be hanging out with people again. And it'll work, right?"

"Right," I said as brightly as I could. "Of course."

"And as long as I have time to spend with my lady at the prom, I'll be fine."

I raised my eyebrows, surprised. "You got a date?"

"Yep," he said, smiling. "Can we go in your limo?"

"Oh," I said, trying to do a head count and then giving up. I was sure it would be okay. Limos were big, after all. That was their whole point. "Sure. Talk to Schuyler. So how'd you get a date?"

"Save the Last Dance," he said happily. "Best website ever. Even better than that betting one."

"What betting one?" I asked, but Brian continued talking over me.

"Even though STLD doesn't let you exchange real names until the day of the prom, and I don't know her name, I know that our profiles were totally compatible. And she's really hot," he added as an afterthought.

"But you don't know her name?" I asked, smiling.

"Not yet," he said, looking unconcerned with this detail. "But what's in a name?"

"'A rose by any other name would smell as sweet,'" Sarah said, appearing and apparently assuming that we were quoting *Romeo and Juliet*.

"Um, I guess," Brian said, shooting me a questioning look.

"Thanks for letting us meet here, Brian," I said as I headed down his front steps, Sarah walking behind me.

"No worries," he called after us. "See you in Marine Bio, Mad."

"Just a second, Mad," Sarah said, taking hold of my arm just as I started toward Schuyler. "I wanted to talk to you about something."

"Yes?" I asked as I caught Schuyler's eye and indicated that I'd just be a moment.

"I'm doing you a favor by helping you with this," she said, not looking at me, but down at the ends of her hair, which she twirled in her fingers.

"I know," I said, wondering what she was getting at. "And I really appreciate it, Sarah."

"Good," she said, "so then you'd be willing to do a favor for me in return?"

"I guess . . ." I said slowly.

"Good." Sarah looked up at me and smiled. "Because like I said in there, I'm going to be president of Thespians next year. And it will be easier for me to do that if you don't run against me."

I stared at her, wondering if I was understanding this. Sarah Donner was blackmailing me? Seriously? "And if I want to run?" I asked. I hadn't decided if I was going to put my name in, but I had definitely thought about it.

"Well," Sarah said. She frowned as though she was thinking hard, but as always, she overdid it. "I'd hate to be talking to a teacher—or Dr. Trent—and find that I'd spilled the beans about this whole plan. Accidentally, of course." She smiled at me pleasantly.

I quelled the urge to yell at her and took a deep breath. "Fine," I said through gritted teeth. "But you have to promise that you're not going to tell. And that this is the only thing you get to hold over me. After this, we're even." I wasn't about to have her tell me next fall that I wasn't allowed to audition for any of the plays so that she could finally have her chance to be the lead.

Sarah stared at me levelly for a moment, and I wondered if she had, in fact, planned on just that. But then she nodded. "Fine," she said. "You don't run, and I won't say anything to anyone, ever. I swear on Meryl." She walked away, then turned back to me. "But you can always try for vice president, Mads," she said. "That would make you . . . why . . . my understudy!" She smiled at me, got into her car, and sped down Brian's driveway.

I headed over to Schuyler and saw that since she was unable to chew her hair, she was making do with her nails at the moment. "Hey," I said, sitting next to her. Schuyler's SUV was so massive, the bumper was practically a ledge, and we could both fit. As I sat, I felt just how tired I was.

"Mad, I'm so sorry," Schuyler whispered, taking her hand out of her mouth. I could see that most of her nails had been bitten to the quick. "This is all my fault."

"It's not your fault," I said, even though it was, kind of. "It's Isabel's fault."

"I just keep thinking, 'Why now?'" Schuyler said. "I mean, why like this? She's had three years to get back at me, and she chooses to do it like this? I don't get it."

I shrugged. I didn't feel up to analyzing the motives of irrational, revenge-driven prom chairpersons. "Who knows?" I said. "I mean, maybe when she saw you at the Hyatt, it triggered something. IDK."

Mika started singing again, and I looked down at Schuyler's phone to see that Connor was calling her. Schuyler bit her lip and looked at the screen, then shook her head. "I'll call him later," she said, putting the phone, the song still playing, into her bag.

"You're going to have to talk to him eventually," I said. "He's going to get worried."

"I know," Schuyler said. "I'll talk to him later. When I figure out what to say."

"Just don't wait too long," I said. Knowing Connor, he was probably only one more missed call away from organizing a search party.

"I owe you, Mad," Schuyler said quietly. "Thank you for doing all this." She looked down at the ground and twirled her keys once around her finger. "Just between you and me," she said in a lower voice, as though we were in danger of being overheard in Brian's deserted drive-way, "will we be able to pull this off?"

I had no idea. I hadn't told Schuyler—or any of the crew—that I'd cribbed most of this plan from James Bond novels. "I think we have to," I said a little bleakly, "or we're all in trouble. Especially me."

Schuyler bit her lip and nodded. We said our good-byes, and she walked around to the driver's seat. I walked to Judy and got behind the wheel. I just sat there for a moment, trying to process everything that had happened that day. Finding this to be not only impossible but also headache-causing, I put my car in gear and headed for home.

CHAPTER 16

Song: Little Lies/Fleetwood Mac
Quote: "An idea that is not dangerous is unworthy of being called an idea at all." —Oscar Wilde

"Hey," Nate whispered to me. He ran his fingers through my hair and kissed me.

I kissed him back. Nate had cut his afternoon classes and had met me in our usual spot to make out during my lunch period. It had been days since I'd seen him, which meant it had been far too long since I'd kissed him, and all I wanted to do was lose myself in our kisses, like always. But today, it just wasn't working. My mind was racing with everything that needed to happen for us to pull off the prom heist.

After a minute, Nate pulled away and looked down at me, his brow furrowed slightly. "Mad, what is it?" he asked.

I looked up at him. I should have known that Nate would be able to tell that something was going on with me. I sighed. "Sorry," I said. "My mind's somewhere else."

"I can tell," he said, tracing my jawline with his fingers. "What's up?"

"Well, it's kind of a long story," I said. There was a part of me that really wanted to tell Nate the whole plan, if only to see if he thought it would work. But another part of me didn't want to interrupt our time together.

"Lay it on me," he said.

I took a deep breath and was about to do just that, when a thought struck me. This whole heist might go disastrously wrong, which would mean major consequences for all of us. And if that happened, and it looked like Nate had been involved at all, he could also get in serious trouble. He was on thin enough ice already at his school, with his acceptance to Yale hanging in the balance. I finally understood why he'd refused to tell me anything about the prank. He was just trying to protect me. And now I'd have to do the same for him.

"I wish I could," I said. "But you know how I'm on a need-to-know basis with the senior prank?"

"Yes," Nate said, looking confused.

"It's kind of the same thing," I said. I saw a flash of hurt in his eyes and hated that I had to do this. I already felt like there was distance between us because of the Melissa/prom night drama, and now I felt like I'd just made it worse. "It's not that I don't want to talk to you," I said quickly. "I really, really do. But if I do . . . and something happens . . . you could get in trouble."

"Don't worry about me," he said. "Seriously. What's going on?"

I bit my lip. "I can't tell you," I said after a moment. "I wish I could. But things might get a little . . . weird at the prom. Just so you know."

"Madison," Nate said, and I stiffened a little, hearing him say my full name. His expression was grave. "Is this . . . about us?"

"No!" I said. The thought was enough to make my stomach plunge, and my heart began to beat faster. "Not at all. I promise." I reached up, took his face in my hands, and kissed him. He rested his forehead against mine.

"I feel like you've been a little . . . distant or something in the last few days," he said.

It would have been the perfect moment to ask him about his prom night, and what he thought I'd meant with the hand gesture, and what he was expecting to happen when we got back to Dave's house. But the thought of having that conversation right now, when things already felt precarious between us, was just too scary. "I know," I said. "I've just had a lot going on. But after the prom, things will go back to normal," I said, fervently hoping that this would be true.

"Okay," he said, kissing my cheek. "But you know that you can always talk to me if you change your mind, right?"

"I know," I murmured. And I did. But I suddenly wondered why he couldn't talk to *me*. Why he hadn't, about the prank stuff, and the Melissa history, and everything else that he kept to himself. I prepared to ask him that very scary question. "The thing is—" I started, just as the bell rang.

"Saved by the bell?" he asked, looking at me closely.

"Something like that," I said. I stretched up and gave him a quick kiss.

"I'll call you tonight," he said. "And we have our date night tomorrow?"

"Of course," I said, smiling. Nate and I always went to the New Canaan Drive-In on Friday nights. After seven weeks, it had just become our routine, and I loved it. The second bell rang, and Nate kissed me again before squeezing my hand and heading across the parking lot to his truck. I watched him go, thinking about that moment when I'd had to confront the thought of losing him, and how frightening it had been. How it had, for a moment, actually taken my breath away. Suddenly, the Hartfield High prom theme no longer seemed quite so stupid.

Roth Mann → the crew Okay! I've got a profile up. Thanks for the website info, Brian.

Grounded_Brian → the crew Save the Last Dance. My salvation.

Dave Gold → the crew We hope.

La Lisse → the crew That was très rapide, Mark.

the8rgrrl → the crew Well, we're getting down to the wire here. . . .

Jimmy+Liz → the crew Um, what's going on? What are you guys talking about? (this is jimmy)

 mad_mac → Jimmy + Liz Don't worry about it, Jimmy. It's just prom stuff.

 Jimmy+Liz → mad_mac Really? Okay. If you say so.

 mad_mac → Jimmy+Liz I'll talk to you in English, okay?

 Dave Gold → the crew Mad, are we all set for tonight?

 mad_mac → the crew I think. Sarah? Can you confirm?

 Shy Time → the crew Um, Mad, isn't she kind of essential?

 Roth Mann → the crew She is essential, right? Because otherwise I can't do my bit, eh?

 Glen → the crew Dude. That's not British, that's Canadian.

Shy Time → the crew Victory! I got that address you needed, Mad.

 Dave Gold → the crew Shy, text it to me. Good work. Unlike *some* people.

 mad_mac → the crew Look, it's not my fault she's gone radio silent. SARAH??

 the8rgrrl → the crew Sorry! Won't happen again. I was getting into character. All set for tonight.

"Okay," I said, turning around in the passenger seat of the Putnam Pizza van and looking into the backseat. "All set?"

Sarah, sitting in the back, nodded. The back of the Putnam Pizza van had been customized to facilitate pizza transportation—only the front row of seats remained, and in the back was a contraption designed to hold a number of pies. It was strapped against the doors, but still had a tendency to bounce around worryingly whenever Dave took a sharp turn. Which was, in fact, every turn that Dave took.

Sarah fluffed up her hair. Ginger had taken over wardrobe and makeup after school, and Sarah looked—for lack of a better phrase—really smoking hot. Ginger had given her glowy skin, lots of lashes, and red lipstick. Her hair was tousled and undone, even though it had taken Ginger over an hour to achieve that effect. And maybe it was the fact that Sarah seemed to be viewing Pizza Delivery Minx as a character she was playing, but she seemed to have a lot more confidence than usual. For wardrobe, Ginger had taken in a Putnam Pizza shirt to the point where several of the buttons seemed in danger of popping off. Dave had turned pale when he'd seen Sarah, and had been expressly avoiding looking into the backseat. That response had been enough for me to begin to think we might actually pull off Operation Mata Hari.

"So Dave and I will be in the van, waiting," I said as Dave slowed to fifty miles an hour—which for him was a crawl—and squinted at the house numbers.

"Mad, can you see what number that is?" Dave asked. He slammed on the brakes, threw the van in reverse, and sped back several feet. "I can't read these. Why can't people just have white mailboxes?"

"Maybe if you slowed down," Sarah suggested faintly from the back. She had the slightly stricken look that people riding in Dave's car tended to have—like she'd just confronted her mortality for the first time.

"Yeah, I don't do that," Dave said, putting the car back into drive.

"We're looking for 1408 Sweetbriar," I said, looking around at the unfamiliar streets of Hartfield. Though Hartfield was only twenty minutes outside of Putnam, I had spent almost no time there, and had no idea where we were.

"I know," Dave said. "I just don't see it, do you?"

"There!" Sarah said, pointing out her window.

I braced myself, and Dave made a highly illegal U-turn in the middle of the road—which was, thankfully, free of other cars. We pulled into the driveway of 1408, and Dave put the car in park just to the side of the front steps and killed the engine. Dave and I both unbuckled our seat belts and turned to face Sarah.

"Ready?" I asked.

She nodded, took three deep breaths, did a quick vocal warm-up, and turned to me. "How do I look?"

Dave glanced at her and turned pale again. "Fine," he muttered to his armrest.

"Great," I said. "Seriously. You're going to be awesome."

Sarah smiled and turned to Dave, who seemed to be making every effort possible to avoid eye contact with her. "Quiz me one last time?" she asked.

"If he asks why Putnam Pizza is delivering in Hartfield . . ." I prompted, since Dave currently seemed to be having trouble swallowing.

"I say that there was a call from his number—"

"This number," Dave said, holding out a piece of paper in her general direction. Schuyler had found all the information we needed on his public Q feed, which was actually a little worrying.

"Right," Sarah said, pocketing it. "And that since Putnam Pizza is so popular all over the area, we deliver outside the customary range."

"Which we don't, but he doesn't have to know that," Dave said.

"Got it," she said. She unbuckled her seat belt, walked

to the back of the van, and selected the two pies we'd brought with us. We had a cheese and a pepperoni, figuring those were safe bets. She pulled open the door of the van, then turned back to us. "What's his name again?" she asked.

"Zach," I said. "Zach Baylor. Good luck." I watched as Sarah sauntered up the driveway—even her walk was totally different—and rang the bell.

Sarah straightened her shirt again, and I just prayed that the buttons would hold out for a few more minutes. Seeing the front door swing open, Dave and I slouched down in our seats. We were doing it as a precaution, but it was probably completely unnecessary, as the guy answering the front door—I recognized him as Zach from Isabel's profile—clearly only had eyes for Sarah. They spoke for a few moments on the porch, and then he opened the door wider and Sarah stepped inside with the pizzas, turning her head and giving us a thumbs-up as she did so. "She's good," I admitted, impressed.

Dave shook his head and we both sat up a little straighter. "You saw that shirt," he said. "The poor guy never stood a chance. This is entrapment or something."

"Isabel stole the Hayes crown," I reminded him. "She deserves it."

He raised his eyebrows. "She didn't steal the Hayes crown," he said.

"What do you mean?" I asked.

"Just what I said," he replied. "She didn't steal it. Schuyler gave it to her. There's a difference, even if she was blackmailed."

I stared at the house, not really wanting to talk about this. "I suppose."

"No, seriously, Mad," Dave said, looking at me. "There's a difference. Schuyler did something really, really stupid."

"I'm not arguing with you," I said.

Dave sighed. "Then I guess I just don't understand," he said.

"Understand what?" I asked.

"Why you'll forgive Schuyler," Dave said, "but not Ruth."

That was *not* what I had expected him to say. "What does that have to do with anything?" I asked slowly.

"It has to do with everything," he said. "Seriously, Mad. Look at where we are. Look at what we're doing."

"Bringing pizza to someone who didn't order it?"

"You know what I mean. You're doing a lot to try and fix Schuyler's mistake. You're still friends with her." I looked away from Dave and stared down at my lap. "I'm just saying. I don't get what the difference is."

"Ruth was out to hurt me," I said. "She hacked my profile—"

"I know that," Dave said. "But Schuyler stole your keys from your locker and broke into your car."

I tried to get my thoughts clear. It was different. For one thing, Ruth had never apologized for the hacking. And . . . also . . . Schuyler wasn't my BFF. Ruth had broken a trust that I had once thought was unbreakable. "Well, I don't see how this is even about you," I said, rather than answering him.

"Because it is," Dave said simply. "Ruth was my friend, too. And I can see what not being friends with her is doing to Lisa—and to you."

His words hung between us in the car, and I looked at the door, thinking that now would be a great time for Sarah to come back. "Anyway," I said, determined to change the subject, "what's going on with you and Lisa?"

"I don't want to talk about that," Dave mumbled. "What's going on with you and Nate?"

"I don't know," I said with a small sigh. Silence fell between us.

"Want to play twenty questions?" Dave finally asked as Zach's door swung open.

We both slid down in our seats again and watched Sarah walk across the driveway toward us, a small smile on her face. She got in, slammed the door, and Dave took off down the driveway. "Well?" I asked, turning to her once we were past the house.

"Mission accomplished," she said, smiling.

"Seriously?" Dave asked.

"It was amazing," Sarah said, looking a little stunned. "He barely even asked about the pizza. And then when I mentioned that our prom was this weekend, and I didn't have a date, he asked me to his. Just like that."

"Wow," I said, thinking that either this guy really liked Sarah, or he really hated Isabel. "Did he mention his current date?"

"Nope," she said with a smile. "He just said that he had a tentative arrangement that he had to undo. But he was texting someone as I left."

"Okay, that's Mark's cue," I said, taking out my phone. "Thanks, Sarah."

"Thanks for not running for president," she said. Dave looked at me, frowning, and I just shrugged, not wanting to go into it. "But you know," Sarah added after a moment, "he really seems . . . nice. And he's really, really cute."

"But you know this isn't a real date, right?" I asked, beginning to get a little worried. "I mean, you're going to have your parts to play during the prom."

"Oh, totally," Sarah said, a little too quickly. "Of course."

I nodded as I updated my status. Operation Mata Hari was completed. Operation Prince William was a go.

CHAPTER 17

Song: Ruthless/Something Corporate
Quote: "Fate is not satisfied with inflicting one calamity."—Publilius Syrus

mad_mac ➔ the crew Mark, you're on.

Roth Mann ➔ the crew Right you are! Off to post my profile, what? Pip pip!

Glen ➔ the crew Is that guy going to keep doing this?

Grounded_Brian ➔ the crew I have Young Investors tonight—but you don't need me, right? Everyone's cool?

Grounded_Brian ➔ the crew Well, except Mark?

Glen → the crew HA. NICE.

 Roth Mann → the crew Well! I say!

 Dave Gold → the crew It's official. I'm working on Saturday night. Big Tony is thrilled.

 La Lisse → the crew Is your petite amie? Um, NON.

 Dave Gold → La Lisse Lisa, can we talk about this off-line?

 mad_mac Still on prom to-do list: Pick up dress from Caitlin's Closet! Must not forget. Or should ask Mom to do it for me . . . hmm . . .

 Roth Mann → the crew Okay, we're set on my end. She seemed kind of desperate. And also kind of furious.

 KitKat → the crew ☺

"Well, I hope you all enjoyed that," Mr. Underwood said as he flipped through our papers at the front of the classroom. When I'd gotten to English that day, he'd announced that we were having a "Quiz. Pop quiz" on *The World Is Not Enough*. I'd been trying to read it all day long between classes, but hadn't finished, because I'd found that A Lunch Period Was Not Enough. As a result, I was pretty sure I'd just dropped my English grade a few points.

Jimmy turned back to me. "How'd you do?" he whispered.

I shook my head. "Bad. Very bad."

"Right there with you," he said.

"So!" Mr. Underwood boomed, turning to the board. "Let's talk about the Fleming double cross. This is paramount in the Bond novels. Our dear Bond never knows who is on his side. Imagine what that must be like . . . . never to be sure who you can trust."

I tuned Mr. Underwood out, leaned forward, and poked Jimmy in the back. "You and Liz are meeting at Dave's on Saturday?" I asked.

"Yes," he whispered, turning his head slightly to talk to me. "At seven, right?"

"You got it," I said.

"And what exactly is going on with your updates?" he asked. "Liz and I are very confused."

"I'll explain on Saturday," I said, hoping that with the excitement of the prom, he would forget. The bell rang, and I shoved my papers into my bag as Mr. Underwood yelled to be heard over the stampede for the door.

"Don't forget to read *Casino Royale* for Monday!" he yelled. "And as you read, remember—you can't ever be sure of anything. Even what you're sure you're sure of."

I headed out of the classroom behind Jimmy, thrilled to be free of Mr. Underwood for the weekend.

"Seriously, what is going on?" Jimmy asked, apparently not wanting to drop the subject of my mysterious status updates. "I can't understand what tons of people are saying these days. Who is in this crew?"

"It's nothing," I demurred as we navigated our way down the hall. "It's just a prom thing. I might actually need your help with it—you and Liz. I'll let you know."

"Sure," he said. "But give me a hint. Is it something to do with that website everyone's talking about?"

"Oh," I said, figuring that he meant Save the Last Dance. "Not really. I mean, Mark got his date there, but—"

"Got his date there?" Jimmy repeated, frowning.

"Save the Last Dance," I said. "The prom date website. Isn't that what you meant?"

"No," he said, still looking perplexed. "I meant Race to the Crown."

"What's that?" I asked. "I've never even heard of it."

"Really?" He looked surprised. "Everyone's talking about it. And my money's on Kittson."

"What do you mean?" I asked, completely confused, as the final bell rang.

"See you tomorrow!" Jimmy yelled, dashing to his class and leaving me wondering what he was talking about, and why nobody seemed to want to tell me about the new websites these days.

Thankfully, I had an open last period, so I headed to the prom committee classroom. Tanner was sitting outside it, playing drums on the door. "Hey," I said. Tanner continued to play on, unawares, until I nudged him with my foot and he pulled his headphones off.

"Hey, Mad," he said. "Did you hear that?" He twirled his sticks with a flourish, causing one to fly in the air and strike the top of his head on its way down.

"Yes," I said. "And it was really . . . loud."

"Thank you," Tanner said, smiling and rubbing the top of his head.

"Did you get those song lists my boyfriend sent you?" I asked.

"Yeah," he said, stopping his roll on the door. "But I have to tell you, Mad, all these songs are lame. They're, like, songs you hear on the radio."

I felt immediately grateful to Nate, since that had been exactly what I'd wanted. "Good," I said. "Tanner, that's the point."

"What?" he asked. "To have a lame prom?"

"No," I said. "To have music that a lot of people will like. Not just Demon Puppets."

"Murderous Marionettes," he said, rolling his eyes. "God," he muttered.

"In fact," I said, "I think that a good rule of thumb is if you hate it, you should play it. That's how you'll know it's a prom song."

"Fine," Tanner said. "Whatevs. I'm going to have to wear earplugs if you want me to play this stuff."

"That's fine," I said. "Just so long as the music keeps playing."

"I don't know if I'd call any of this music," he said. "But if you change your mind, I still have the good playlist—the one with *real* music on it—on my iPod. Just in case, come Saturday, we need to get the party started."

"I'll keep that in mind," I said.

"And I was thinking," he said, drumming again, "that if things get really lame, I can always bring my drum kit. Again, just in case. And then, when it's necessary, I can just bust out a drumroll like so. . . ." Tanner demonstrated on the carpeted hallway, which, thankfully, killed some of the effect.

"That's great, Tanner," I said, pulling open the prom classroom door. "Thanks. See you tomorrow!" I headed into the room, where Kittson was already waiting. I wasn't sure if she also had an open, or had simply stopped going to classes so that she could devote all her attention to the prom. I thought it might be best if I didn't ask.

We stuffed the favor bags for an hour. It was mindless work: Each gift bag got a light-up pen, a sparkly silver flash drive, a small photo frame, and a handful of confetti. As I assembled bag after bag, I couldn't help wishing we'd just gone with candles and hired a real DJ instead.

When we finally finished, I followed Kittson out of the classroom, hitting the lights behind me on the way out. I waved goodbye to Kittson as she got into Turtell's car, which was waiting for her at the front entrance. Turtell honked and waved at me, and the two sped off. I headed to the junior parking lot, looking forward to my Nate date, feeling lighter than I had in days.

As I got closer to Judy, though, I saw someone standing next to it, waiting. Someone with a perfect ponytail. Someone who'd once been my best friend.

I forced myself to keep walking to my car, my mind racing as I tried to figure out what Ruth could be doing there. Had Dave called her or something?

She spotted me and raised a hand in greeting. "Hey," she called. She sounded nervous, and she was playing with her gold *R* necklace, sliding the letter back and forth on the chain.

"Hi," I said, walking over to the driver's door and dropping my bag at my feet. I raised my eyebrows, hating once again how awkward things were between us. "What's up?"

Ruth stuck her hands in her pockets and looked over her shoulder quickly. I followed her gaze, but there was nothing there—just the empty lacrosse field. "I wanted to talk to you about something," she said, her voice strained. Ruth looked tired, like she hadn't slept in a while. I'd seen her during her worst phases of insomnia, but she'd never looked quite this worn-out.

"Okay," I said cautiously.

"It's about the prom," she said.

Immediately, I felt my defenses go up. "Oh?" I asked, trying to sound as neutral as possible.

"Yeah," she said. "I'm worried that there might be . . . something going on during it."

I wondered who had talked to her. Or if she'd just been reading our status updates and had been able to guess this herself. "Why would you think that?" I asked, still trying to sound neutral. Beige. Switzerland.

"I've just heard some things," she said. She looked at me. "Mad . . . I'm worried."

I wondered if Jimmy had been talking. "It's just rumor," I said, trying for a breezy tone. "Nothing at all out of the ordinary is going to be happening at the prom."

She stared at me and seemed to be trying to decide whether or not to say something. "I think there *is*," she said finally. "And I think you need to be ready."

"I'm fine," I said firmly. "But, um, thanks for the heads-up."

She nodded, and her shoulders slumped a little. "Okay," she said. "Sure."

We stood in silence for a moment, the tension between us palpable. I stared down at the keys in my hand. Dave's comments kept replaying themselves in my head. If I'd been willing to forgive Schuyler, *should* I think about forgiving Ruth? But would it even make a difference? Would things between us ever go back to how they had been? I guessed there was only one way to find out. "Listen, Rue . . ." I started.

"I have to go," she interrupted. I looked up and saw a coldness in her eyes that hadn't been there moments before. "I have some stuff to do before tomorrow."

"Okay," I said, a little jarred by this change. But I supposed it was just par for the course with us these days. "I'll see you tomorrow," I said.

"You will." She nodded. "Talk to you later." The words lingered in the air for a moment, and it was almost like I could see them in a cartoon bubble. Two months ago, I would have replied, "Talk to you soon," our habitual BFF goodbye. But we hadn't said that to each other in a long time now. Ruth flushed slightly, as though she'd just realized what she'd said. "I mean, bye," she added quickly, turning and walking across the parking lot.

"Bye," I called to her retreating form. I unlocked Judy and got in, putting on the most upbeat Stockholm Syndrome song I could find for the drive home. I was determined not to let the encounter drag me down. Sure, it had been strange, and maybe there were rumors going around that something out of the ordinary was going to be happening at the prom. But with a crew of ten, somebody was bound to talk to someone. All would be fine. Probably. But in the meantime, I had a date with my boyfriend to get ready for.

As I walked through the kitchen, I saw that my mother was in full-on preparation mode, getting ready to leave for South Carolina in the morning. "Hey, Mom," I said. I didn't have time for small talk, but I also wanted to appear responsible and trustworthy, so that she wouldn't change her mind at the last moment and hire a sitter.

"Hi, hon," she said, looking up from the to-do list on her BlackBerry while simultaneously cleaning out the fridge. "How was school?"

213

I decided that honesty was not the best response to this question. "Oh, fine," I said casually. "You know," I added, very glad that she didn't.

"Are you going out with Nate tonight?" she asked.

"Yes," I said. I looked at the microwave clock. "And I should actually get ready for that. He'll be here before too long, so . . ."

"Well, then, go primp," my mother said, smiling at me.

I smiled back at her. "Thanks, Mom," I said, heading for the stairs.

"Oh, and one more thing," my mother called to me. I paused, foot hovering over the bottom step. "I stopped by Caitlin's Closet to pick up your dress, but they didn't have it. They said that your friend Isabel had picked it up earlier."

CHAPTER 18

Song: Everything You Ever/Dr. Horrible's Sing-Along Blog
Quote: "It's only words . . . unless they're true."
—David Mamet

 mad_mac wait, what? WHAT?!?!

I walked upstairs in a daze. I'd nodded dumbly when my mother had gone on about how she wanted to meet this new friend of mine, and how nice it was that I was making new friends, since it seemed like I hadn't been spending much time with Ruth lately.

I sat on the edge of my bed, trying to process this. Isabel had stolen my dress? My phone, sitting next to me on the bed, began to ring. I picked it up and looked at the caller ID. I didn't recognize the number, but it had a local area code.

"Hello," I said numbly.

"Well, Madison," the voice on the other end said, sounding very pleased with itself. After a second, I recognized it as Isabel and felt my hand tighten on the phone. "How *are* you?"

"How did you get this number?" I asked.

"Oh, I have ways of getting lots of things," she said airily. "Like your dress, for example. I gather that you found out about that. It's just lovely."

"How did you know I'd found out about that?" I asked, stunned. I wasn't asking the questions I really wanted to ask—like why the hell she had done this—but I also wanted to know how she knew these things.

"Madison," she said, her voice condescending, "you just updated your status."

"And how do you know that?" I blurted. A second later, the answer hit me. "Are you following me on Status Q?"

"Of course I am," she said. I blinked, stunned. It was one thing for Travis to follow me. But the thought that Isabel was reading my status updates made me feel . . . spied upon, almost. I tried to remember what I'd posted recently, and if any of my updates would give our plan away if she read them. "After all," she continued, her voice losing its mocking edge and becoming harder. "I make it my business to keep track of the people who are trying to sabotage me."

"Where's my dress, Isabel?" I asked, slowly growing more furious.

"Where's my prom date, Madison?" she snapped. "I know that you had a hand in that."

"How?" I asked, wondering—on top of everything else—why she was talking to me. "Why are you even doing this to me? Isn't it Schuyler that you have a problem with?"

"We both know Schuyler didn't contrive to have my prom date dump me *two days* before the prom," she said, and I could hear the anger in her voice now. "From everything I've heard, you're the brains of the operation."

"Heard from who?" I asked, genuinely baffled. Isabel didn't respond right away, and I could have sworn I heard some muffled whispering in the background. I strained to hear. Was I on speakerphone?

"That's irrelevant," she said, but she sounded a little less sure than she had a moment earlier. "The point is, you can't do something like that and not expect retaliation. I'm thinking I might cut up your dress and make . . . oh, a wrap out of it. Think that would work?"

"The only reason we did that to you," I said, trying to keep my voice level, "is because you blackmailed Schuyler into giving you our crown. You can't do something like *that* and not expect retaliation."

"Fair enough," Isabel said. "But anyway," she added, smugness returning to her voice, "your little ploy to have me go dateless didn't exactly work. I have another date already. And he's *really* cute. He's *British*."

"Wow," I said, trying to keep my voice expressionless. "Is that so?"

"Yes," she snapped. "So just give up, Madison. I've got your crown. I've got your dress. I've got a date. I *won*. I'll see you tomorrow."

With that, she hung up. I closed my eyes, trying to think. Isabel had just stolen my prom dress. She was status-stalking me. I needed to talk to someone about this immediately. I turned on my computer and waited for it to boot up, praying that Schuyler would be online. I knew that calling her was never the best way to achieve instant connection. But Schuyler was online, I saw with relief, and I iChatted her. A moment later, she was staring back at me, looking confused.

"Hey, Mad," she said. "What's up? Shouldn't you be at your drive-thru right now?"

"Drive-in," I corrected automatically. "And yes. But listen. We have a problem."

"What is it?" Schuyler asked, frowning.

"Isabel stole my dress."

"What?"

"Isabel," I said with a renewed sense of rage, along with the feeling that I might burst into tears. "She stole my prom dress."

"Oh my God," Schuyler said, looking stricken. "Why would she do that?"

"She's mad about the Sarah date-stealing," I said.

"But why is she going after you?" Schuyler asked.

"My thoughts exactly." I looked at Schuyler and saw that she was wearing a white tank, her hair pulled back in a sloppy ponytail. "Shy, aren't you going out with Connor tonight?"

"Oh," she said, looking down. "No. I told him that I was sick."

"Schuyler," I said, "have you been avoiding him this whole time?"

"No," she protested. "I e-mailed him last night. To tell him I was sick."

"Shy," I said, "you can't keep doing this to him. You have to . . . hold on," I said as my iChat dinged with an invitation from Kittson. I clicked over to her.

"We have a problem," Kittson said from inside her very pink bedroom. Behind her, I could see Turtell pacing back and forth.

"I do, too," I said. "Listen—"

"Me first," she interrupted me. "Have you heard about some new prom website?"

"Kind of," I said. "But nobody will tell me what it's about."

"Did you know about this, Mad?" Turtell asked, sticking his head into the camera's view.

"No!" I said. "I don't even know what this website is!"

"It's trouble," Kittson said, frowning.

"Yes, but what is the content?" I asked as my computer dinged with another chat invitation—from Sarah Donner, of all people. "Hold on," I said, switching over to Sarah.

"Madison," Sarah said as soon as she appeared on my screen. "We have a problem."

I closed my eyes for a second and hoped that I would never have to hear those words again. "Oh?" I asked, bracing myself for the bad news.

"Yeah," she said, looking worried. "Did you know that the Hartfield prom is eighties themed?"

Well, that threw a big neon wrench into our plan. "No," I said, trying not to panic. "No, I didn't."

"I only found out because Zach wanted to make sure

I had the right kind of dress to wear. Which is totally sweet, and so like him, but I *don't,* and I don't know where I'm going to find an eighties dress by tomorrow."

"Hold on a second, Sarah," I said. I brought up Kittson and Schuyler as well, and looked at them all. "Okay. So there are some problems," I said, going for understatement.

"We need to contain this. Now," Kittson said, and Turtell, behind her, nodded.

"I agree," I said. I looked at everyone looking to me for answers and knew what I had to do. "I hope nobody had ironclad plans tonight. Schuyler, would you see if Ginger's free tonight? We're going to need her. And Dave, too."

"Sure," Schuyler said, looking confused. "But what about your date?"

I sighed. "That's not going to happen," I said.

"In war, there are casualties," Kittson said.

"Thanks," I said, picking up my phone to call Nate. "That's very comforting right now."

****

An hour later, I was back at school. I pulled into the junior parking lot and parked next to Schuyler's SUV. The back hatch was up, and Schuyler sat inside, her legs dangling over the edge. I got out of my car, locked it, and headed over to her.

"Did Nate understand?" Schuyler asked as soon as I was in earshot.

"He said he did," I said with a shrug, "but I don't think he was happy about it."

I'd called Nate as soon as I'd closed out the chats. "Hey, you," he'd said when he picked up. Making matters worse, he'd sounded really happy to hear from me. "I was just out the door to get you."

"Right," I'd said heavily, hating that I was doing this, and at the last minute, too. "About that . . ."

When Nate had spoken again, his tone was much more subdued. "You can't make it," he'd said, like he'd been expecting this.

"I'm so sorry," I'd said in a rush. "There's just a prom thing that's come up at the last minute, and I need to take care of it."

"It's okay," he'd said, but his voice was a little flat. "I understand, Mad."

"I hate to cancel our date night, and I really wanted to see you. It's just . . . I have to take care of this."

"It's fine," he'd said. "I promise. Go take care of whatever you need to take care of, and I'll see you tomorrow."

"Okay," I'd said. I suddenly didn't want to get off the phone with him. I was worried that things were changing between us, and canceling this date was just making things worse. "I just . . ." My voice had trailed off. I wasn't sure what I wanted to say.

"Mad, it's *fine*," Nate had said, his voice a little gentler now. "Look, want me to call you later?"

"Yes," I'd said. The promise of a conversation raised my spirits a little. And then tomorrow we'd go to the prom together, and then after tomorrow, the prom would be over, thank God. We'd said our goodbyes and I hung up, wondering when all the constants in my life had started to get so shaky.

"Anyway," I said, focusing back on Schuyler. "Let's get this figured out. Where is everyone else?"

"En route," she said, looking at her phone. "If their GPS locations are anything to go by, that is."

Sure enough, as she said this, three cars careened into the parking lot, followed by the Putnam Pizza van. Sarah got out of one, Ginger out of the second, and Kittson and Turtell out of the third car. Dave got out of the Putnam Pizza van, looking stressed.

"I can't be here long," Dave said as he got close to Schuyler's SUV, where everyone was congregating. "I'm going to have to go out on deliveries soon."

"If you need to, you can take my car," I said. "But we're going to need the van to transport the clothes." I noticed Kittson's outfit for the first time, and saw that it consisted of black leggings and a black tank top. "What are you wearing?" I asked.

"We're breaking in," Kittson said. She pulled a thin silver laptop out of her purse. "This is what you wear for that."

"We're breaking in?" Schuyler asked, turning pale.

"No," I said quickly. "Not really. We have keys."

"How many people need outfits?" Ginger asked. Out of all of us, she looked the least stressed. She was slipping into her professional-costumer mode, and I was happy to see it.

"Well," I said. I paused and thought about it. "Me, Sarah . . ."

"Mark," Kittson added.

"Mark?" Schuyler asked, frowning. A moment later, her expression cleared. "Oh! Right. I keep forgetting about him."

"So three," Ginger said, making notes on a piece of paper and nodding. "That should be doable."

"Isabel stole my prom dress," I said, hoping that if I said it enough times, it wouldn't keep threatening to make me cry. "So I might need two dresses, if we can find something."

"We will," Ginger said, with such confidence that I believed her. "Don't worry."

"How'd she do that?" Sarah asked.

"Because she's a liar and a cheat," Kittson said angrily. "Oh, I am so looking forward to taking her down."

"She knew where it was because I had it on my Q," I said. "She's following mine. She's probably following Kittson, and who knows who else. Also, we know Dr. Trent is following Glen—"

"Damn the Man!" Turtell muttered.

"Right. But he's following me, too," I said. "So we're not going to be able to use the updates like we thought. We don't want to give stuff away."

"But isn't that a huge part of it?" Dave asked, frowning. "I mean, how are we supposed to communicate?"

"We're going to have to figure out some codes," I said. "I'll work on that tonight. But for the moment, just be careful what you say."

"You never know who's listening," Turtell said darkly.

"It's true," I admitted, still not quite able to believe that he'd been right about this.

"So there's one more thing," Kittson said. She gestured for Schuyler to move, and Schuyler immediately jumped up and walked to the side of her car. Kittson placed her laptop down where Schuyler had been sitting and opened it. "There's a website," she said.

"Oh, I've heard something about this," Dave said. "I think."

"What is it for?" I asked, thrilled to finally get an answer to this mystery.

"It's a betting site," Kittson said, leaning over her computer and typing in an address.

"Betting on what?" Ginger asked.

"On who's going to win prom king and queen," Kittson said grimly. "Look."

"Okay," I said, straightening up. "Is it just me, or is that really weird?"

"Super weird," Ginger said. "Who would even bet on this?"

"A bunch of people, apparently," Sarah said, pointing to the bottom of the screen. "There's twelve hundred dollars already in play." She looked up at me, then back at the screen again. "Mads, your odds are really bad. Like, shockingly bad."

"Dave's, too," Ginger pointed out.

"Thanks," Dave muttered.

"This has to be illegal, right?" I asked, trying not to focus on the fact that I had terrible odds. Which seemed, actually, kind of odd. I mean, it wasn't like I was a social

Race to the Crown

Putnam High School   "A Night to Remember"   Saturday, May 25th

Welcome to Race to the Crown—your opportunity to get in on the action of one of the most hotly contested Prom Royalty elections!

Adding to the drama are Putnam's new voting rules, which PROHIBIT nominations! The field is wide open, and anyone could walk away a queen, with the famous Hayes crown!

How it works:

$100 minimum bet. Use PayBuddy link at bottom.

Choices for King AND Queen must be correct to win.

Play the favorites or go for a dark horse candidate! Either way, if you win, you win big! Good luck, and good betting!

FAVORED CANDIDATES

QUEEN	KING
KITTSON PEARSON	JUSTIN WILLIAMSON
Odds: 2 to 1	Odds: 3 to 1
ROBERTA BRIGGS	BRIAN MCMAHON
Odds: 6 to 1	Odds: 8 to 1
LIZ FRANKLIN	JIMMY ARNETT
Odds: 12 to 1	Odds: 15 to 1
MADISON MACDONALD	DAVE GOLD
Odds: 100 to 1	Odds: 60 to 1

pariah or anything. How were these being calculated, anyway? "I mean, can you just bet on people like this?"

"I want to know who's behind this," Turtell growled. "I mean, someone is betting on my girlfriend? Not cool."

"Not at all," I said, frowning at the screen. "I'm sorry, but I don't understand these candidates."

"You mean you?" Sarah asked.

"No," I said. "Well, yes, that's part of it." I could understand why Roberta Briggs had made the cut; she'd been considered the hottest girl in our class since approximately fourth grade. "But they just seem so random. And why even put me and Dave down if our odds are so bad?"

"Lisa isn't going to like this," Dave said in a small voice, shaking his head.

"*I* don't like it," Turtell said. "Someone is going to be making money off of my girlfriend."

"But I don't understand how anyone *is* going to make money off this," I said, bending down and looking at the screen again. I tried to remember everything my father had told me about sports betting sites. None of the factors that made those profitable—point spread, buy money, return rate—were in place here. Whoever was running this stood to lose a huge amount of money, unless . . . "It's like they already know who's going to win," I said slowly.

Kittson wrinkled her nose. "But that's impossible," she said. "Nobody's even voted yet."

"I know," I said. "That's what worries me."

"Well, nobody can get to the voting program," she said. "The codes are going to be texted to us ten minutes before the crowning. And they've been secured on Dr. Trent's computer."

"Well, I don't know," I said, shaking my head. "But something's off about it."

"Can we get this going?" Dave asked. "I might need to leave soon."

"Right," I said, trying to focus on the task at hand. I looked at Ginger, then Turtell. "You guys ready?" They nodded.

"Dave, you should probably drive the van around to the theater door," Ginger said. "And it might be a good idea to kill your lights."

"I'll meet you guys over there," Dave said, getting into the van.

The rest of us followed Turtell around the back of the school, to an entrance I'd never paid any attention to before, a single unmarked door near the back gym. "How did you find out about this?" Schuyler whispered, looking around nervously.

"You'd be amazed at how much wisdom janitors are willing to share," Turtell said with a smile. He rubbed his hands together and took a huge key ring out of his pocket. He selected a key and moved toward the door.

"Wait!" Sarah yelped before he could put the key in. We all turned to look at her. "You're sure this door isn't alarmed, right?"

Turtell lowered the key. "I'm sure," he said. "They missed this door when they updated the security system a few years ago. It's our only way in."

"And there aren't any cameras, right?" she asked.

"I can answer that," I said. "And the answer's no. We asked Dr. Trent about it a few months ago, when my locker was broken into."

"Are we doing this?" Turtell asked, sounding impatient.

"Yes," Kittson said. "Go for it, baby."

I held my breath as Turtell put the key into the lock and turned it. He pushed the door open and I closed my eyes, bracing myself for an alarm to start wailing and the cops to descend on us. But nothing happened. The door just swung open silently. I let out a breath and saw Schuyler and Sarah doing the same.

"We don't want to attract attention to ourselves," Turtell said in a low voice. "Just in case. So I'd say silence unless absolutely necessary. Don't turn on any lights. And let's do this as fast as possible. Get in and get out. Okay?"

We all nodded and followed Turtell through the door and into the deserted high school.

CHAPTER 19

Song: Keep The Car Running/Arcade Fire
Quote: "Everybody breaks the law."—Joseph Cotten,
The Steel Trap

We walked down the dark, silent hallway. I tried my best to concentrate on being quiet, mostly so I wouldn't think about how much trouble we would all be in if we were found there. It was eerie being in the school at night. There were strange shadows everywhere, and a dense quiet that was never there when classes were in session.

The group of us crossed the student center in silence. It looked absolutely huge, and there was something creepy about seeing it so deserted—almost like a ghost town. When we got closer to the theater, Ginger took the lead, and we walked down the stairs single file, with me bringing up the rear. She led us to the door of the costume vault and took out her keys to open it up. Again, I held my breath, but the door swung open quietly, no alarms tripped.

She stepped in, and then came back and looked at

Turtell. "I need to turn on the light," she whispered. "I can't see anything in there."

"No light," Turtell said. "I don't know if it's true, but I've heard a rumor that the lights are all on a grid. If one goes on, there might be a record of it."

"I can't do this without light," Ginger said. "We might as well leave."

"Wait," I said, getting an idea and heading for the stairs. "I'll be right back."

"Mad, where are you going?" Schuyler hissed at me, but I just kept walking.

I hurried upstairs, across the student center, and to the prom classroom, finding my way by the dim emergency lights and moonlight streaming in through the windows. To my relief, the door was unlocked, and I stepped inside. The prom favors were right where we'd left them. I plundered three gift bags, taking out the flashlight pens, then dropping them into one bag. I closed the door quietly behind me and headed back down to the theater.

The group was still standing outside the costume vault door, and Schuyler was chewing her hair. Everyone seemed slightly more nervous than they had when I'd left them. I handed out the flashlight pens, and Kittson nodded.

"Excellent," Ginger whispered, clicking hers on. Sarah and Schuyler each took one and turned them on as well. Ginger stepped inside and we followed, the small flashlight beams barely cutting through the cavernous darkness of the costume vault. But it didn't seem to bother Ginger. She was utterly in her element. She pointed to one of the rolling metal clothes racks and indicated where she wanted it. I nodded, and Turtell and I wheeled it outside the door.

Ginger began moving at warp speed, rushing around and grabbing clothes off racks, seemingly at random, then tossing them to Sarah or Schuyler. They would then transfer whatever Ginger had just tossed them to the rack outside. In just a few minutes, the rack was filling up with short tutu-style dresses, white suits with pastel T-shirts, a powder blue tuxedo, and lots of lace.

When the rack was almost full Ginger came back out with accessories. She separated out an armful of jewelry—strands of pearls and cross necklaces—and draped them over Sarah's head. She handed me three pairs of black lace gloves, and I raised my eyebrows, confused. Ginger mimed cutting the fingers off, and I smiled at her.

"Are we done?" Kittson whispered, checking her watch.

Ginger shook her head, holding up one finger. She turned to me, looking at me closely, her head tilted. Then she disappeared into the vault again, her tiny beam of light leading her way. She emerged a moment later with something pink over her arm and nodded at all of us. "Done," she whispered.

She locked the costume vault behind her, and we wheeled the rack down the hall. When we got to the stairway, we lifted it as a group and maneuvered it up the steps and into the student center. The six of us crossed the student center, moving quickly, Turtell doing the lion's share of the work, pulling the rack behind him. When we passed the office, I paused. Kittson slowed as well.

"What?" she whispered.

"You said the voting program was on Dr. Trent's computer," I said quietly.

"Yes," she whispered back. "So?"

"So," I said, "this is our opportunity to find out if someone's messed with it."

"Madison," Ginger called softly. She and the others were several feet in front of us, and everyone had stopped moving. "We should go."

"We'll be there in one minute," I called in a low voice. "Start loading the clothes into the van, okay?"

Ginger looked worried, but nodded, and the group continued down the hall, Schuyler turning back to look at us one more time before they disappeared from view.

"Why me?" Kittson asked, looking very much like she wanted to join them.

"Because you're good at this stuff," I said. Kittson was great with computers. Even though I didn't like it, the scrapbook-themed prom website was amazing, and she'd set it up in less than a day.

"You want us to break into Dr. Trent's office?" Kittson hissed.

"Of course not," I said, gesturing toward the door. "We won't have to do that. It's open."

Kittson's jaw dropped and she turned to look at the door to the office, which was propped open. And I could see that Dr. Trent's office door was unlatched. He probably assumed that since the whole school was alarmed, the office was pretty safe. But then, Dr. Trent had also assumed that it was a good idea to put Turtell on janitorial detention. Kittson stared at the door for a moment, then turned to me and nodded, prom-chairperson determination back in her expression. "Fast," she whispered.

"Well, yeah," I whispered back, and I led the way as we tiptoed in. I paused at the threshold to Dr. Trent's office, looking at his desk in the moonlight, wondering if we were really going to do this. It felt like we were crossing a line. I looked up and saw the poster of the exhausted-looking eagle and the motto underneath it. *Dedication: Keep trying until you just can't try anymore . . . then try a little harder!* This was probably not how Dr. Trent had meant that motto to be taken, but it worked for me. I stepped inside his office, still expecting alarms and sirens to go off. But there was only the silence and the gentle whirring of the computer. A green light blinked on and off at the base of the monitor.

Kittson reached out a hand to wake the computer from sleep, and I grabbed her wrist, pulling it back at the last minute. She raised her eyebrows at me, and I handed her a pair of the black lace gloves. "Just to be on the safe side," I murmured.

Kittson rolled her eyes, but put the gloves on, and I did the same. She touched the mouse, and the computer came to life, bringing us right to Dr. Trent's desktop, which displayed a picture of Putnam High School.

"He didn't have a password?" I whispered, surprised.

There was probably no need for us to keep our voices down, but something was compelling me to.

"I guess not," Kittson whispered back. She took a breath and started typing on the keyboard, searching. I looked around the office. I couldn't shake the feeling that we were being watched, or that someone was going to come in at any moment.

"Hurry," I whispered, even though I knew that wasn't helping.

"That's not helping," Kittson murmured, concentrating on the screen. "Okay, found it."

"And?" I asked.

She shook her head. "I can't tell anything from this right now. I need to analyze the program and how it's set up. I need to get this off his computer and spend some time with it. It's too big to e-mail, and plus, that would leave a trail."

I felt my shoulders slump. I had hoped that Kittson would be able to see right away if the voting program was properly functioning, and then we could leave. But if we needed to get something off the computer . . .

"Wait," I said. I reached into the gift bag I was still carrying and took out the flash drive. I held it up to her, and it glinted in the moonlight. "Will this work?"

Five minutes later, Kittson had copied the program onto the flash drive, and we tiptoed out of Dr. Trent's office, careful to leave behind no trace that we'd been there. We walked into the hallway, moving faster and faster as the exit door got closer, and both of us breaking into a run as we reached it. We stepped outside, back into the cool night and fresh air, and I took a deep breath. Everyone—including Dave, standing on the running board of the van—looked very relieved to see us.

"Where were you?" Schuyler asked around a mouthful of hair.

"Hair," I reminded her. "We had to stop by the office for a minute," I said as casually as possible. I glanced at Kittson, who gave me a small nod. I didn't want to tell the others what we'd just done. It seemed safer that way.

Schuyler tucked her hair behind her ears and twisted her hands together. "But is everything okay?"

"Hopefully," I said, looking at Kittson, who started to pocket the flash drive before realizing that she was only wearing leggings, and palmed it instead. "Are we all set?" I asked Ginger, looking at the van. The rack of clothes had been placed into the back, next to the pizza carrier.

She nodded. "I might have to make some last-minute alterations, but I'll just bring my kit with me tomorrow and do it on-site."

"Great," I said, a little shocked we had managed to pull this off.

"So we're good?" Dave asked. "Because I just got an order. And if you need me to be working tomorrow, it would help if I didn't get fired tonight."

"I think we're good," I said. "Thank you, guys."

"Meeting at Dave's tomorrow at seven," Kittson reminded everyone as there was an exodus toward the cars. "Don't be late!"

"I'm never late," Sarah said as she got into her car.

Dave started the van and rumbled out of the parking

lot, not turning on his headlights until he was back on the main road. Sarah followed him, and Schuyler, waving goodbye to me, followed her.

Kittson walked up to me as Turtell locked the door again and headed to his car. "I'll see what I can find out tonight," she said, indicating the flash drive. "And let you know tomorrow."

"Great," I said. "Thanks."

"It was a good call," she said, turning over the flash drive in her hands. "Something's going on with this, and I don't like it. I want to win fair and square, you know?"

"Right," I said with a small smile. Kittson gave me a wave and got into Turtell's car, which veered out of the parking lot with more speed than I might have advised, given that we were trying to be incognito.

I headed to Judy and saw that Ginger was still in the parking lot, leaning against her car. "You okay, G?" I called to her.

Ginger nodded and walked over to me, holding the pink thing she'd brought out last from the costume vault. "Got something for you," she said.

"What is it?" I asked, squinting.

She held it up. It was the gorgeous fifties-style dress that she'd had me try on to model the crown. "It's your prom dress," she said, smiling. "Like it?"

CHAPTER 20

Song: Existentialism on Prom Night/Straylight Run
Quote: "There could be no honor in sure success, but
much might be wrested from a sure defeat."
—T. E. Lawrence

"*What* are you wearing?" Travis asked from across the kitchen, smirking at me.

"What?" I asked. I looked down at my dress. I was absolutely in love with it. I was thinking I was going to have to buy Ginger a pony or something to thank her. It fit like it had been made for me, and the pink went perfectly with the silver heels I'd planned on wearing with my original dress. It wasn't a typical prom dress, but that was exactly what I liked about it.

Trying to catch my reflection in the microwave, I smoothed my hair down. I hoped it would hold out against the humidity. I'd gotten it blown out, surrounded in the salon by other girls getting their hair and nails done for the prom. I'd been running around all morning—picking up Nate's boutonniere, getting my nails done in a soft pink to match my dress—and it had made me excited for the prom in a way I hadn't been since this whole mess had begun.

I still didn't know what was going to happen with Nate once the prom was over and we got to Dave's. But right now, I was trying not to think about that. It wasn't actually that difficult, since there was a part of me that didn't believe we were going to make it through the prom. After all, there was a possibility I might be spending the night in jail, which would make the whole sex-or-no-sex question moot.

My parents had left early that morning in a flurry of activity. My mother had given me a laminated card with all their South Carolina contact information on it, reminded me to take lots of pictures, and handed me a pamphlet about the Cinderella Project, telling me that we would talk about my lack of charitable work when she got back. She also told me to be nice to my brother, which at the moment was proving particularly challenging.

Once the microwave showed me that my hair was still fighting the good fight against the humidity, I straightened up and walked past Travis to the fridge, where I took Nate's boutonniere out of the vegetable crisper. "I'm wearing a prom dress," I said, placing the boutonniere on the kitchen counter and examining the long pearl-topped stickpin that had come with it, wondering what I was supposed to do with it. "What are *you* wearing?"

I had said it from force of habit, but Travis's face clouded and he looked down at his suit, worried. "Why?" he asked. "Is something wrong with it? Does it look stupid? Mom picked it out, but I thought it looked kind of stupid. . . ."

"No," I said quickly. "I was just kidding. You look fine. Olivia will love it."

"Really?" he asked, smoothing down his dark blue tie, then his hair, then pushing me aside and checking his own reflection in the microwave. "Because lately, she's been . . . I don't know. Different or something."

"What do you mean?" I asked.

Travis sighed and stuck his hands in his pockets. "She has all these exes she's still hanging out with. And whenever I ask her about it, she says they're just friends. Like *that's* true."

I wondered what it was about the Pearson girls' DNA that caused guys to get all crazy and protective around them. "Travis," I said, "you have to trust her. Why would she lie about that?"

"I dunno," he muttered. He reached out absent-mindedly to play with Nate's boutonniere, and I moved it before he could accidentally destroy it. "But listen, Mad," he said, suddenly looking grave. "You're not going to say anything to her, right? About any of that stuff that you said you wouldn't? And you won't send her that picture, right?"

"I promise," I said. "As long as you promise that as far as Mom and Dad are concerned, I came home from the prom and stayed here with you tonight."

"Deal," Travis said. He held out his hand and we shook quickly, just as the front doorbell rang.

I could feel my heart start to beat more quickly. It thrilled me that Nate had come to the front door. He always knocked on the side door when he picked me up.

239

But it was like he had somehow known that the front door was reserved for special occasions. I started to hurry toward it, and my heel slid slightly on the kitchen floor. I slowed my steps, smoothing down the fabric of my dress, hoping that Nate would like it.

I got to the front door and smiled involuntarily. Nate was standing on the top step, a clear plastic box in his hand. He was wearing his tux easily, as though he wore one every day. It looked like maybe he'd just gotten his hair cut—the curls seemed a little more under control than usual. I noticed that the tux wasn't black—it was a very dark blue and it brought out his eyes. I had never seen him look more handsome. I unlocked the door and pulled it open.

"Hi," I said, smiling wider.

Nate looked at me in silence for a moment, then stepped inside, his slightly crooked smile appearing. He touched my hair and then the waist of my dress carefully, as though he was afraid of messing them up. Then he touched my cheek lightly, his smile growing. "You look so beautiful," he said. "This dress is incredible." He shook his head. "I can't believe you're my girl."

I was thrilled to hear that he liked the dress, but all the same, I felt my cheeks get hot. "*You* look beautiful," I said. "I mean, handsome. I like this tux."

"Oh," he said casually, "it was just something I had lying around the house." He opened the jacket, showed me the cummerbund—which was a slightly lighter blue than the rest of the tux—and pretended to model it.

"Ooh, very nice," I said, laughing. I stepped close

to him, reaching my hands inside the jacket and stroking the fabric of his tuxedo shirt. As I did so, I could feel the muscles of Nate's stomach beneath the shirt, and I moved my hand around to his back. Suddenly, things didn't seem quite so funny anymore. Under the pretense of straightening his already straight bow tie, I rested my hands on his chest, trying to get control of myself. Because suddenly, all I wanted to do was kiss him, even though we were ten feet away from my little brother, in my front hallway, and I'd just put on my lipstick.

I looked up at Nate. His expression had turned serious, and he was breathing a little harder than usual. He spanned his hands around my waist and murmured, "Mad . . ."

That was all I could take. I threw myself at him, kissing him hard, and Nate stumbled back a few steps before he bumped into the foyer wall, the plastic box in his hand clattering to the ground. He tightened his arms around my waist and kissed me back, matching the intensity in my kisses. He was backed up against the wall, and I leaned into him, and it was like I couldn't touch him enough—running my hands inside his jacket, over his chest, up his back. He seemed to feel the same way, cupping my face in his hands, encircling my waist, tracing a slow line down my side that made me shiver.

We continued like that for . . . well, I actually have no idea how long. Not nearly long enough, in my opinion. I felt as if I couldn't get enough of him, and rather than sating this, every kiss just made me want him more. This was a level of intensity we'd never experienced before, and I wondered if it was the formal wear. If that was the case, maybe Bond had been onto something after all.

We broke the kiss, and I caught my breath, which was coming a lot more shallowly than usual. I tried to compose myself, suddenly scared of what I was feeling. The prom, the crown . . . none of it seemed to matter anymore. I just wanted to stay there with Nate, kissing him and . . .

For the first time, I truly entertained the idea of what it might be like not to have to stop. What it might be like if we decided to go all the way. Possibly tonight. The thought didn't terrify me, as it usually had. Instead, right then, it seemed like an intriguing option.

"Wow," Nate murmured, blinking down at me.

"I know," I said, looking up at him. Neither of us was smiling. Something had just happened between us that felt . . . serious.

Nate sighed and kissed my forehead, then pushed himself off the wall he'd been leaning—okay, where I'd leaned him—against. "Well, if that's what happens when we get dressed up, I think I should break out the tux more often," he said, arching an eyebrow.

"That's just what I was thinking," I said, smiling up at him.

"Hey!" Travis yelled from the kitchen. "Um, shouldn't we get going? I don't want to keep Olivia waiting."

I rolled my eyes at Nate and took a moment to straighten my dress and smooth my hair down. Nate retrieved the fallen plastic box, and I saw that there was a beautiful corsage inside.

"Sorry about Travis," I said.

"He didn't do anything," Nate said, handing me the corsage box.

"Oh, he will," I assured him. "That was just preemptive." I opened the box and took out the corsage, which was a perfect white rose. "It's beautiful," I said. "Thank you."

"Let me," Nate said, and slipped it over my wrist. He held my hand for a moment, and I stretched up and gave him a quick kiss.

"Okay," I said, squeezing his hand and taking a deep breath. "Let's do this."

****

As we got close to Dave's house, I could see a line of cars stretching down the driveway and onto the street. Parked a little way up the street was the white Putnam Pizza van, and the sight of it was enough to remind me that this was not going to be an ordinary prom night. We parked at the back of the car line and headed up the driveway, Travis walking a few feet behind us, as though he wanted to pretend he'd somehow gotten there on his own.

Everyone had assembled on Dave's back lawn, by his pool and the rock wall that overlooked the Long Island Sound. My friends were lined up, with the water behind them, posing for pictures. I squeezed Nate's hand, and we walked closer. Travis joined a petite blond girl who I assumed was Olivia, since she looked like a mini-Kittson.

I smiled as I took in the sight of all my friends dressed in their prom finery. Lisa was in a strapless black dress

243

that hit the floor and hid the fact that she was wearing four-inch heels. Dave was standing next to her, wearing a tux and looking a little bulkier than usual. Schuyler looked stunning in a tiered green dress with a Gerbera daisy corsage. She was next to Connor, but the two of them weren't standing very close, and neither looked particularly happy. Jimmy and Liz were gazing into each other's eyes and, as usual, appeared to be in their own world. Kittson looked amazing in a light yellow dress that almost matched her hair. And if it wasn't for Turtell's gazing at Kittson adoringly, I wouldn't have recognized him. In his tux, hair combed neatly, he looked beyond clean-cut.

Brian was standing alone, looking down the driveway and checking his watch, presumably waiting for his internet mystery date. Lisa smiled and waved at me, then seemed to remember she was still mad, and lowered her hand and glanced away. I made it a priority tonight to talk to her, and do what I could to fix the fact that she was still upset.

"Amazing dress, Mad," Liz said, tearing her eyes away from Jimmy for a moment and smiling at me.

"Thank you," I said.

"Where's it from?"

"Um . . . the Vault," I said, thinking quickly.

"I've never heard of it," she said, frowning.

"It's new," I said. "Just opened."

"Well, be sure to give me the info," she said. "I'd love to check it out!"

"Absolutely," I said as convincingly as I could.

"Is the limo here yet?" Nate asked Dave as they did their ridiculously complicated guy handshake.

"Any minute," Dave said, checking his watch.

"It should be here," Schuyler said, coming over to us. She looked beautiful, but also exhausted and worried. "I confirmed with them this morning." Connor trailed behind her, and I saw that he had a daisy boutonniere to match her corsage. It looked like she'd had better luck putting it on than I'd had with Nate's, which, after three attempts, still kept slipping to a forty-five-degree angle on his lapel.

"I'm sure they're coming, Shy," Connor said, smiling at her. "You were very clear on the address and directions." Schuyler looked down and nodded, not making eye contact with him.

"Dude," Brian said, seeing Nate and coming over. The two of them then did a different complicated guy handshake, this one involving a shoulder bump at the end. "Good to see you."

"You too," Nate said. "Nice to see you've been released into the world again. When do we get to meet your date?"

"Should be any minute now," Brian said, his face clouding slightly as he looked down the driveway again.

"How was Young Investors?" I asked, trying to distract him.

"Oh," he said, and his expression became even more troubled. "Not so good."

Apparently, that had been the wrong topic to bring up. "Sorry," I murmured.

245

"We were supposed to invest in something, and have a return by Monday," he said. "But I kind of forgot. They're meeting tonight to pick something."

"It's a Saturday," I said, shocked. "And it's prom night."

"Well, most of them don't have lives," Brian said matter-of-factly. "Otherwise, they wouldn't be in Young Investors."

"You are," Nate said. "What does *that* say?"

"Listen, Ellis . . ." Brian said, and I had a feeling a guy insult-fest was about to begin.

"I need to talk to you," Kittson said, taking my elbow and drawing me away from the rest of the group. When we stopped, I saw her take in my outfit, her eyes widening. "Nice," she said offhandedly after a moment. I knew Kittson well enough to realize she'd just given me a very big compliment.

"Thanks," I said. "You too."

"I know," she said, smoothing down her dress. "Of course, I hadn't planned on spending my prom night with my sister."

"I hear that noise," I said, shaking my head. We both looked toward Olivia and Travis, who were still standing off to the side and appeared to be having an intense discussion.

"But listen," Kittson said, leaning closer and lowering her voice. "It's about what we got off Dr. Trent's computer. The prom voting is seriously messed up."

"What do you mean?"

"I mean you were right in thinking that whoever was running that site was rigging it. The election's totally fixed." Kittson looked furious, and I had a feeling that the election wasn't fixed in her favor.

"How?" I asked as Turtell came over to us.

"Sup, Mad?" he asked.

"Hi, Glen," I said. I looked at Kittson, hoping we could get back to our conversation, but she gave me a tiny, subtle shake of her head and smiled at Turtell.

"Something's up with Olivia," Turtell said, pointing toward Travis and Olivia, who were now standing apart from each other, both with their arms crossed.

"Ruh-roh," I said. "Trouble in middle school paradise." This did not look good. I turned to say something to Nate when I noticed someone walking up Dave's driveway.

It was a very pretty girl in a beautiful light blue prom dress. She was very petite— she and Lisa, without heels, would probably have been around the same height. But unlike Lisa, she was curvy, and her dress accentuated this. Her hair was dark brown and glossy, and up in a perfect twist. Seeing this, I ran my hand over my own hair.

"Who is that?" Kittson asked, frowning.

"Brian's date, I assume," I said. The girl approached us, and I saw that she was even prettier up close, with bright blue eyes and porcelain skin.

"Hi," she said, glancing at the guys in tuxes. "I'm looking for someone. . . ." she said tentatively. Her glance

247

fell on Nate, who was still busy insulting Brian. Her eyes lit up and she smiled. *"Nate?"* she asked, sounding surprised and thrilled.

Nate turned to her and his eyes widened. "Mel?" he asked, sounding stunned. "What are you doing here?"

"Who's Mel?" Kittson hissed at me.

"I . . . don't know," I said. I was hoping with every fiber of my being that what I was afraid was happening was not actually happening, that Mel was actually short for Melinda. Or Melvin.

As I watched, horrified, Mel and Nate hugged. It looked like she hung on for just a moment longer than he did. I saw Schuyler and Lisa take this in, and both immediately made their way over to me.

"I'm here to meet my prom date," Mel said, laughing.

"I think that would be me," Brian said, bounding forward and looking elated. "I'm Brian."

"Melissa," she said, and they shook hands.

"Melissa?" Schuyler whispered to me, appearing at my shoulder.

"*Sex* Melissa?" Lisa whispered, arriving behind her.

"Don't call her that," I murmured. "Maybe it's just a coincidence."

"Why did you call her Sex Melissa?" Kittson asked.

"Yeah," Turtell said, looking very interested in the answer.

"This is so funny," Melissa said, turning back to Nate. She laughed and rested her hand on his arm. "I can't believe this!"

"You two know each other?" Brian asked.

"Well, we, um . . ." Nate said, glancing over at me.

"We used to date," Melissa said.

"You're *Nate's* Melissa?" Dave asked, sounding flabbergasted. He looked over at me, brow furrowed.

"Well, not anymore," Melissa said. "But at one time . . ."

"Mel, you haven't met Madison, have you?" Nate said, cutting her off. "My girlfriend. Mad?"

I pressed my lips together and walked over to Nate, who threaded his hand through mine. I smiled at Melissa, trying to pretend that she was just some random gorgeous girl I was meeting and not someone who might have slept with my boyfriend. "Hi," I said, forcing myself to smile.

"Madison," Melissa said, smiling easily. "I've heard so much about you. It's so nice to finally meet you!"

"You too," I said.

"Nate and I had been talking about all of us getting together soon, and now we can! We can hang out together all night!"

"Hooray," I said faintly as she gave me a bright smile. It shouldn't have surprised me that Melissa seemed nice. I wouldn't have expected Nate to have dated someone who wasn't. But I really, really didn't want her here, attending my prom with me and Nate. There was far too much going on already.

"Have you met everyone else?" Brian asked, stepping closer to Melissa and beginning to make the introductions.

"Mad," Kittson whispered, tipping her head to the side slightly. I let go of Nate's hand and walked a few steps away with her. I forced myself not to look at Melissa and tried not to notice how Brian—and most of the guys—were staring at her. I tried to focus on Kittson.

"The prom voting," she said urgently. "I don't know how, but it's been fixed. The codes have been corrupted, so people's votes aren't going to go to the right person. Any vote for Justin is going to count as a vote for *Dave*, of all people."

"*Dave* is going to be prom king?" I asked.

"That's not all," she said darkly. "Any vote for me—since whoever did this was assuming, rightly, that I would win—is also counted as a vote for someone else."

"Who?" I asked.

Kittson looked at me in silence for a long moment, then finally spoke. "You," she said.

CHAPTER 21

Song: Jesse Buy Nothing . . . Go To Prom Anyways/
Hellogoodbye
Quote: "Bam, said the lady!"—Nathan Fillion

"But that makes no sense," I whispered to Kittson as I climbed out of the limo at the Hyatt. It had not exactly been a relaxing ride. Travis and Olivia had spent the entire time sniping at each other; Schuyler and Connor appeared to be barely speaking; and Jimmy and Liz had spent the whole ride making out. Kittson had glowered at me the whole time, as though trying to determine if I would be capable of rigging a prom queen election in my favor. Nate and I had ended up squeezed in next to Melissa and Brian, and Melissa kept leaning across Brian to talk to us. Needless to say, I had been very happy when we'd finally arrived.

We'd been stuck in a limo line for fifteen minutes, and as we got out, I could see the cars stretching back as far as I could see. The limos were mostly black, but there were a few white ones and one stretch Hummer that appeared to be blocking the fire entrance. All around me, people were getting out of limos, dressed to the nines. I saw that it was going to be easy to tell the Putnam and Hartfield prom-goers apart. The Putnam people were dressed in normal prom clothes. But the Hartfield people had clearly embraced their eighties theme—I saw neon, crimped hair, and dresses with big puffed sleeves.

As I straightened my dress, I saw the white Putnam Pizza van rumble past. Back at Dave's house, Dave and Lisa had ridden with us down to the bottom of the driveway, then had gotten out of the limo and driven to the prom in the delivery van. I watched the van disappear around the back of the hotel, heading for the service entrance.

I walked up the steps, still trying to talk to Kittson. I glanced behind me and saw that the rest of our group was moving more slowly. Melissa was talking to Nate as Brian hovered nearby.

"I know it doesn't make sense," Kittson snapped as we reached the lobby. I looked nervously toward the desk and saw that Mr. Patrick was working, speaking on the phone and frowning at the line of high school students filing past him. I tried to see if the door behind the desk—the one that led to the safe—was open. It didn't appear to be. The wall behind the desk looked solid, completely hiding a room behind it. So presumably, the Hello Kitty crown was very secure.

"Kittson, I didn't do this," I said as we stopped to wait for the rest of the group. "I don't want to be prom queen!"

"You certainly looked happy wearing the crown," she said sourly. "I saw the pictures on Q-pic, Mad."

Had *everyone* seen Ginger's pictures? "But that doesn't mean I want to be prom queen," I said. "I don't. I promise."

Kittson looked at me a moment more, then nodded. "I believe you," she said, a little grudgingly. "But somebody wants you to be prom queen. God knows why."

"Or they *don't* want you to be queen," I said. Turtell was crossing the lobby toward us, and I looked at him closely. "How jealous *was* Glen about the fact that you might dance with someone else?" I murmured.

"Not possible," she murmured back, but didn't sound entirely sure. As Turtell joined us, she switched into prom-chairperson mode. "I'd better go make sure everything's set up," she said, hustling down the hall to the Rosebud Ballroom, Turtell following behind her.

"That way?" Jimmy asked, pointing to where Kittson was heading.

"That way," I confirmed, and Schuyler and Connor also began making their way down the hallway. "Travis," I said as my brother stomped up the stairs, "your ballroom is that way, down a very long hallway. . . ." Olivia stormed past us without a word and headed toward the bat mitzvah ballroom. "What's going on?" I asked Travis.

"What's *going on* is that Olivia just broke up with me," Travis said, his voice quavering.

"Oh, Travis," I said. I suddenly felt bad about all the times I'd teased him about his relationship. After all, Olivia was his first girlfriend, and he was only thirteen. "I'm so sorry."

"Well, not as sorry as you will be," he said. His voice wasn't quavering anymore. It was just very cold. "I have no reason now to keep lying for you, do I? I might just call Mom and Dad and tell them you're not coming home tonight."

He might have only been thirteen, but he was pure evil Demon Spawn. And I never should have let myself forget it. "Travis," I said in my calmest voice. "You don't want to do something like that."

"Why not?" he said. "What's to stop me?" He headed toward the endless hallway. "Have a good prom," he called over his shoulder. "I'll tell Mom and Dad you say hi." I watched him go, cursing once again the fact that I had been saddled with him as my brother.

"There you are," Nate said, coming up to me and taking my hand. "Ready?"

"Yes," I said, trying to smile at him as we made our way down the hallway. I looked back and saw Brian and Melissa following behind us.

"Can you tell me why Dave and Lisa left our limo and got into a van?" Nate asked as we headed toward the Rosebud Ballroom.

I smiled at him. "Need-to-know," I said. "I wish I could."

"Got it," he said. "But just so you know, I'm intrigued."

"Oh, are you?" I asked. I couldn't help laughing at that. If he thought the van was intriguing, I could only imagine what he would say if he knew about everything that was happening: the Plan, the crown stealing, and the fact that someone was apparently pulling strings to make me prom queen. Which was actually really, *really* strange.

"I am," Nate said as we rounded the corner to the entrance of the ballroom.

I stopped, stunned, staring ahead at what was in front of me. It looked like a security checkpoint had been set up at the doors that led to the sitting area outside the Rosebud Ballroom and the grand staircase that led to the Lily Ballroom. The checkpoint was a long table, with Dr. Trent, Stephanie, and the woman who I assumed was the Hartfield High equivalent of Dr. Trent sitting behind it. People were being separated by school and having their tickets and IDs checked by the school administrators before they were allowed past. As I watched, every student was given a plastic bracelet before going through the doors and to their respective proms. Hartfield students were getting red; Putnam students were getting blue.

"What's going on?" Nate asked me.

"I have no idea," I said. I couldn't stop staring at the bracelets. We'd had multiple meetings about prom security with Dr. Trent, and he had never mentioned bracelets. If they were to prevent people from moving from one prom to the other—and I assumed they were—our plan was suddenly in serious jeopardy.

"Hello, Madison." I turned and saw Isabel standing behind me. She was wearing a long gold dress, tight-fitting but with exaggerated shoulders—clearly designer eighties wear. Her dark hair was in a complicated updo on top of her head.

"Isabel," I said flatly. She smiled at me and adjusted the shoulder bag she was clutching, and I saw that there was a scarf tied to it. I looked more closely and realized to my horror that it looked very familiar. It was my dress. She'd cut up my *dress* for an ugly purse accessory.

"Nice dress," she said, frowning. She was clearly wondering how I'd managed to get another one—and, frankly, a better one—on such short notice. "Where's it from?"

"The Vault," I said.

"Let me introduce you to my date," she said smugly. She tugged on the hand of the guy standing behind her, who turned around to face us.

"Wot? Oh, yes, quite. Ever so charmed to meet you. I'm Marcus." I bit my lip hard to keep from smiling. It was Mark Rothmann, almost unrecognizable in a tux with a neon blue bow tie, his hair parted sharply down the middle, and a very exaggerated English accent. Mark smiled at us pleasantly.

"Hey there, good to see—" Nate started. I squeezed his hand tightly, and he stopped in midsentence. "Meet you?" he amended quickly, looking at me. I nodded as subtly as I could.

"Darling, you can tell them your whole name," Isabel said, threading her arm through Mark's and smiling up at him. "He's just modest. It's so *English* of him."

"Oh, rather," Mark drawled. "Well, it's all a bit . . . you know. Top-drawer, wot? But the whole bit is Marcus James Selwidge Rothschild. Bit much, eh?"

"Third earl of Essex," Isabel said with a self-satisfied smile. "So we should actually be calling him Lord Rothschild."

"The Honourable Marcus Rothschild, actually, luv," Mark amended. "That's how it goes in the *Debrett's*, wot?"

"Oh, of course. Of course," Isabel said quickly.

"Really." I stared at Mark hard. We hadn't planned any of that. Mark had been told specifically to keep his real name. Whenever Mark starting going off book, disaster inevitably followed. "Selwidge, huh?" I asked. "Wow. That doesn't even sound like a real name at all."

"Well, he's *British*," Isabel said, as though I was very dim. Her eyes shifted to Nate. "And who's this?"

"Nathan," I said quickly. Nate shot me an incredulous look, and I just squeezed his hand again.

"Yes, I am Nathan," Nate said to Isabel and Mark. "Nice to meet you both. For the first time."

"It's a pleasure," Isabel said. Her purse slipped off her shoulder, and she grabbed for the chain, righting it. Her hand gripped the bottom of the bag a little too tightly. And now that I looked at her outfit, the bag seemed wrong for it. It was too bulky or something. . . . I watched her carefully adjusting the bag, and then it hit me: It was where she was keeping the crown. It had to be. If Mark could get to the bag immediately, this all might go more easily than I'd imagined.

"We should be going," Isabel said, smiling at me again.

"What's with the bracelets?" I blurted out before they could walk away. "They weren't on any of our security plans."

Isabel's smile grew. "Oh, I know," she said. "But when I told my headmistress that I was afraid of people trying to prom jump, she thought we'd better partner with your headmaster—"

"Assistant," I said automatically.

"To make sure that everything ran smoothly. So now nobody gets a bracelet unless they have a date from that school. I hope that's not a problem for you, Madison."

I gritted my teeth. "Why would that be a problem?" I asked.

"Well, exactly. Why indeed? Enjoy your night," she said, heading over to the Hartfield line, hand still clutching her bag.

"Awfully nice to have met you chaps. Cheers, eh?" Mark drawled, staying in character. Then he broke it for a moment, giving me a grin and a thumbs-up before trotting after Isabel.

"Okay," Nate said, turning to me. "Please explain. Why is Mark pretending to be an earl?"

"Nate—"

"And if I'm going by Nathan, can I have an accent, too? Maybe this Nathan character, he is Russian. *Da?*"

"Nyet," I said, trying not to laugh. "I can't tell you. But thanks for playing along. You were brilliant."

"You're going to have to explain this to me later," he said as we moved forward in the Putnam line. "Because things are getting weird."

I didn't have the heart to tell him they were probably only going to get weirder. "Speaking of weird," I said, "it's strange Melissa's here."

"I know!" Nate said, shaking his head. "Small world, right?"

"I mean . . . " I stopped, not sure how to put this. "It's just that you've never really talked about her."

Nate frowned. "You want me to talk about my ex-girlfriend?"

"No," I said as we got closer to the table. "I mean, yes. I just want to know more about your relationship. I want to know . . ." I hesitated. *Did you sleep together? Did you love her? Are you over her?* But I couldn't quite get the words out.

"Well, we can talk about it if you want, Mad," Nate said. "But it's the past. And I'm not sure it does any good to look back."

"But—"

"Names?" Stephanie asked. I looked up and realized we'd made it to the table.

"Oh, hi," I said. I handed her our tickets. "Madison MacDonald and date."

"Hi there," Stephanie said, smiling at me, taking my tickets, and crossing my name off a list. "Wrists," she said. I held out my right wrist, and so did Nate, and she snapped the blue plastic bracelets around them. "I am to officially remind all students that there should be no wandering around to other areas of the hotel," Stephanie recited, a little wearily. "No going to the Hartfield prom. No hanging out by the hotel pool. Any student found in an area they're not supposed to be in will face serious consequences, including suspension or possible expulsion." I stared at her, a little stunned by this speech.

It had just made our night *so* much harder. "Enjoy the prom," she added. "Next!"

Nate and I stepped to the side and headed for the doors that led to the ballrooms. "You go ahead," I said, trying to appear like I was not currently experiencing a meltdown. I needed to figure out how to get around this bracelet thing. If I couldn't, I should just surrender and turn myself in to Dr. Trent. "Official prom business," I said, giving him my best attempt at a smile.

"See you in there," Nate said, squeezing my hand and continuing in to the prom.

I wondered what I was supposed to do now. The plan depended on the assumption that we would have access to both proms. And apparently, eighties formal wear was no longer going to be enough to get us in. I forced myself to try to think clearly. Only people with Hartfield dates were being given red bracelets. Which meant . . .

Which meant I'd need a Hartfield date.

I scanned the Hartfield line—girls in bubble-gum-pink dresses and guys in baggy white suits. My eyes fell on a guy standing alone, and I took a deep breath and made my way over to him. He was cute, I saw as I got closer. He was wearing a houndstooth check bow tie with matching cummerbund and was medium height, with spiky black hair and killer cheekbones. A little stunned that I was actually going to do this, I tapped him on the shoulder.

"Hi there," I said, with a big smile.

He turned to me, looking confused. "Um, hi."

I held out my hand. "I'm Madison MacDonald." He

tilted his head to the side, as though he recognized the name and was trying to place me.

"Andy Lee," he said, shaking hands with me.

"Do you have a date?"

"Um." He looked around, as though trying to make sure I was talking to him. "No."

Jackpot. "Wow, that's too bad, Andy."

"It's not exactly my fault," he said a little defensively. "I just moved from Minnesota, and it's not like I know that many people yet."

"Oh, totally understandable," I said, nodding. "So, since you don't have a date, I was wondering if it would be possible for me to go with you. Would that be cool?"

Andy was staring at me like I'd grown an extra head. "Is this some kind of dare or something?" he asked. He looked around again, this time as though someone might be recording us. "Is this going to end up on YouTube?"

"No, no," I said as we moved closer to the front of the Hartfield line. I turned my back to Dr. Trent's end of the table. "I just really want to go to this prom. And you seem . . . nice."

Andy pointed at my bracelet. "Aren't you going to the Putnam prom?"

"Yes," I said quickly. "Well spotted, Andy. But I wanted to go to this one, too. I just really . . . love proms." Andy didn't say anything but, incredibly, seemed to be considering it. "Look, I'll pay for my own ticket, and I promise that I won't bother you or anything."

"Well . . ." Andy looked around one last time, as if making sure that he wasn't being punk'd. "I guess so."

"Thank you," I said, incredibly relieved. "I really appreciate it."

"Sure," Andy said, giving me a smile for the first time. "I mean, the prom's more fun with a date, right?"

Oh, crap. "Well," I said, trying to backpedal a little, "it's not going to be like a *real* date, exactly. . . ."

"Name?" The woman working the Hartfield list looked up at us.

"Anderson Lee," Andy said. "And, um, date. But I need a ticket for her. I guess."

"That'll be eighty," the woman said, checking off Andy's name.

I dug in my purse and located the money that my mother had given me to buy food over the weekend. Travis and I would just have to make do with ramen, or something. "Here," I said, counting out four twenties. The woman frowned at me, and I tried to act like this was completely normal behavior.

"Wrists?" she finally asked. I tucked my blue-braceleted wrist behind my back and held out my other hand to her. She snapped a red bracelet over my wrist and did the same for Andy. "I am to officially remind all students that there will be no . . ." she started.

"Got it," I said, not wanting to have to listen to the speech again. She appeared relieved to be able to skip it as well, and waved us inside.

"Enjoy the prom," she said. "Next!"

I walked around to Andy's other side and kept my head down to avoid being seen by Dr. Trent. When we made it through the doors without anyone yelling at me

262

to stop, I let out a small breath and looked around, happy to see that the résumé kids had followed through on their one job. The area in front of the Rosebud Ballroom had been transformed since I'd last been there, with balloons and streamers in our prom colors—silver and blue—everywhere. There was a hotel employee standing outside the doors to the Rosebud Ballroom, checking bracelets as people went in.

Andy gestured to the staircase, which had white and gold balloons—presumably Hartfield's prom colors—tied to the railings. "Should we go up?" he asked.

"Um," I said, glancing toward our ballroom. "I'll meet you up there in a minute. Just have to . . . check in on the other prom."

"Okay," he said, smiling at me again. "This might actually be fun, Madison. I'll see you soon." He gave me a wave and headed up the staircase, showing a hotel employee standing on the stairs his red bracelet. As I watched him go, it hit me that I probably should have mentioned that I had a boyfriend.

Well, I could do that later. I showed my blue bracelet to the employee at the door and entered the ballroom.

For all of Kittson's tyrannical methods, I had to give her credit. All the errands and lectures and extra work had truly paid off. She had pulled together a beautiful prom. The ballroom was stunning—silver and blue balloons covering the ceiling, silver and blue soft swirling lights over the dance floor, and streamers everywhere. The tables that surrounded the dance floor were covered in silver sparkles that picked up the light, making the entire ballroom seem like it was underwater. Which was ironic, considering the theme. But it was magical. I allowed myself a moment to stand there and just take it all in.

"Madison!" I turned to see Kittson hurrying toward me.

"Hey," I said. "Congratulations. This is amazing. It's just—"

"We have a problem," she interrupted me.

Oh, dear God. "What now?" I asked, afraid of the answer.

"Look around, Madison," she said. "What's missing?"

I looked around. Everything seemed to be perfect. People were milling about the tables; the decorations were immaculate; the lights were in sync; it was very quiet. . . .

"Where's the music?" I asked.

"Exactly," she said. "Tanner was your responsibility. He better not have flaked, or you're DJing this prom yourself." She took a breath and looked down at my wrist, her eyes widening. "You got a red bracelet," she said, looking relieved. "How'd you manage it?"

"I got a date to the Hartfield prom," I said. "Don't tell Nate."

"Well played," Kittson said, looking at me with more respect than I'd ever seen from her before.

"I'm going to find Tanner," I said. "Um, if you see Nate, tell him I'm on my way."

"Sure," Kittson said, heading back across the ballroom. I looked in the direction she was walking and saw that she had commandeered a table off to the side. Normally, it never would have been the table Kittson—or anyone else, for that matter—would have chosen. It was tucked away, almost pushed against the wall, not well lit, and near an exit door. So for our purposes, it was perfect.

I walked out of the ballroom toward the checkpoint area. I was worried that the hotel employee guarding the door might stop me, but he was busy examining a bracelet and didn't notice me. As I looked around for Tanner, I saw that the person currently at the front of the line was Ruth.

She looked great, I noted with a flicker of former BFF pride. Her dress was lovely, a simple cream-colored gown that suited her perfectly. Her hair was up, and she carried a small evening bag in one hand. But she was standing alone, and I wondered if she'd driven herself over. Then I wondered if she'd had to shop for the dress by herself. The thought made me sadder than I was prepared for. I looked down at my own dress, then across the room at hers, and felt a pang, thinking of the picture of us in our prom dresses that we would never take. Ruth got her bracelet, and I forced myself to look away and get back to searching for Tanner.

He was nowhere to be found, but standing off to the side was a guy clearly too old to be a student, texting on his phone. He was wearing a black T-shirt that read *Play That Funky Music!* and was carrying a bag that appeared to be filled with electronic equipment. He looked so professional I was immediately ashamed of Tanner. Clearly, this was a DJ who understood what someone meant by "prom music." He also looked lost, and I took pity on him.

"Hi," I said, walking up to him. "Are you the DJ?"

"Yes," he said, closing his phone and looking relieved to see me. "I'm Chris, from Play That Funky Music Entertainment. Are you from the prom? I'm supposed to talk to someone named Isabel so I can get set up."

"Mad!" I turned toward the voice and saw Tanner running full speed toward me. "I'm so sorry I'm late. I kept trying to find this place, but the hotel people kept directing me to this bat mitzvah. And there was this really long hallway, and I don't know why they kept sending me there. . . ."

It might have had something to do with the fact that Tanner looked about Travis's age in his T-shirt and backpack. It was kind of depressing to see the contrast of Tanner standing next to a real, professional DJ.

A terrible, devious idea suddenly occurred to me. It was going outside the plan, but it would fit nicely with Kittson's revenge initiative. But I dismissed it. I couldn't do that to Isabel.

But a second later, I remembered the sight of my mangled dress hanging off her bag, and the way she'd smiled when she'd taken our crown from a crying Schuyler. She *deserved* this.

"Well!" I said brightly. "So glad you're both here. Sorry about the confusion. We have two events here tonight, so things are a bit hectic. Chris, you're going to be doing the Putnam prom."

"What!" Tanner said, looking affronted.

"And, Tanner, your special skills are going to be used to entertain the Hartfield students."

"All right," Chris said. "Where do I set up?"

"Just go to that table," I said, gesturing to where Dr. Trent was sitting, "and tell him that you're here to DJ the Putnam prom. And they'll tell you where to go!"

"Great," Chris said, shouldering his bag. "Thanks." He headed straight up to the table, walking around the line, and as I watched, Stephanie snapped a blue bracelet on his wrist, and he headed through the doors toward the Rosebud Ballroom.

"Thanks a lot, Mad," Tanner said, his voice cracking a bit. "I really worked hard on this gig. And then you replace me at the last minute with a total sellout like that? I thought we were friends."

"We are," I said, turning to Tanner, "which is why I need you to DJ this other prom. Because they're the ones who can appreciate your unique . . . vision. Do you still have that playlist you made? The one with Satan Muppets?"

"Yes," Tanner said slowly. "And it's *awesome*. But I don't know what . . ."

"I think you need to play what's on that playlist," I said. "And *only* that. And even if people tell you to play other things, you should stand strong. Don't take any requests. Stay true to your vision!"

"Yeah," Tanner said, his eyes lighting up. "I can do that."

"Great. Go up to that table," I said, gesturing to the Hartfield side, "and tell them that you're Chris the DJ from Play That Funky Music Entertainment. Can you do that? Or should I write it down?"

"No, I'll remember," he said excitedly. "Is that, like, my DJ alias?"

"Exactly," I said. "You'll do great, Tanner. Go rock out!"

"Thanks, Mad!" Tanner said, beaming at me. "Catch you on the flip side!" I watched long enough to see him walk up to the table and get a bracelet; then I slipped back inside and headed to the Rosebud Ballroom.

Chris was setting up his professional-looking equipment, and I smiled as I headed to our table. It was overcrowded, which was funny, since it was clearly the worst table at the prom. But wedged around it were Nate, Jimmy, Liz, Schuyler, Connor, Kittson, Turtell, Brian, and Melissa.

I caught Liz's eye as I got closer to the table, and she came over to meet me. "Hi, Liz," I said as we walked together toward the table. I handed her my small prom purse. "How's it going?"

"Oh, fine," she said. She handed me her bag. "How are you?" she asked.

"Can't complain," I said as we reached the table. Nate stood up and smiled when he saw me. It looked like he'd been sitting next to Melissa, and my heart gave a funny little twist.

"Where's Tanner?" Kittson asked me as I approached.

"DJing the Hartfield prom," I said quietly.

"Madison, I think I underestimated you," Kittson said

in an awed voice. I felt the bag in my hand vibrate and saw that the phone was lit up with an update. Schuyler, Kittson, and Turtell looked down as well, and I knew it must have been heist-related.

 Dave Gold → the crew Getting all set up in the greenroom before the show. Ready when you are.

I caught Schuyler's eye and nodded. She whispered something to Connor, who shrugged, arms folded. Then she followed Kittson and Turtell as they got up and headed for the back exit, the one near our table.

"Hey," Nate said, coming over to me. "Where've you been?"

"Prom stuff," I answered. I sighed. "And I'm afraid I have to go again."

I saw a look of annoyance cross Nate's face. "Mad, you just got here," he said.

"I know," I said. I looked toward the door and saw Schuyler holding it open, waiting for me. "I'll be back soon, okay?"

"Okay," he said, and gave me a smile, but I could tell that his whole heart wasn't in it. I gave him a quick kiss, then hurried to meet Schuyler at the door.

It was go time.

CHAPTER 22

Song: Let's Make This Moment A Crime/The Format
Quote: "It's an ill plan that cannot be changed."
—Anon

I followed Schuyler outside the Rosebud Ballroom. This exit was at the other end from the hotel employee checking bracelets, and it looked like he hadn't even heard the door open. We crossed to the door that led to the service staircase and went through it. I grabbed the door to slow its momentum so that it wouldn't slam, and let it latch quietly.

I turned to Schuyler, who looked pale and a little bit sick. "Ready?" I asked her.

She didn't look ready, but she nodded. "Ready," she said.

We crept down the service stairs one flight, to the level of the hotel where the conference rooms were. Kittson had checked—there were no conferences taking place tonight, so we'd have the whole floor to ourselves. We rounded the corner, heading for Conference Room B.

Standing outside it were Kittson, Turtell, Ginger, Sarah, Lisa, and Dave. Dave was still wearing his bulky-looking tux, standing next to a rolling silver service tray covered with a white tablecloth.

"Where's Brian?" Dave asked, looking around.

"Making excuses for us at the table," Schuyler said. "I thought it would be good to have ears up there, in case people start asking questions."

"Good idea," I said. I turned to Turtell. "Ready, Glen?"

Turtell nodded, opened his jacket, and pulled a small pouch from the inside pocket. He knelt in front of the locked door of the conference room. "Lookout?" he asked.

"Oh, right," Schuyler said, hustling down the hall. "Sorry." A moment later, all our phones beeped at the same time.

 Shy Time → the crew Glen, you're crystal.

"Excellent," he said, unrolling the pouch, which was filled with small picks of varying sizes. He selected one and brought it up to the lock. Just a few minutes later, he'd worked his magic, and the door swung open. "Done," he said. He rolled up the pouch, placed it back in his jacket, and stepped into the room. He grabbed a sign from the corner that read MEETING IN PROGRESS and placed it outside the door. Everyone filed into the room, and I sent an update for Schuyler.

promgirl → the crew Shy, Meeting in Progress.

 Shy Time → the crew What? Who is this? I have no idea what you're referring to.

 promgirl → the crew Shy, it's ME. We talked about this.

 Shy Time → the crew Oh, right. Sorry.

Schuyler returned to the conference room and closed and locked the door behind her. Then we got to work. Ginger hung up a sheet across one corner of the room, which would function as a makeshift changing area. Dave whisked the white tablecloth off the serving cart, which contained no food. Instead, it was filled with the clothes and equipment we'd brought with us. I took my Hartfield outfit from the pile and hung it on the back of a chair. Dave took off his tux jacket and unbuttoned his tux shirt, revealing his Putnam Pizza T-shirt underneath. Kittson opened her laptop and began typing on it, frowning at what she saw on the screen.

"Okay," I said, turning to the group. "Let's synchronize phones." I looked down at the one that was mine for the night. "I've got eight forty-five." Everyone else, looking at their phones, nodded. "And just remember

272

to use the codes as much as you can, and don't let your updates be too obvious."

"You don't know who's reading them," Turtell added.

"Glen's right," I said. "Also, anyone who is at the Hartfield prom," I said, looking at Dave and Sarah, "you can't have any contact with Mark. As far as Isabel knows, you've never seen him before."

"I'm an *actress*," Sarah said dismissively. "I think I can handle that."

"Also, he's pretending to be an earl," I said. "Just BT-Dub."

"Why?" Dave asked.

"He's building a character," Sarah said, as though this was completely understandable.

"So is everyone clear on the Plan?" I asked, looking around the room. Everyone nodded. Nobody looked totally confident, but nobody was leaving, either. "Great," I said. "Just keep in communication. Especially if things start to go wrong. Which they won't," I added quickly, seeing Schuyler's stricken expression.

"We should probably get back," Lisa said, checking the time on her phone.

"Right," I said, realizing how quickly time was passing, and getting a little nervous about everything that had to happen before the prom was over. "So let's leave one by one, just to be safe."

"And we're meeting here at the end, right?" Ginger asked.

"At ten-forty-five," I confirmed. Nobody moved. "Come on, guys," I said, trying to rally morale. "Let's make it a night to remember."

Kittson looked up from her screen and glared at me as Sarah slipped out the door. "I can't believe you're still making fun of my theme," she said.

"I'm not making fun of it," I said as Schuyler headed out the door. "That was an homage." Lisa breezed by me, very pointedly not looking in my direction. "Lise," I said, trying to catch her arm.

"Non," she said without stopping, keeping her eyes focused straight ahead. "Not talking to you, Mad."

"Lisa," I said, frustrated, feeling that this had gone on much too long. But she ignored me and left. Before the door closed, I could see her slinking down the hall, *Alias*-style.

"Ready, Mad?" Ginger asked, standing by the curtained area, holding up my dress.

"Ready," I said, letting out an angry breath. "Dave," I said, turning to him, "could you please talk some sense into your girlfriend? Why is she still angry at me?"

Dave spread the tablecloth over the now-empty serving cart and pushed it toward the entrance. "Mad, believe me, I don't know why she's still acting this way. But if you think I'm getting in the middle, you're crazy."

Turtell held open the door for Dave, and Dave looked around and pushed his cart out into the hall, whistling in what I'm sure he thought was a nonchalant manner, but actually made him look incredibly suspicious. Turtell let the door close and looked at Kittson. "Coming, baby?" he asked her.

Kittson looked up from her screen and paused in her typing. "I'll be there in a sec," she said. "Save me a seat."

Turtell nodded, pushed the door open slowly, looked out, and left. It closed and Ginger held up my dress again. "Mad?" she asked.

"Right," I said, focusing on the task at hand. The clock was ticking, after all. I ducked behind the curtain and stepped out of the pink dress. "Kittson, what's with the laptop?" I called through the curtain.

"I am going to reverse this voting thing," she said, and I could hear her keyboard clicking.

"How?" I asked.

"Dell's not the only one who knows how to hack people," she said, sounding grim.

"Seriously?" I asked.

"Seriously," she said. "It's just that some of us don't choose to use our powers for evil."

"What are you guys talking about?" Ginger asked.

"Nothing that's not fixable, hopefully," Kittson said.

"Ready," I said, reaching over the curtain. Ginger handed me what she was calling my Hartfield dress. I looked at it for a moment, mentally preparing myself to put it on. It was black with flashes of hot pink across the bodice, strapless, and short. The skirt flared out, tutu-style, with taffeta netting underneath. I sighed and stepped into it. Of the eighties dresses Ginger had pulled, it fit me the best and had been the easiest to get into and out of. But it would never have been my choice to wear in front of everyone I knew. I zipped it, stepped out, and saw Kittson raise her eyebrows at me. "What?" I asked, looking down. "Is it bad?"

"No," she said, turning back to her computer. "It's just a little . . . short."

"I know," I said. I tried to tug it down but found I couldn't do that without the top being in danger of slipping too low. Whoever this dress had been designed for, I had a feeling that she was not as tall as me.

"You look great," Ginger said. "Accessories." She draped several long pearl necklaces over my head and handed me a pair of the now-fingerless black lace gloves.

"These, too?" I asked.

"It's the details that make it," Ginger said firmly, and I knew better than to argue with her. Plus, we didn't have time. I put on the gloves and she took a step back.

"Well?" I asked.

Ginger smiled at her handiwork. "Very early Madonna," she said. "You look great."

"Thanks," I said, straightening the gloves.

"You know who else looks great?" she asked as she hung my real prom dress over the back of a chair. "Ruth Miller." Then she seemed to realize what she'd just said and looked at me, stricken. "Um, sorry, Mad."

"No, it's fine," I said. "We're friends, after all. Kind of."

"Well, her dress is fantastic," Ginger said as she straightened up the wardrobe area and made her way to the door. "Though I guess it makes sense that she can afford a dress like that."

"What do you mean?" I asked.

"The betting website," Ginger said, sounding surprised I didn't know what she was talking about. "The one you showed me yesterday. It's registered in her name."

CHAPTER 23

Song: Prom Theme/Fountains of Wayne
Quote: "Every exit is an entry somewhere else."
—Tom Stoppard

The door slammed behind Ginger, and I turned to Kittson, stunned. "What?" I asked her.

Kittson typed rapidly for a few moments, then nodded and looked up. "Ginger's right," she said. "It is registered in her name. That is so weird."

"Why would Ruth rig the election so that *I* would win?" I asked.

"Maybe she thinks that it would make you two friends again," Kittson said. She shook her head. "Oh, I'm going to kill her."

"But how would she even have gotten to the voting program?" I asked. I started to sit on the edge of the table, before realizing that the length of my skirt made that problematic.

"Or," Kittson said, still typing, "maybe she thought you'd get in trouble. Maybe this is, like, her revenge."

"Why would I get in trouble?" I asked.

"Well, come on," Kittson said, looking up long enough to give me a small smile. "I think once *you* and *Dave* were crowned, there might have been an investigation into what the hell had gone wrong. Not to mention the fact that Lisa would probably kill you." She hit a key and smiled. "Done," she said.

"Really?" I asked as she closed her laptop.

"Yes," she said. "All votes are now going to go to the people they belong to. Which means that if there's any sense in the world at all, I'm going to win."

"And Justin?" I asked as we headed for the door.

"Probably," she said, shrugging.

"Is Glen still going to beat him up?"

"Probably," she said with a small frown. "He'll be dancing with me, plus there's the fact that he's my ex. Not sure that's going to go over too well."

"Poor Justin," I said.

"Poor me," Kittson said. "I almost had my rightful title taken away from me."

I shook my head and checked the time on my phone. "Okay, you go first," I said. Kittson nodded and slipped out the door. I waited a moment, looked down at my ridiculous outfit, and sighed. Nate was probably wondering what had happened to me. Either that, or Melissa was keeping him company. I tried to push that thought away, but it wasn't going easily.

I hit the lights in Conference Room B and slipped out the door, looking around the deserted hallway. I walked quickly around the corner, holding my strands of pearls in one hand so they wouldn't click together. I pushed the door to the service stairs open and ducked inside. I walked up one flight and pushed the door open slowly, stepping into the area by the Rosebud Ballroom. I crossed toward the staircase and started to climb it.

"Hey!" I heard someone say. I turned and saw the hotel employee who was checking Putnam bracelets looking at me. "Where are you going?"

"Up to my prom," I said, holding up my red bracelet, pulling my glove over my blue one, to cover it.

"Well, you shouldn't be down here," he said. "Try to stay in your area, okay?"

"You got it," I said, heading up the staircase quickly. I showed my red bracelet to the employee on the staircase, who was busy texting and appeared very uninterested in me. I walked to the landing, and my ears were immediately assaulted by screeching that sounded a little bit like a dying cat. I smiled, very proud of Tanner. Before I entered the ballroom, I took out the phone and updated my status.

promgirl → the crew I Love The 80s. Looking for the Package.

Dave Gold → the crew Ready with the Pickup Truck.

Shy Time → the crew All Quiet on the Putnam Front.

I pulled open the doors to the Lily Ballroom and looked around. It was a nicer ballroom than ours, and clearly the Hartfield budget had been bigger than ours. The decorations were fancier, but they also seemed a little overdone. Maybe it was all the hours I'd spent making streamers, but I thought that ours had more charm than these clearly store-bought decorations. There were white and gold balloons everywhere and white and yellow roses on every table, and *Top Gun* played on a screen, silently, behind Tanner's DJ station. Nobody was dancing, and the few people who had ventured near the dance floor were covering their ears and glaring at him. But if Tanner noticed, it wasn't apparent. He had his headphones on and a goofy smile on his face, moving to a beat that only he seemed able to hear.

I looked around the room, searching for Mark. In the back of the ballroom, I saw Dave with his cart, organizing the hors d'oeuvres that were set up along the back table. He caught my eye and shook his head. On the other side of the room, I saw Sarah sitting very close to Isabel's former date. I had to admit that even at this distance, he did look pretty cute. And it looked from Sarah's expression like she was pretty into him.

"There you are!"

I turned around and saw Andy smiling at me.

"Oh. Hi!" I stammered. I'd almost forgotten about him.

"Did you change?" he asked, frowning at my dress.

"Oh, well," I said, tugging at the bottom of it as much as I dared, "I just thought . . . since your theme is the eighties . . ."

"Where did you even get it?" he asked.

"Gift shop," I said quickly.

"Wow," he said, smiling at me, looking impressed. "So, do you want to dance?" he asked.

"Um," I said, looking at Tanner. This song was even worse than the last one, since now there was someone wailing tonelessly along with the screeching. "I'm not sure this is really dancing music."

"Yeah, I guess not," Andy said, looking at Tanner as well and shaking his head. "I don't know why they hired this guy."

"I know," I said. "It's weird. Hey," I said, gesturing to the back, where Dave was still standing with his cart, "let's get something to eat." I pulled Andy toward the tables at the back and pretended to be examining the bruschetta as I leaned close to Dave. "Did you get it?" I whispered.

Dave straightened a platter. "Nope," he murmured.

I checked my phone. We weren't out of time yet, but the clock was certainly ticking. "Mark," I muttered under my breath, taking out my phone and updating my status.

promgirl → the crew SELWIDGE. Where's the package???

I waited a moment for a response, but nothing came. I looked around the ballroom but didn't see Mark anywhere.

"Did you want something, Madison?" Andy asked, holding a plate filled with appetizers.

"Who is that?" Dave muttered to me as he passed Andy a stack of napkins.

"My date," I muttered back.

"Your *what*?" Dave asked at a normal volume.

"You know, I don't think I want anything after all," I said quickly as Andy looked over at us.

"Oh," Andy said, looking down at his plate. "Okay . . ."

"But you should sit and eat. It's, um, better for your digestion. Find a seat and I'll join you in a minute."

"Okay," he said a little doubtfully. "Well, when you do, there's something I wanted to ask you. . . ."

"Sure!" I said as brightly as I could. "In just a minute!"

Andy nodded and wandered away with his plate, looking for an empty seat.

"Your *date*?" Dave asked as soon as Andy was gone.

"It's a long story," I said, scanning the ballroom for Mark again. I finally saw him sitting at one of the biggest tables, next to Isabel. I tried to catch his eye, but he seemed to be involved in telling a story, making lots of hand gestures. Isabel's smile was a little fixed, but she appeared to be listening. "What is he *doing*?" I asked. He looked up and caught my eye, but he must have stopped midstory, because Isabel followed his glance and looked at me, eyes widening.

"You've been made," Dave murmured.

"That's okay," I said. "Now Mark can tell us what's going on. But you might want to get out of here so that the Pickup isn't compromised later on."

"If he can get it," Dave said, grabbing his cart.

"He has to," I said, realizing that perhaps a plan that gave Mark so much responsibility was not the best way to go. Dave nodded and wheeled his cart out of the ballroom.

Isabel stood up and started walking toward me, and to my dismay, she took her purse with her. As soon as her back was turned, Mark took out his phone and began typing frantically on it. Isabel was moving toward me at a rapid pace, her face set.

"Madison," she said, frowning at me, taking in the fingerless gloves and the pearls. "What are you doing here?"

"I'm attending your prom," I said, holding out my bracelet for her to see.

She blinked at it for a moment, then looked at me, eyes narrowed. "How?" she finally asked.

"My date," I said, pointing out Andy, who was sitting at a table by himself. "Really nice guy."

"What about Nathan?" she asked.

"What about him?" I asked pleasantly.

Isabel didn't seem to know what to say to this. "Well . . . fine," she said after a moment. "I'm glad you got to see how a *real* prom is run."

"Absolutely," I agreed. "It's very enlightening. Interesting DJ you've hired."

Her face darkened. "Did you have something to do with this?"

"With what?" I asked. "I happen to love this song."

"I think there was a mix-up with the DJs. And I tried to get down to your prom to see, but they wouldn't let me in without a bracelet."

"Oh, that's too bad," I said. "You know, I did hear that

284

they're cracking down on people trying to jump proms. Now, who told me that?"

"You *did* have something to do with this," she snapped. "I knew it!"

"I have no idea what you're talking about," I said. "Of course, if you wanted to just give us our crown back, I might be able to fix the situation. And maybe your fellow classmates would actually be able to dance at their prom."

Isabel stared at me, and for a moment it looked like she was considering it. I watched as her hand involuntarily gripped the bottom of her bag. Then she shook her head. "Not a chance," she said.

"Okay," I said. "Well, nice to talk to you, Isabel. I'll see you around." I turned and headed for the exit. I saw Mark watching me, and I stepped outside the ballroom and checked my phone.

Marcus → the crew Package not delivered. Bollocks!

KitKat → the crew Have you found it yet?

Marcus → the crew Righty-o. Location confirmed. Just a matter of delivery.

promgirl → Marcus I'm waiting outside the Lily, Earl.

A moment after I stepped outside, Mark stepped out, too. "Well?" I asked.

"I simply can't stay long, Mad," Mark said, his accent thicker than ever. "The crown's in her bag, in a jewelry box. But she's not letting the bloody thing out of her sight, is she? It's a right mess."

"Well, we need to get it away from her somehow," I said. "Right? Selwidge?"

"Oh, quite, quite," he said. "It's just . . . might be a bit of a sticky wicket, wot?"

"But we need it," I said. "If we don't get it, I'm dead, Schuyler's dead, and if Isabel finds out you're not a count—"

"Earl, luv," Mark said, looking offended.

"If Isabel finds out you're not an *earl,* you're dead. So we need to get the crown." I checked my phone, beginning to panic when I saw how much time had passed. "And soon. Okay?"

"Tally-ho!" Mark said a little weakly, heading back to the ballroom. I hurried back down the stairs and started toward the Putnam prom, thinking of all the time I wasn't spending with my boyfriend. But then I looked down at my outfit and realized I'd have to change first unless I wanted to do a lot of explaining. I went down the back stairs to the conference room. Once I'd slipped inside, I froze, looking around.

The lights were on—and I'd left them off. And I saw what looked like someone standing behind the curtain. "Hello?" I called, heart pounding, hoping that it was someone who was a part of all this, not someone who had the power to expel me.

Lisa stepped out from it, looking surprised to see me. She had her black prom dress draped over one arm and was wearing black pants and a Putnam Pizza T-shirt. "What are you doing here?" she asked.

"I'm changing for our prom," I said, grabbing my dress off the back of the chair and ducking behind the curtain. "What are you doing?" I heard Lisa sigh as I stepped out of one dress and into another. Ginger had been right about one thing—this dress really was easy to get out of. Maybe because there wasn't much to it. I pulled the pink dress on, zipped it, and stepped out from behind the curtain.

"Je ne sais pas," Lisa said, tucking in her T-shirt. "I guess I realized that it's just not the prom unless I'm going to spend it with Dave. Even if that does mean that I have to help him with catering."

"That's really nice," I said, realizing how much I wanted to get back to Nate. I looked at her and sighed. "Lisa, can we talk? You've barely spoken to me in days."

"I know," she said. She gave me a small smile. "I'm sorry, Mad. It wasn't about you."

"But what was it about?" I asked. "I'm sorry that I brought up the sex issue with Dave. I didn't know that it would turn into a whole thing."

"I know," she said. "And *je suis désolée.*"

"What's going on?" I asked. We probably didn't have time for this, but I needed to make things okay again between the two of us.

"I guess I just got scared," Lisa muttered, looking down at her hands. "I mean, I've wanted to sleep with Dave for a while."

"Really?" I asked, surprised. She'd never mentioned it to Schuyler or me.

"Oh, *oui*," Lisa breathed. "*Depuis longtemps*. But I started getting afraid that was the only reason that he was still with me. I mean, what if we did it and then he broke up with me right afterward?"

"Lisa, that's crazy," I said. "Dave's in love with you."

She shrugged one shoulder. "It's just what I was thinking," she said. "I know it doesn't make sense. But I am sorry for taking it out on you."

"It's fine," I said, just relieved that this tension was behind us. "But the next time you're mad at me, just talk to me. Relationships are about communication, you know."

Lisa laughed at that. "*D'accord*," she said, and we hugged quickly.

"I'd better get back," I said when we stepped apart.

"Me too," she said, checking her phone. "You can go first."

"Roger that," I said, heading for the door. Then something occurred to me and I turned back to Lisa. "You are going to change back, right?" I asked. "For the Mona Lisa diversion?"

"*Mais oui*," Lisa said. "I know the plan. See you out there."

I walked out the door and up the stairs, toward our ballroom. I smiled and held up my wrist for the employee

288

at the door, who just stared at me. I looked down and saw that I'd forgotten to change accessories. I was still wearing the gloves, one of which was covering my blue bracelet. I peeled the glove off to show him my bracelet, and then took the other glove off as I passed him. I'd just have to pretend I'd decided to accessorize my dress with some ropes of pearls. Midprom.

I waved my blue bracelet at him. He frowned at my wrist, but nodded, and I stepped inside. The prom was now in full swing, with most of the dance floor covered with my classmates, who were getting down to music that had actual lyrics, just like I'd always hoped. As I watched everyone having fun, I felt a pang, because I was missing so much of it. I headed over to our table, and to my dismay, Melissa and Nate were sitting close to each other and laughing. As I got closer, I saw that she was touching him—her hands were on his lapel. I stopped in my tracks.

"There!" Melissa said, leaning back, and I saw that Nate's boutonniere, which I'd failed at affixing, finally looked secure.

"Hi," I said, feeling a little bit like I was interrupting something.

They both looked at me, and Nate smiled, though he also seemed a little exasperated. "Mad, finally," he said. "Where have you been?"

"Prom business," I said vaguely. "You know . . . this and that."

"I like your necklace," Melissa said. "Did you have that on before?"

"Um, no," I said. "It's . . . new."

"It's cute," she said with a smile.

"So where's Brian?" I asked, looking around. I didn't see him anywhere, but I did see Schuyler and Connor dancing together, both of them looking unhappy.

Melissa gestured toward the doors. "He's been making phone calls all night," she said. "Talking to people about an investment, or something."

"Ah," I said. I really wasn't sure what the Young Investors Club hoped to find that they could invest in at this point and see a return from by Monday. But they should really blame whoever had decided to give Brian that much responsibility.

"Can we dance?" Nate asked, standing up and taking my hand. "Finally?"

"Yes," I said, smiling at him. "Please." The song slowed down as I said that, which made me very happy. And it was one I'd always liked, too—Hellogoodbye's "Oh, It Is Love."

"Nate!" Melissa said, smiling. "Listen!"

"I hear," he said, nodding but not smiling back.

"It's our song!" she said with a sigh. She waved us away. "Go dance, you two!" she said. "Have fun!"

Nate led me by the hand to the dance floor and pulled me close and I pressed my lips together and tried not to cry. "This . . . was your song with Melissa?" I asked when I felt I could speak again.

"Mad, are you okay?" Nate asked, leaning back a little and looking at me with concern.

"I just . . ." I started. I looked at all the couples around me, girls resting their heads on their dates' shoulders, people swaying together in time to the music. I just wanted us to be one of those couples, enjoying their time together without complications. The way we had been, until a few days ago. "I just wish we had a song. And Melissa seems nice and all, but I can't help thinking that you still like her, and it's hard for me to see you two together."

"Wait a sec," Nate said, raising his eyebrow. "Why would you think that I still like Melissa?"

"I don't know!" I said, more emphatically than I'd meant to. "Maybe because your relationship was significant, but I don't know anything about it. Sometimes I feel like there's a whole side to you that you don't tell me about." I said that all in a rush, before I lost my nerve. I looked up at him, waiting for his response, my heart hammering.

"I can see that," Nate said after a moment. "And I can work on it. But I feel like you have to tell me things, too."

"What do you mean?" I asked.

"Like what's been going on tonight?" he asked. "What's been going on this whole week? You need to trust me with this stuff, Mad."

I wasn't sure what to say to this, so I just nodded. Air Supply's "All Out of Love" came on, and I moved a little closer to him. He wrapped his arms around me and kissed the top of my head, and we moved together to the music. I closed my eyes and breathed in the Nate smell

I loved so much—and the woodsy scent of his cologne that he must have worn for the occasion—and wished that we could stay like that forever.

"Madison," I heard Schuyler whisper in my ear. I turned my head and saw her standing to my side, tapping my shoulder. "We have a problem."

CHAPTER 24

Song: All Falls Down/Kanye West
Quote: "If you ever catch on fire, try and avoid seeing yourself in a mirror. Because I bet that's what really throws you into a panic."—Jack Handy

 promgirl → the crew Heading back to the 80s. Do we have the package? Selwidge?

 Marcus → the crew Afraid not. Think we're going to have to draw the dragon from the lair. Eh?

 promgirl → the crew Dave, ready for an outside pickup?

 Dave Gold → the crew The chosen people are choosing their entrees at the moment. Give me 20.

 Shy Time → the crew If we're drawing the dragon from the lair, we might need Operation Abercrombie & Switch standing by. JIC.

KitKat → the crew Good call. I'll ask. Thank God Abercrombie doesn't have a date.

 Gingersnap → the crew I still think that's weird, though, don't you?

 La Lisse → the crew Focus, people!

 La Lisse → Gingersnap But yeah, it is weird. But good for us . . .

 promgirl → the crew Sarah, are you warming up?

 promgirl → the crew Sarah???

"And nobody's been able to get in contact with her?" I asked, trying to yank down the hem of my eighties dress as Schuyler and I hurried back up the stairs.

"She's not responding to texts or calls and hasn't updated her status all night," Schuyler said. "But . . . um . . . maybe her phone's broken."

I doubted it. If Sarah had gone radio silent, there was a reason for it. But we really didn't need this tonight. We hadn't scheduled in any time to talk people out of going rogue. "I'll find out what's happening," I said. We made it back to the Putnam ballroom, and I led us a few feet down the hall, away from the grumpy guy guarding the door. "How are you doing?" I asked. "You and Connor don't look so happy."

Schuyler shrugged and tried to smile, but I could tell she didn't mean it. "I'll be happy when this whole thing is over and I won't have to keep secrets from him," she said.

"Or you could just tell him," I suggested.

Schuyler shook her head. "It would be the end," she said simply. "The end of us. And I can't face that."

I nodded. "Okay," I said. I didn't know how to tell Schuyler that it looked like Connor wasn't about to forget the way she'd been acting as soon as the prom was over. I straightened my dress and smoothed down my hair. "How do I look?" I asked.

"Good!" Schuyler said. "But . . . um . . . aren't you cold in that dress? It's kind of short."

"I'm fine," I said, putting the gloves back on. "Just keep things running in there, okay?"

Schuyler gave me a thumbs-up, and I walked up the staircase and into the Hartfield ballroom. Inside, the situation seemed to have deteriorated. What was playing now could barely be called music, and the students did not look happy about it. Most were standing around, talking angrily, arms crossed. But a group of guys wearing tuxedo T-shirts, moshing in front of Tanner's DJ station, appeared thrilled with the choice of music.

I looked around the ballroom and spotted Sarah exactly where I'd last seen her, deep in conversation with her date. I crossed over to her, making sure to give the moshers a wide berth.

Sarah looked up as I arrived and gave me a vague smile. "Madison, hi," she said. "Have you met Zach?" She gestured to her date, who smiled at me briefly before returning his attention to Sarah.

"Hi, Zach," I said. "Sarah, can I have a moment?"

"Actually, we're talking," Zach said, gazing at Sarah.

"It'll just be a second," I said, taking Sarah's arm and pulling her toward the side of the ballroom.

"Back in a minute!" Sarah called to Zach.

"Miss you!" he called back.

Sarah turned to me, starry-eyed, when we were out of earshot. "Oh, Mads," she said, looking happier than I'd ever seen her. "Isn't he the best?"

"He seems great," I said. "Really. But are you still with the program?"

"Oh," she said, glancing toward Zach again. "About that . . ."

I closed my eyes. "Sarah, please," I said. "Please tell me you're still on board."

"The thing is," Sarah said, "I didn't know that I was going to like him this much. And I really do like him. And you can do this without me, right? It's not necessary."

"Of course it's necessary!" I said, louder than I'd intended. I saw several pairs of eyes swing over to me—including those of my second prom date, who waved at me and started to head over. "Sarah, please," I said quickly, seeing Andy making his way toward us, but getting tangled up in the mosh pit en route. "We need you to do this. You have to delay the Hartfield crowning. It's really essential to the plan."

"But . . ." Sarah said, looking back toward her table. "But Zach . . ."

"Help!" I heard from the direction of the mosh pit, and I turned to see Andy struggling to free himself from it. "Help me!"

I turned back to Sarah. "Think of this as a test of Zach's feelings for you," I said, grabbing wildly at straws. "If he still likes you after you do it, you know he's a keeper."

"Huh," Sarah said, looking pensive.

"We need you, Sarah," I said. I glanced over and saw Andy emerging from the pit, looking distinctly worse for wear. "Please," I said quietly. Sarah looked at me for a moment, then nodded and practically ran back to her date.

I watched her go. I still wasn't sure that she was with us. Meaning that the whole plan might be in jeopardy. Yet again.

"Hey," Andy gasped as he made his way over to me. "Wow. That was . . ." He turned and looked back at the guys in front of the stage, who were now forming a circle pit and tossing someone around in it. "You guys certainly throw interesting proms here."

"You have no idea," I said, smiling involuntarily.

"Listen," Andy said, sitting down on one of the chairs that were pushed against the back wall, still trying to catch his breath. "There was something I wanted to ask you. There was a girl from Putnam that I used to date . . . but then I went back to Minnesota and we lost touch. But I was wondering if maybe you knew her." He looked at me, his face hopeful.

"Um, maybe," I said. "What's her name?"

"Erm . . . sorry to bother, wot?" I looked up and saw Mark standing behind Andy. "Just wondered if I might borrow Madison for just a mo? Won't be but a second. Right quick! Jolly ho! Pip-pip!"

Mark's accent seemed to be taking its familiar tour of the British Isles, and it seemed the strain of keeping it going for this long was causing him to lose control of his colloquialisms. "Sure!" I said, jumping up. "Andy, I'll be right back. Okay?"

"Stay away from the moshers!" he called after us as Mark and I crossed the ballroom and headed toward the door.

"Who was that bit of stuff? Hm?" Mark asked, raising his eyebrows at me.

"Never mind," I said as we headed outside the ballroom.

"Oh, right. Very good. Aces," he said. We left the ballroom and both leaned on the staircase railing, a little apart from each other. If someone came by, it would appear as though we both just happened to be getting some fresh hallway air at the same moment.

"So we're going to make it an outside play," Mark said. "I'm going to ask her to come outside to have a bit of a chat. Brill, eh? Dave'll be standing by, with Lisa in position for the double-decker. And then we grab the crown, she's none the wiser, and Bob's your uncle!"

"You do realize," I said, feeling my phone vibrate and reaching down for it, "that when this is over, you're going to have to drop the accent?"

"I don't know what you're meaning, I don't," he said, sounding affronted. And a lot like Daniel Day-Lewis.

"Watch the accent," I said. "That was pretty Irish, Your Lordship."

"Blimey," Mark muttered.

 La Lisse ➜ promgirl From what I can see at the mitzvah, I think that the Demon Spawn might be in need of some help.

"Oh, God," I sighed. I'd pretty much forgotten about Travis and the fact that I might, at that very moment, be in major trouble with my parents. I checked my watch. I might have time, if I ran very quickly down the world's longest hallway. "Bye, Mark," I said.

"Cheerio," he called, and I dashed down the stairs.

I rushed to the doors that led to the checkpoint. This was where things might get tricky. If there were still people working the door, it might be hard to convince them to let me cross the hotel to talk to my brother. And if they were people who worked at my school, it might be hard to explain why I was sporting early Madonna. Not to mention two different bracelets. I pushed the door open slowly and saw that while the table was still there, it was, at the moment, deserted. I hustled past it, trying to look like I was going somewhere totally kosher. Which, ironically, I probably was.

When I reached the Hallway of Eternity, I sat on one of the benches and took my shoes off, then ran flat out. Time was a-wasting. I thought I might have to ask for directions to Heidi Goldwater's bat mitzvah, but once I got close, it would have been impossible to get lost. There were signs every few feet that read *HEIDI Au+H_2O!!* The signs, for some reason, were printed on black, with blood-red lettering. As soon as I stepped inside the ballroom, I understood why.

The theme of this bat mitzvah was vampires. There were red and black rose flower arrangements, with rose petals scattered on the floor and on all the tables. There were apples and red ribbons everywhere, and fang centerpieces on every table. It seemed a little morbid to me, but it didn't appear to be bothering any of the guests, most of whom were on the dance floor. They all looked like they were having much more fun than the people at the Hartfield prom were. As the "Cupid Shuffle" started up, prompting cheers from the crowd, I spotted Travis sitting by himself in the corner of the room.

Trying to look like I'd been there the whole time, and just had a very peculiar sense of fashion, I Cupid Shuffled my way over to Travis. He was slumped in his chair, his tie askew and his hair, so carefully plastered down a few hours earlier, sticking up in many directions, like he'd been running his hands through it. On the table in front of him were five empty Dr Pepper bottles.

"Hey," I said, sliding into the seat next to him.

He looked over at me and blinked in surprise. "Mad?" he asked. "What are you doing here?"

"Just checking on you," I said. It sounded strange once I said it out loud, but I realized to my surprise that it was true. That was exactly what I was doing. "Are you okay?"

"No," Travis muttered. He looked at me again and frowned. "Why are you dressed like Cyndi Lauper?"

"Never mind," I said. "Want to talk about it?"

Travis shook his head, picked up a white T-shirt from the table, and tossed it to me. "Want this? It sparkles in the sunlight."

I set the T-shirt aside, trying not to think about how much time was going by, and trying to focus on my little brother. "Come on, Travis," I said.

Travis shrugged and reached for a new bottle of Dr Pepper, but I moved it out of his reach, cutting him off. He sighed and stared down at the tablecloth. "What's there to talk about?" he asked. "Olivia dumped me. End of story."

"Well, what happened?"

He shrugged again. "I don't know. She said that I was too jealous, and that I didn't trust her. But she was always hanging out with her ex-boyfriends! What was I supposed to do?"

I looked at Travis and wondered if there was something in the MacDonald DNA that caused us to be irrational and insecure in relationships. Because his relationship issues were basically mine in miniature.

"Listen," I said. I snuck a look at my phone and realized I had only a few moments to impart whatever little wisdom I might have to give. "Go apologize."

"What!" Travis said, looking shocked. "Me?"

"You," I said. "Do you want to get your girlfriend back?"

"Yes," he muttered after a long pause.

"Then go apologize. And in the future, just remember that she likes *you*, not her exes. She wouldn't be dating you if she didn't like you."

"Yeah?" Travis asked, looking hopeful for the first time since I'd sat down.

"Yeah," I confirmed. "Though God knows why," I added, and was rewarded when Travis rolled his eyes at me, a sign that he was coming around. "I should get back."

"Okay," Travis said. "Thanks, Mad."

"Sure," I said as I got up from the table.

"And don't worry," he said as I prepared to leave. "I didn't call Mom and Dad. I won't tell them anything."

I let out a sigh of relief; at least something was going my way tonight. "Thanks," I said. "Good luck."

Travis nodded, straightened his tie, and got up. I Electric Slid my way across the dance floor and headed for the exit. "Don't forget your gift bag!" a woman said to me as I left, pointing to the sparkling red and black bags stacked on a nearby table.

I nodded and, figuring it was easier than raising suspicion, grabbed one and headed for the hallway. At the first bench, I took my shoes off again and ran for it.

302

Dave Gold → the crew Are we set?

 Marcus → the crew I'm set. Dragon's in her den.

 La Lisse → the crew I'm set. And très uncomfortable. What are we using as bait?

 Shy Time → the crew I'll do it.

 KitKat → the crew Really? I can handle it.

 Shy Time → the crew No, it's something I need to do. It's important to me.

 KitKat → the crew Roger that. Abercrombie is standing by.

 Marcus → the crew Good luck! God save the prom!

 Shy Time → the crew Mark, text me her digits, okay?

Marcus → the crew Righty-o!

 promgirl → the crew I'm in position. Good luck, everyone!

I made it back to the area outside the Putnam ballroom just in time, beyond thankful that the checkpoint table was still deserted. I threw myself into one of the high-backed armchairs that faced away from the area where the main event would be taking place. For this to work, it was imperative that Isabel not see me, but I still wanted to be nearby, just in case things went horribly wrong.

I slipped my shoes back on and pulled my legs up underneath me, hoping that I was totally hidden by the sides of the armchair. I looked to my left and saw that the door to the service stairs was pushed open slightly. I saw a flash of silver from the serving cart and knew that Dave—and Lisa—were ready and in position.

"Fine," I heard Isabel snap. I fished a compact out of my purse and held it in front of me to get a glimpse of what was going on behind me. Isabel was descending the staircase, clutching her purse, talking on her phone. "I'm coming down now. Okay?"

The hotel employees on the stairs and in front of the Putnam ballroom were gone, probably figuring they weren't needed anymore now that the proms were getting close to ending. So there was nobody to question

Isabel as she stopped in the middle of the room. I slid down farther in my armchair, even though I knew there was no way that she could see me.

"Darling," I heard a plummy British accent say from above me. I looked up and saw Mark leaning over the railing. "Where are you going?" he asked Isabel. "Shall I come as well? I can be down in just a mo!"

"No," Isabel snapped. "Just stay up there, okay, Marcus? I'll be back in a minute."

"All right, darling, as you wish," Mark said. "I shall count the minutes until you return!"

I saw a look of irritation cross Isabel's face, and she rolled her eyes dramatically. Clearly, Mark was beginning to wear on her nerves. Which suited our purposes perfectly.

"I'm here," Isabel said, closing her phone and crossing her arms. "What do you want?"

I turned the compact to the side and saw Schuyler standing in front of her. Schuyler looked terrified and seemed to be trembling slightly. But she also looked more determined—and more angry—than I'd ever seen her before.

"Isabel," she said. It came out as a squeak, and I saw Isabel smirk. Schuyler cleared her throat, and when she spoke again, her voice was steadier. "What you're doing to me and my friends is not okay. And you're going to regret it."

Isabel's smile just widened. "What is this?" she asked. "A last-ditch effort to get me to give your crown back? Well, it's not going to work, so you can just stop now and save yourself the embarrassment." She folded her arms and looked around theatrically, causing my heart to start beating extra fast as I slid down even farther in the armchair. "I'm surprised *you're* doing this," Isabel said. "Where's Madison to fight your battles for you?"

"Your problem is with me," Schuyler said. "This isn't about my friends."

"That's what you think," Isabel said, and I frowned, wondering what she meant by that.

"You never should have hurt my friends," Schuyler said, sounding fiercer than I'd ever heard her. "This was about you and me. But you crossed the line."

"Your *friends*," Isabel said scathingly. "I'm sure, Schuyler. I'm sure you have supertight *best* friends at Putnam. And they'd do anything for you."

"Actually," Schuyler said with a smile, "I do. And they would. In fact, they are. Right now."

Isabel seemed thrown by this, and she narrowed her eyes slightly. "What is that supposed to mean?" she asked, looking around.

"Oh," Schuyler said, taking a step closer to Isabel, forcing her to take one step back, then another. While she was moving her backward, into position, she'd taken out her phone, her finger poised on the screen. "I think it'll hit you soon."

"And just what do you mean by—"

My phone vibrated.

 Shy Time → the crew GO NASCART!!!!!

I held up my compact to watch as Dave burst out of the service entrance and ran full speed behind the cart that he was pushing with a great deal of effort. He was heading straight for Isabel and Schuyler, and I saw Isabel's eyes widen in shock, as it looked like a collision was imminent. At the last moment, Schuyler grabbed her arm and yanked her out of the way, with enough force that both she and Isabel hit the ground, and Isabel's purse went flying. Dave wheeled the cart in front of the purse, and I saw an arm—Lisa's—reach out from the tablecloth that covered the bottom. She pulled the purse underneath for a few seconds, then tossed it out again, and Dave wheeled the cart away.

"I'm so sorry," he gasped at Isabel as he pushed the cart toward the main lobby. "I think there's a problem with the wheel. My bad . . ."

"Wow, that was weird," Schuyler said, a little too loudly. She pushed herself off the ground and dusted off her dress, then looked down at Isabel. "I just wanted to tell you how I felt. I'm not scared of you anymore. And you're going to regret doing this for a long, long time." Then she headed into the Putnam ballroom, head held high, and I had to bite my lip hard to keep from cheering.

"WTF?" Isabel muttered, pushing herself up to her feet, which apparently took some doing in her skintight dress. She grabbed for her purse just as someone else picked it up. I smiled. Abercrombie had come through for us.

I angled the mirror and saw Justin giving her the smile that had made me almost fail gym.

307

"Hi there," he said. "Is this yours?"

Isabel's expression softened, and a blush colored her cheeks. "Um, yes," she said with a high-pitched giggle that made me wince. "Thank you." She held out her hand for it, but if Justin noticed this, he didn't let on, and continued to hold on to the bag.

"Are you okay?" he asked. "That looked like quite the accident."

"Oh, I'm fine," Isabel said, a little breathlessly. "Thank you for asking."

"Can I help you carry this somewhere?" Justin asked, lifting the bag slightly. "I don't want you trying to lift anything too heavy."

"Oh," Isabel said, giggling again. I saw her look at Justin with a smile of contented calculation. "That would be *so* sweet of you. I actually need to drop it off backstage."

"Then why don't we go there together?" Justin asked. "May I ask your name?"

"Isabel," she said, straightening her bangs.

"That's beautiful," Justin said, holding eye contact with her for just a moment too long, causing Isabel to blush and smile again.

"Isabel? Dearest?" I heard Mark call from above my head.

"Someone calling you?" Justin asked, raising an eyebrow.

Isabel shook her head. "Just this silly English boy who's been following me around all night," she said dismissively. "Don't worry, I'll get rid of him."

"Well, then," Justin said, offering her his arm. "Shall we?"

Isabel smiled in triumph and they headed up the stairs together arm in arm. A moment later, I heard a despairing "Wot? *Wot?*" from Mark, above me. I heard Mark running down the stairs. I waited ten seconds, then cautiously poked my head around the side of the armchair. Mark headed over, a triumphant smile on his face.

"It's over," he said, accent still holding strong. "I mean, I say."

"Sorry, Mark," I said.

"I'm not," Mark said. "I mean, she bought it, wot? The whole bit! She thought I was English!" He grinned at me. "I have been vindicated, eh? The drama critic can suck it!"

My phone vibrated, and I looked down at it.

 La Lisse → the crew We have the package, and it's safe and sound.

 promgirl → the crew I'll pick it up before Goodbye Kitty.

 La Lisse → the crew You got it. T minus 30.

"So am I done?" Mark asked. "Can His Lordship retire for the evening?"

"Maybe not quite yet," I said. "Just in case, maybe—"
My eyes widened as, over Mark's shoulder, I saw a girl
in a cream-colored dress coming out of the service staircase. "Be right back, Mark."

"Jolly good!" Mark said as I beat feet toward Ruth.

I had some questions for her, and I was going to get
some answers. Right now.

CHAPTER 25

Song: 10:15 Saturday Night/The Poems
Quote: "You can get all hung up in a prickle-ly perch.
And your gang will fly on. You'll be left in a Lurch."
—Dr. Seuss

"Hey," I said, striding up to her. She looked surprised to see me, and let the door close behind her.

"Mad!" she said, sounding flustered. She was holding her phone in her hand, and her other hand went to her throat, where her *R* necklace usually was. "How's it going?" She took in my dress and looked up at me, frowning. "Why are you wearing that?"

"Never mind," I said impatiently. "I need to talk to you. In here." I pushed the service staircase door open. Ruth took a step inside, and I pulled the door closed behind us.

"Sure," she said. "I've been wanting to talk to you too—"

"Oh, sure you have," I snapped. "Listen, I don't really have time to do this. I just want you to know that your little plan isn't going to work out."

Ruth stared at me for a long moment. "What little plan?" she asked.

"The betting website," I said, amazed that she was going to play dumb. "Race to the Crown? I know you rigged it so that I would win prom queen. The site's registered in your name. But you should know that Kittson fixed everything. I'm not going to win, which means your site's going to lose, so you can just give up your little game."

"Maddie," Ruth said gravely, and my eyes widened at the use of my nickname, which only she was allowed to use, and only in very serious situations. "I have absolutely no idea what you're talking about."

****

Ten minutes later, we stepped outside the staircase, my head still spinning with what she'd just said. "All right?" I asked her, and she nodded.

"All right," she said. She gave me a tentative smile, and we crossed the lobby area together. I checked my watch and realized that it was almost time for the crown swap—the make-or-break aspect of the whole plan.

"Madison! There you are!" I looked up and saw Andy descending the staircase. But he stopped short when his eyes fell on Ruth.

"Rue?" he asked, sounding shocked, but also delighted.

"Andy?" she asked, eyes widening. She smiled, staring at him. "What . . . what are you doing here? Why aren't you in Minnesota?"

"We just moved," he said, walking to the bottom of the staircase. "I'd been hoping that I would see you. . . ."

"How do you two know each other?" I asked, still trying to put this together. *Ruth* was the girl from Putnam that Andy had dated?

Ruth blushed slightly, still smiling at Andy. "Science camp last summer," she said, and Andy smiled back, nodding.

Andy was Ruth's Mystery Science Boyfriend! He did exist, after all. I made a mental note to tell Lisa that she owed me ten bucks.

"But what are you . . ." Ruth said, looking from me to Andy. "How do you know Mad?"

"She's my prom date," Andy said.

"What?" Ruth asked incredulously, and I heard surprise—and great hurt—in her voice. "Seriously, Madison?"

"No," I said quickly, not liking the expression on Ruth's face at all. "Not like a real date. I'm here with Nate. My boyfriend," I said to Andy, who looked totally lost. "Sorry. I should have mentioned that earlier."

"Wait, what?" Andy asked, frowning, as my phone vibrated.

 Dave Gold ➔ the crew Take the Chevy to the levee.

 La Lisse ➔ the crew In Paris, the cafés are many. The Mona Lisa is in place.

 promgirl ➔ the crew I'm on the move.

"I have to go," I said, turning and heading toward the lobby. "I'll see you later?" I tried to catch Ruth's eye, but she was looking at the ground. I wanted to stay and sort the situation out, but there simply wasn't time. It was ten fifteen already, I wasn't in the lobby yet, and I had two phone calls to make.

I called Kittson, thrilled when she answered right away. "Listen," I said, speaking as fast as I could. "You need to hack the voting system again."

"No!" she said, sounding appalled. "Madison, I have worked too hard for this for too long—"

"Not you," I said. "You can win fair and square. But you have to change who's going to win prom king."

"To who?"

"Think about it," I said. "Who's the one person Glen won't beat up?"

There was a long pause, and then Kittson said, "Okay. I'll do it, but I have to hurry. Codes are going out in ten minutes."

"Thanks," I said, hanging up with her and calling Brian immediately. "Brian," I said as soon as he picked up, "I have an investment for you, but you have to do it now. But I guarantee a return. And tell everyone else the plan, okay?"

I hung up with Brian as I reached the main lobby and stopped at the designated armchair, the one near the harp, where Lisa was sitting, waiting for me. She was back in her black dress and had added red lipstick, which made her look very sophisticated—and hopefully nothing like the girl who had been helping out with catering all night.

"*D'accord?*" she asked.

"Kind of," I said, holding open my bag. Lisa looked around and placed the Hayes crown inside. I let out a huge sigh of relief when I saw it, safe and sound, back in our possession again. "Is it okay?" I asked.

"*Oui,* as far as I can tell," Lisa said. "Isabel didn't check her bag to make sure that it was there?"

"Justin's very distracting that way," I said as I pulled the edges of the bag closer together. "Ready?"

"When you are," Lisa said with a small smile. She tilted her head toward the desk. "Bring this home, Mad. *Allez-y.*"

I took a deep breath and crossed over to the desk, which had gotten no less intimidating. In fact, it even seemed a little more so, now that I was wearing a very skimpy Reagan-era dress. I saw Mr. Patrick raise his eyebrow at me as I approached.

"Ah, Miss MacDonald," he said. "You're here for the crown?"

"Yes," I said, hoping that he would take it out before Dr. Trent arrived.

"Well, I know that your headmaster is going to be here as well, to inspect that the crown has been kept safe. But," he said, checking his watch, "we can get the process started." I let out a breath as he disappeared behind the secret door and, a moment later, returned, reverently holding the dark blue jewelry box. The one that contained a plastic Hello Kitty tiara.

I took out my phone and updated my status as subtly as possible.

"Your headmaster isn't here yet, but I don't suppose it would hurt to take a look, would it?" Mr. Patrick asked, hand on the lid.

"Well, um," I said, trying to think quickly, "actually . . ."

"Allô?" I turned and saw Lisa standing at the other end of the desk, banging her palm on it. *"Où est le concierge? Je suis très déçu! Qui est le responsable ici?"*

"Oui, mademoiselle?" Mr. Patrick asked. He turned to Lisa, and I reached out for the box—but his hand remained firmly on it.

"Qui êtes-vous?" Lisa demanded, taking a step away, trying to draw Mr. Patrick farther down. He took a step but—I saw, my hopes plummeting—he kept his hand resting on the box.

"Qu'est-ce que c'est le problem, mademoiselle?" he asked, frowning.

"Oh," Lisa said, looking to me. I could see the panic in her eyes. *"Erm. Donc . . ."*

I felt my shoulders slump. It was over. It was done. Dr. Trent was going to arrive in a moment, and Hello Kitty would be in the box. We had come so close. But it was over.

"Mon Dieu!" Lisa screamed, pointing away from the desk.

She was clearly trying to get Mr. Patrick to turn around, but even *he* had to be able to see through that one—

At that moment, a streaker ran through the lobby.

It wasn't a true streaker, I saw as the guy ran through the lobby doors and out into the car circle, frightening the limo drivers, who jumped out of his way. It looked like he was wearing a pair of tan boxers. But still. It had worked.

There was pandemonium in the lobby. The harpist seemed particularly unsettled, and Lisa was having some kind of French panic attack. In the confusion, Mr. Patrick let go of the jewelry box. I reached out for it, whisked out Hello Kitty, tossed it into my bag, and replaced it with the Hayes crown. Then I pushed the jewelry box away from me, down the counter, my heart hammering. Had we pulled it off? Had we done it?

"What is this?" I turned and saw Dr. Trent striding up to the desk. "What's going on here?"

"So . . . sorry," Mr. Patrick said, turning from where he had been trying to calm Lisa down, in French. Her eyes widened when she saw Dr. Trent, and she turned her back on him and slunk away. "Just attending to a guest." Mr. Patrick turned back. When he saw that Lisa was gone, his frown deepened. "I'm afraid," he said, mopping his brow, "that we've had some . . . irregularities tonight."

"Yes, well . . ." Dr. Trent said. He seemed to notice me for the first time, and frowned at my dress. Then he shook his head and turned back to Mr. Patrick. "I trust our tiara has been kept safe?"

"Oh, yes, sir," Mr. Patrick said. He opened up the jewelry box, and there sat the Hayes crown, looking completely innocent and unharmed.

"Well," Dr. Trent said, adjusting it slightly, "that seems to be in order. Thank you for taking such good care of it."

"Of course, sir," Mr. Patrick said.

"Well, I should take this back and prepare for the crowning. You'd better get back, too, Madison," he said. He checked his watch. "The codes should be going out now."

"I wouldn't miss it!" I said as cheerfully as possible.

Dr. Trent tucked the jewelry box under his arm and headed back to our ballroom. I let out a breath, wishing that I had time to collapse for a few hours. But I didn't. My phone beeped with the voting number, and I texted back my choices, crossing my fingers that we might actually be able to pull this off.

Then I turned around and made my way back to the area outside the Putnam ballroom. As I headed down the service staircase, I found that I couldn't stop smiling. Schuyler was standing outside the door to Conference Room B, twisting her hands together.

"Shy!" I yelled gleefully, running toward her, not really caring that all night we'd tried to keep our voices down. Who cared about that now? We were home free. "Shy, guess what? We did it!"

"Um, Mad," Schuyler said, her voice quavering. She pointed behind me, and I followed her gaze.

Dell was standing there.

CHAPTER 26

Song: Right Back Where We Started From/Maxine Nightingale
Quote: "Boom goes the dynamite."—Brian Collins

I stared at him. It was unmistakably Dell, wearing a tuxedo and a satisfied smile. The dreads were gone, and his hair had been cropped short, but it was him.

"Hello, Madison," he said, taking a step toward me. I forced myself not to take a step back, and even made myself stand up straighter, as I was a few inches taller than Dell in my prom heels.

"What are you doing here, Dell?" I asked. I looked over at Schuyler, who was just staring at Dell like she'd seen a ghost, her bottom lip trembling.

"I think I could ask you the same question, Madison," he said. "I don't think you're supposed to be in this area of the hotel, now, are you?" Involuntarily, I looked back at our conference room, filled with nothing but incriminating evidence—the clothing and props and equipment we'd used to get through the night. Dell nodded. "I didn't think so."

"Why are you here?" I asked again.

Dell stuck his hands in his pockets and smiled at me. "Now, you disappoint me, Mad," he said. "I thought you would have figured it out by now. Because that's your little hobby, isn't it? Solving mysteries?"

"Maybe you should explain it," I said. I looked at Schuyler, expecting her to step behind me as usual. But she was standing next to me, showing no signs of moving.

"I am disappointed," he said again, even though his smile stayed in place. "This is an easy one, after all. And frankly, I'm amazed you weren't expecting it. You certainly should have been. One word. Seven letters." He took another step closer to me and lowered his voice. "Revenge."

"What do you mean?" I asked.

"You didn't expect me to let you get *away* with what you did to me, did you?" he asked. He gave a short laugh. "Come on, Madison. You got me expelled. That carries consequences."

"You hacked my profile!" I said, incredulous. "You stole from people, and made copies of databases. . . ."

Dell waved these allegations away with one hand. "I performed a job I was hired for," he said, his voice cold. "Hacking you was nothing personal. When you tried to ruin my life, you made it personal. And I got my revenge."

"And, um, how did you do that, again?" Schuyler asked, looking from me to Dell.

"Well, I didn't do it alone," Dell said. "I had some help from my cousin." He turned to look around the corner, and Isabel stepped out, smiling pleasantly. Dell looked at Schuyler and me. "I assume you all have met?" he asked.

"Your *cousin*?" I asked, stunned.

"Yes," Isabel said, and I could see from her expression how much she was enjoying this.

"When you had me sent to boarding school, I called up the one person I knew who'd gone," Dell said. Now that they were standing next to each other, I could see a family resemblance. The same dark eyes and hair. The same warped moral compass. "And just imagine how thrilled I was to find out there was someone who hated one of your little friends as much as I did. And so we began planning."

"I got to help a family member in need *and* get my revenge on you," Isabel said, glaring at Schuyler. "Even though I had to wait three years. But it was so worth it."

"And now, the moment I've been waiting for," Dell said to me, pulling out an iPhone. "I get to see the look on your face when I destroy your life. It's only fair, after all, Madison. You have to admit that."

"What are you doing with that?" I asked, looking at the iPhone.

"Oh, we're about to watch streaming video of the Hartfield crowning," he said. "We're about to see the Hartfield queen get crowned with your precious Hayes crown. The one you had responsibility for. The one that, if you misplaced it, would get you expelled. And I get to watch your face while you see that."

"How could you do all this?" I demanded. "How

321

did you even know that I'd been put in charge of the crown?"

"Well, for God's sake, Mad, you update your status constantly with all the details of your precious life. It wasn't that hard." Dell tapped the screen and sent a text, then looked up at me and smiled. "But as it turns out, I had someone giving me some help."

"Who?" Schuyler asked, brow furrowed.

"One second," Dell said. He turned to look around the corner again, and a moment later, Ruth came out.

She gave me a hard look and stood next to Dell, her arms folded. Dell smiled at me. "It's nice to have loyal friends," he said. "Ruth was invaluable."

"It's time," Isabel said, checking her watch.

"Oh, excellent," Dell said. He tapped his iPhone and held the screen out to me. I could see the stage of the Lily Ballroom, but nobody was being crowned. Instead, Sarah was holding center stage, grabbing the mic with both hands and belting out, for all she was worth, "Don't Cry For Me, Argentina."

I couldn't help smiling. She'd come through for us. And she was on pitch, too.

"What's going on?" Isabel asked, staring at the screen. "What is that?"

"Andrew Lloyd Webber," I said. "*Evita.*" I raised my eyebrows at Isabel. "I'm surprised you don't know it."

"Get her off the stage," Dell snapped, looking at Isabel.

"What am I supposed to do from down here?" she asked sharply.

322

"Well, in the meantime, why don't we watch *our* crowning?" I said, turning to Schuyler, who was pulling out the ShyPhone. She tapped it, and streaming video of the Rosebud Ballroom appeared.

A tiny Dr. Trent was standing on the stage, announcing the prom royalty. "By a landslide, Kittson Pearson is your prom queen! And by . . . four votes . . . Glen Turtell is your prom king!" The ballroom burst into applause and shocked whispers, and Dr. Trent placed the Hayes crown on Kittson's head.

"Wait . . . no . . ." Dell murmured, growing pale.

"Not what you were expecting?" I asked. "You were right about one thing," I said. "It is nice to have loyal friends." Ruth smiled at me and came to stand by my side.

"No," Dell said, looking at the two of us. "*No.* What is going on here?"

"Should we tell Sarah to stop?" Schuyler asked, looking down at Dell's iPhone, which had started to shake in his hand.

"Sure," I said. "Unless she wants to do an encore."

Schuyler typed something on her phone, and a moment later, the Sarah on Dell's screen looked at her phone, took a deep bow, and ran offstage.

"What did you do?" Isabel asked, looking from Schuyler to me, her face mottled with rage. "How did you . . ."

"We just took back what was ours," Schuyler said. "What you tricked me into giving to you."

"But how?" she asked weakly. "I had it with me the whole time. . . ."

"Did you?" I asked.

"Give it a sec," Schuyler said. "It'll hit you."

Dell was still staring at me and Ruth. "The prom results," he said, his voice cold. "How did you do that?"

"How did *you* do it?" I asked. "That's the question. You rigged the texting codes so that Dave and I would win. And then you set up a betting website, on which we had terrible odds, so that you could make a huge profit."

"Yes," Dell said, frowning at both of us. "So?"

"So you registered the site in my name, you jack-ass," Ruth said, her voice shaking with fury. "When it was looked into—and maybe you would have been the one to get Dr. Trent to look into it; I wouldn't put it past you—Madison would have gotten in trouble for rigging the election. And I would have gotten in trouble, again, for profiting off of it. You know that I would have been expelled. And unlike some people, it's not like I can buy my way out of trouble."

"Was that your backup plan?" I asked. "In case I didn't get into enough trouble when the crown went missing? You wanted to be sure that I'd get expelled?"

"Something like that," Dell said, his voice hard.

"Your mistake was registering it in Ruth's name," I said. "When we talked about it, it became clear. Ruth is terrible with computers, and never would have been able to do it herself. And who would want to make it look like she'd done something like that? It was simple. One word," I couldn't help adding. "Four letters. Dell."

"But you weren't *supposed* to talk," Dell said, his voice rising. "You two hate each other!"

I looked at Ruth and smiled at her. Ruth had explained in the stairwell what she thought was going on, and it turned out she'd been right. We had been here before—me, her, Dell—and it was much nicer to be on the same side. "It's time you learned something about real friendship," I said to Dell. "It's stronger than almost anything. And it's certainly stronger than you."

"I wasn't helping you," Ruth said. "I was pretending to so that I could try and find out what you were up to. I tried to warn you, Mad. . . ."

"You did," I said, remembering the conversation in the parking lot, when I'd dismissed her warnings. "Sorry I didn't listen to you."

Isabel was looking from us to Dell, furious. "What is happening?" she spat. "How did they do this to you *again*?"

Dell glared at me. "I can prove you've been prom hopping," he said. "I know that you weren't where you were supposed to be, all night—"

I shook my head. "It's not going to work, Dell. Let it go."

"Let it go?" he asked, his pitch and volume rising. *"Let it go?"*

The door to the service staircase opened, and Sarah, Dave, and Lisa stepped out, midconversation, arriving at the rendezvous point. But their conversation died as they took in the scene in front of them. "Whoa," Dave said, looking around. "Um, what's going on?"

The door opened again, and Mark, Brian, and Ginger stepped out.

"Marcus?" Isabel asked, staring at him. "What are you doing here?"

Mark smiled at her. "Right," he said in his normal accent. "About that . . ."

"You mean," Isabel said, realization dawning, "you're . . . you're not an earl?"

"Of course not," Dell snapped. "He's one of Madison's *friends*." He looked around at everyone and seemed to be barely containing his fury. "Oh, you all have no idea what you've just done. I have information on you. On *all* of you. And I know what to do with it. You're going down, all of you—"

"Enough," I said firmly. "No. We're done."

"Really?" Dell asked, his voice getting more strangled. "Oh, *really*?"

"Really," I said quietly. "No more, Dell. You're out a lot of money tonight on your site."

"I'm aware of that!" he snapped.

"No, I'm not sure you are," I said. "Brian?"

"I'm happy to report that the Putnam Young Investors Club made a ten-thousand-dollar profit tonight," he said. "Much obliged."

I watched the color drain from Dell's face.

"Here's what we propose," I said. I looked around at the group, and they all nodded. Clearly, Brian had gotten the word out. "We'll give you half. You can use the rest to pay off the people who used the site. And if we give it to you, it means we're done. No more revenge. No more schemes. You walk away. And we're finished."

"Fini," Lisa added helpfully.

326

Dell looked like he was considering the alternative. But after a moment of staring down at the ground, his hands clenched into fists, he nodded. "Fine," he muttered. "Fine."

"And how do we know you're not going to go back on your word and do something else next month?" Dave asked, crossing his arms.

"Because I won't," Dell said, shaking his head. For the first time ever, he looked defeated. And it didn't seem like an act, either. "I promise. We're done."

"What?" Isabel asked, looking at Dell, furious. "That's *it*?"

"That's it," he said quietly. Isabel glared at him, then at all of us, then turned on her heel and stomped up the staircase. Dell looked at me for a long moment, then dropped his gaze and headed for the stairs himself, walking slowly away in silence.

"Oh my God," Schuyler breathed when the sound of his footsteps faded away. "So that's it? We did it?"

"It looks like it," I said, not quite able to believe it myself. "So who was the streaker?" I asked, looking around at the various guys. "Come on."

"There was a *streaker*?" Sarah asked as my phone vibrated.

 mad_mac ➜ the crew Look out. The Eagle is flying.

So much for thinking we were home free. "Guys," I said, "we're not out of the woods yet. Get this stuff out of the conference room and into the van and get back to the prom ASAP."

"What's going on?" Ginger asked.

"Dr. Trent," I yelled as I pushed open the door to the stairs. "He's on his way."

CHAPTER 27

Song: Do You Wanna Dance?/The Beach Boys
Quote: "And say my glory was I had such
friends."—William Butler Yeats

I ran up the stairs and stepped into the area outside the
Putnam ballroom just in time to see Dr. Trent heading
toward the service stairs. Trying to intercept him,
I increased my pace.

"Hi, Dr. Trent," I said cheerfully.

"Madison," he said, looking surprised, and maybe—
was I imagining it?—a little disappointed to see me there.

"Great prom, huh?" I asked. I realized that as he was
facing the staircase, he would have a clear view of everyone as they came up. So I walked around to stand next
to him, forcing him to turn his back on the staircase to
keep facing me. "I was really happy that Kittson won.
It's just fitting, right?" I babbled as I saw the door to the
service entrance open slowly and Schuyler slink out.
"I mean, she worked so hard and all."

"Yes, well . . ." Dr. Trent said. He turned to look at
the staircase just in time to see the door close, and he

329

frowned. "I have to go check on something downstairs. Don't go anywhere, Madison. I want to have a talk with you."

"Yes. But!" I yelled, forcing Dr. Trent's attention back to me as the door opened again and Ginger and Sarah slipped out.

"What?" Dr. Trent asked, looking perplexed.

"Um," I said. Dr. Trent turned to look at the door again, only to see it slam closed once more. While his back was turned, I quickly updated my status.

 promgirl → the crew GO OPERATION PDA!!!!

"Madison, what is going on?" he asked, looking at me over the top of his glasses.

"Going on?" I asked, stalling. "I don't know what you could possibly mean. What do you mean? What does that mean, precisely?"

"Oh, for heaven's sake," Dr. Trent said, looking at something behind me. I turned and saw Jimmy and Liz stumbling through the ballroom doors, arms around each other, kissing madly. "That is not appropriate," he said, heading up to them. "Excuse me!"

 promgirl → the crew CLEAR NOW RUN!!

The staircase door opened and Mark, Ruth, Dave, Lisa, and Brian made a run for it, slinking behind armchairs until they made it to the ballroom doors. There, they slowed down and walked more casually.

"Can you hear me?" Dr. Trent yelled to Jimmy and Liz, who were still making out furiously. "This is your assistant headmaster! And this is not acceptable behavior!"

"Come on, Liz," I said, tapping her on the shoulder. She immediately stopped kissing Jimmy and turned to look at me.

"Hi, Mad," she said. "Hi, Dr. Trent. I—oops!" She dropped her bag, and I immediately bent down to pick it up, placing the one I'd been carrying all night on the ground next to it. Liz picked up that one. "Thanks," she said.

"No, thank *you*," I said emphatically, and she smiled at me.

"Please," Dr. Trent said, looking at Jimmy and Liz. "Have a little more respect for where you are. This isn't a video arcade."

Jimmy frowned at that, but Liz nodded emphatically. "Right you are, Dr. Trent." She pulled Jimmy back into the ballroom and Dr. Trent turned to me.

"Now, Madison," he said. "There's something I need to check downstairs. But I want you to wait here. I need to speak with you."

"Sure," I said easily, hoping that they'd gotten all the evidence removed from Conference Room B. I looked at the ballroom doors, where Lisa, Dave, and Schuyler were still lingering, watching. *Are we okay?* I mouthed to them, and Lisa gave me a thumbs-up just as Dr. Trent came

331

back, looking out of breath and annoyed. "Something wrong?" I asked him.

"No," he said, though he didn't look happy about it. "Everything appears to be . . . in order." He looked down at me. "Now. Madison. I have heard some very disturbing reports over the course of the night that you have not been where you were supposed to be. That you've been wandering the hotel, even though you knew the consequences of this. I'd hate to have to punish you, especially since the prom was carried off successfully. But I'm afraid those are the rules."

"Who said I was where I wasn't supposed to be?" I asked. "Do you have any proof?"

"I think I will," he said with a faint smile. "Do you have your phone with you?"

"Of course," I said, taking it out of my bag.

"Pull up your Status Q page, please," he said. I did, smiled at what I saw, and handed him the phone.

 mad_mac I love the prom!!

 mad_mac aren't proms fun?

 mad_mac Jimmy looks so cute tonight!

 mad_mac I mean, Nate.

mad_mac yay for the prom!

These continued on for a page or so, a new update every ten minutes, all with my location embedded in them, putting me inside the Rosebud Ballroom the whole time. Dr. Trent stared down at my phone in his hand, looking perplexed.

"Is there a problem?" I asked.

"Yes," he snapped. "I've heard reports—that you weren't at our prom. From a reliable source. That you weren't with your boyfriend, Nathan, but flitting about the hotel. . . ."

Nathan. Well, that told me exactly who his source was. "The source can't have been that reliable," I said, "because my boyfriend's name is Nate. And my updates place me in the prom the entire time. Don't they?"

"Yes . . . but . . ." Dr. Trent looked down at my phone, then at me, angrily, and I realized that Dell hadn't been the only one who'd been hoping to get me expelled tonight.

"Is there a problem?" I looked over and saw Nate striding out of the Rosebud Ballroom. He did a double take at the eighties minidress but kept on walking toward me and placed his arm around my shoulders. "Hi, Mad."

"Hello, Nate," I said, for Dr. Trent's benefit.

"I know you've barely left my side the entire night," he said, looking right at Dr. Trent as he said this, "but I miss you already. Coming back in?"

I looked at Dr. Trent and raised my eyebrows. "Was there something else?" I asked.

Dr. Trent looked very much like he wanted to say something else, but then he just shook his head. "We're finished," he said, giving me something that was probably meant to approximate a smile. "Go enjoy the prom." He turned and headed back into the ballroom.

I waited until the doors had closed behind him, then turned to Nate and wrapped my arm around his waist. "Thank you," I said.

"Is everything okay?" he asked.

"Everything's great," I said, smiling at him.

"Good. Because I'm going to need some answers. Like this dress. Is it my imagination, or were you wearing something else before?"

I stretched up and kissed him. "I'll tell you everything," I said, realizing that I now could, and feeling the weight of having to keep this secret lift. "I promise."

"Well," he said, "why don't you start with the dress?"

"Dude!" I looked over and saw Dave standing in front of the ballroom doors, motioning for Nate to join him. We started to head over when something caught my eye. It was Justin, sitting in one of the armchairs and staring into space.

"Meet you in there," I said to Nate, who squeezed my hand and headed toward Dave. I heard Nate ask him, "Did it work?" before the two of them entered the ballroom.

"Hey," I said, walking back to Justin. "Thanks for helping us out before. That was awesome of you."

Justin looked up at me, his brow furrowed. "What was that about, Mad?" he asked. "I had no idea what was going on—Kittson just told me to distract that girl Isabel, and then come back to our prom after a few minutes."

"There was a whole situation," I said, feeling that it was probably best not to go into details. "But you really helped us."

Justin stood up, frowning. "So you just used me?" he asked.

"No," I said quickly. "It wasn't like that."

"Then what was it like?" he asked.

I tried to think fast, but couldn't come up with a response. Justin looked at me for a moment longer, then shook his head and walked away. I started to head after him when someone called my name.

"See you, Mad!" I looked away from Justin and saw Andy descending the staircase. "It was nice to have met you and all."

"You too," I said. But I saw that Andy wasn't listening to me anymore—he was looking at the ballroom doors, where Ruth was coming out, pulling a wrap around her shoulders.

"Ready?" Andy asked her, and she nodded.

"Ready." She looked at me and then down at her small drawstring bag. "So that was . . . interesting tonight, Mad."

"A night to remember?" I asked, and she laughed.

"Definitely." She seemed like she was about to say something else, but then just gave me a small smile. "Talk to you later."

She turned back to Andy, and they headed toward the lobby. I watched her go, thoughts flooding my head—about what had happened this past spring, about what had happened tonight, about nine years of friendship, and about a picture that we never got to take. Just before she and Andy were out of earshot, I made my decision. "Ruth," I called, and she turned back to me. "Talk to you soon."

She looked at me, surprised, but with a hopeful smile creeping over her face. Then she nodded and turned back to Andy, and as I watched, he took her hand and they disappeared from view.

****

"All right!" Chris yelled over the microphone from his DJ station as I stopped dancing for a moment to catch my breath. I had been beyond thrilled that the dancing wasn't over when Nate and I had headed back to the ballroom, and that there was enough time for me to spend some of my prom actually *at* my prom. "Putnam High, let me hear you make some noise!" All around me, everyone yelled, and I smiled as Chris did some fancy DJ scratching, then cranked up Beyoncé, causing everyone to yell again and start dancing with renewed energy.

I turned in a circle and saw my friends dancing like crazy all around me. Lisa and Dave were getting down, Lisa with her head thrown back, singing along with the song. Kittson was showing off her moves—which were quite impressive, if somewhat R-rated—as Turtell shuffled his feet from side to side next to her. She was still wearing the crown, which caught the light from the chandelier and reflected it against the walls. Jimmy and Liz were slow dancing, wrapped in an embrace, and gazing into each other's eyes. I'd realized pretty quickly that this was how they danced to every song, no matter what the tempo. Sarah had brought Zach down to our prom, and they were dancing enthusiastically, Sarah's arms flailing so wildly that people around them were giving them a wide berth. Ginger and Josh were dancing next to Brian and Melissa, and Mark was pulling a Billy Idol, and dancing with himself, but not appearing very upset about it.

Tanner was there, looking a little worse for wear — he'd been forcibly ejected from the Hartfield prom and replaced with an iPod. But he'd told me between songs that it was cool; the guys from the circle pit had crowd surfed him out. In the exodus, his shirt had gotten torn, and I'd given him the T-shirt from the bat mitzvah gift bag. He'd been grateful for it, and I didn't have the heart to tell him that on the back, it read *Today I Am An (Immortal) Woman.*

Even Justin was there, standing off to the side, watching everyone dancing. If he was disappointed that he hadn't won prom king, it wasn't showing.

"Dipping you," Nate said. He spun me around and, in one smooth movement, bent me backward over his arm and whipped me back up again. I smiled at him as he grabbed my hand and spun me into him, then twirled me out. It turned out that Nate hadn't been lying about having moves. My boyfriend could *dance.* I tipped my head back, threw my arms in the air when the song told me

337

to, then dropped them, shimmying my shoulders at Nate and making him laugh. My feet hurt in my prom heels, but I didn't care. The lights were flashing, the music was loud, my friends were dancing all around me, and my boyfriend was spinning me into his arms. It was what I'd always wanted the prom to be.

I turned my back to Nate, and he put his hands on my hips and we moved together, prompting some faux-scandalized whoops from my friends—which was ridiculous, really, because Kittson had been grinding with Turtell for the last three songs. I was about to turn back to Nate so we could dance face-to-face for a while, when someone standing in the doorway of the ballroom caught my eye. My feet slowed.

It was Isabel, just standing there, staring into the ballroom. I watched her take it all in—the crowds of dancing people, the decorations, the DJ we'd poached playing actual prom music. Her eyes moved around the room and stopped on my group of friends. With a sinking feeling, I watched her face as she stared at them—Kittson wearing the Hayes crown, Dave and Lisa twirling madly, Sarah laughing with Isabel's original date, Mark getting down, Tanner grooving to his own beat, Justin standing apart, looking lost in thought but clearly with us. It was as though she was putting the events of the night together and was now watching us celebrate our victory.

Then she looked at me, and we made eye contact. No longer moving, I held her gaze for a long moment, and she stared right back at me. I didn't like what I saw on her face. It wasn't Dell's acceptance of defeat. It was pure, unadulterated rage. And it was directed right at me.

"Mad, you okay?" Nate asked, probably wondering why I'd stopped moving altogether. I turned to look at him and nodded, then glanced back at the doorway. But Isabel was gone.

"Okay, it's the last song," Chris said, prompting boos from the crowd. "So we're going to slow it down a bit for all you sweethearts out there."

Again I looked at the doorway where Isabel had been, trying to shake her expression, or at least figure out why it was bothering me so much. Then I gave up, determined not to let her ruin what was left of the prom. I turned back to Nate, who smiled at me. I stepped close to him and slid my arms around his neck. Nate wrapped his arms around my waist as Pete Townshend's "Let My Love Open the Door" began to play.

"I love this song," I said, looking up at him.

"Me too," he said, leaning down and kissing me. We lingered like that for a moment, then he pulled away and smiled at me. "Our song?" he asked. "What do you think?"

"It's perfect," I said, smiling back at him.

"And we're getting to dance to it at the prom," he said. "Just like you wanted."

"I know," I said. I leaned my head against his chest and closed my eyes, savoring the moment and wishing that it could last forever.

CHAPTER 28

Song: If My Heart Was A House/Owl City
Quote: "It was hell at the time, but after it was over, it was wonderful."—Billy Wilder

An hour later, our limo finally pulled into Dave's driveway, following the Putnam Pizza van. It had been a very long ride. It had taken us half an hour just to leave the hotel, stuck in a line of limos that had seemed never ending. And Travis and Olivia, reconciled, had spent the entire ride making out, much to my—and Kittson's—disgust. But most troubling were Schuyler and Connor, who were clearly not doing well. They hadn't exchanged a word the entire ride, and Schuyler's eyes were red-rimmed, and she wasn't looking at me or Lisa.

When the driver stopped in front of Dave's house, I flung open the limo door and stepped out, thrilled to be free of it. Everyone else piled out, and I noticed Schuyler and Connor walk over to the edge of Dave's driveway and begin what looked like a serious conversation.

Olivia and Travis exchanged anguished—and sloppy—goodbyes before she got into the car that was waiting for her, and Travis walked up to me. "Home," I said, pointing to the limo. "The driver will drop you off, and I want you to go right to bed."

"Okay," Travis said, looking too dazed to put up a fight. "Thanks a lot, Mad. For what you said before."

"Sure," I said. "I'm glad it worked out."

"Me too," Travis said fervently. "Listen," he added, lowering his voice and taking a step toward me. "You tell Nate that if he ever hurts you or anything, he's going to have me to answer to. Okay?"

I couldn't help smiling at that, but seeing how serious Travis looked, I bit my lip and nodded. "Thanks, Travis," I said. "I appreciate it."

"See you tomorrow," he said as he got back into the limo.

"I'll be back in the afternoon," I said. Travis nodded and slammed the door, and the limo began backing down Dave's driveway.

Everyone else had headed up to the afterparty, which I could already hear from the driveway. I took off my prom heels and walked across Dave's lawn, past the pool, heading for the rock wall. I glanced behind me into the French doors that opened out from Dave's kitchen and saw the party, already in full swing. But I just wanted to take a moment to myself. I sat on the edge of the rock wall and looked out at the water, thinking about the night and everything we'd done. Then I heard someone coming up behind me. I turned and saw Nate and realized that the night wasn't close to over yet.

****

"This is nice," I said, stepping inside the main bedroom in Dave's guesthouse. It really was—big windows that looked out onto the Sound, reflecting water and moonlight; a flat-screen TV; and a really, *really* big bed. I found that I couldn't tear my eyes away from the bed. It seemed to be taking up the whole room, and it was all I could focus on.

"I know," Nate said, looking around. He sat on the edge of the bed and held out his hand to me. "Come here."

"Um," I said. I walked a step closer to him, but remained standing. Then I took a deep breath and finally said what I should have said to him five days ago. "I think maybe we should talk."

"I think so, too," Nate said. He gave me one of his half smiles, but there was a seriousness to his voice that made me blink in surprise.

I nodded and sat next to him on the bed. The time had come. It had hit me, as I'd watched everyone updating their status during the limo ride to Dave's, that constant communication wasn't the same as actually talking. Just because Nate and I were never out of touch, it didn't mean that we'd been talking about the things we should have. Those things were scarier, and harder, and they took more than 150 characters to say. I drew another deep breath, preparing to have a real conversation with him.

"Okay," I said, tucking my hair behind my ears. I felt like I was about to do the most frightening thing I'd ever done. Scarier than breaking into the school and

342

stealing something off Dr. Trent's computer. Scarier than facing the possibility of expulsion. But there was no going back now. "I've kind of been freaking out all week, because I wasn't sure what . . . you had thought I meant when I talked about prom night on Monday. I thought that maybe you thought I meant that I wanted us to sleep together," I said. "But . . . that's not what I meant." I looked up at Nate, to see what his reaction was, but he just nodded, and I continued. "I still feel like there's a lot we don't know about each other. And . . . I just don't think that I'm ready yet."

Nate tucked that one lock of hair behind my ear, then held my hands in his. "Mad," he said, "I hadn't planned on us sleeping together tonight. But then after what you said on Monday . . ." He smiled at me. "It did get me thinking about it. And you're right. We aren't ready yet."

I felt relief flood through me, and I squeezed his hand. "But . . . you have . . . done it, right?" I asked, wondering why this was so hard to talk about and why every answer was so terrifying.

Nate nodded. "Last year," he said. "With Melissa."

So Brian had been right. "Oh," I murmured, trying to keep breathing normally and not let the disappointment and jealousy I was feeling show on my face.

"But it was a mistake," Nate said, surprising me. "We weren't ready, and it put too much pressure on things. It was the reason we broke up, really." Nate stared down at our hands, entwined together, and said, "And I don't want that to happen to us."

"Me neither," I said, leaning over and kissing him.

He kissed me back, and then rested his forehead against mine.

"Are we okay?" he asked, stroking my hair.

"We're great," I said, smiling at him. And it felt true. Maybe now we'd be able to talk about these difficult things, instead of both of us keeping our own secrets.

"In that case," Nate said, raising an eyebrow at me, "I want to hear what was going on tonight. Seriously. Start at the beginning and spare me no details."

"Okay," I said, pulling my legs under me on the bed. "So the story actually begins a couple years ago, at Choate. . . ."

"Oh," Nate said, leaning back on the pillows piled against the headboard, "I think it's going to be a good one."

I smiled at him. "You have no idea."

CHAPTER 29

Song: We Used To Be Friends/The Dandy Warhols
Quote: "I think this is the beginning of a beautiful friendship."—Humphrey Bogart, *Casablanca*

"So then what happened?" Lisa asked, leaning across the Stubbs table. I held out a napkin to Schuyler, but she waved it away.

"I'm okay," she said. She looked pale and tired, but she had stopped crying, and she gripped her latte and managed to give us a faint smile. "So then he told me that if I wasn't going to talk to him—if I wasn't going to trust him—then we couldn't be together." Her voice shook, and she looked down at the table.

"I'm so sorry, Shy," I said, mentally cursing Connor Atkins. I wanted it to go on the record that I had never liked him. But I thought that now might not be the moment to bring it up.

"*Les hommes,*" Lisa said, shaking her curls. "*Beaucoup stupide.*"

"It's my own fault," Schuyler said. "He's right. If I'd just talked to him, all of this could have been avoided."

"If he was really worth it, that wouldn't matter to him," I said. I'd always known that Connor saw things in terms of black and white, but this seemed to be taking it a little too far.

"Anyway," Schuyler said, "let's talk about something else. Is it true that there was a streaker?"

"There was," I said, taking a sip of my own latte. We'd already recapped my night with Nate, and I was eager to get to the gossip. "Kind of. He was wearing boxers."

"Boxer briefs," Lisa said, looking down at her phone.

Schuyler and I both turned to her. "Oh, really?" I asked. "And how would you know that, Lisa?"

Lisa looked from Schuyler to me, her cheeks growing red. "What? Nothing. *Rien*. I . . . um . . . saw at the hotel."

"No," I said, shaking my head. "Because I was there, and he was moving too fast for me to see."

"Oh my God, was it Dave?" Schuyler asked eagerly. Lisa's blush deepened. "OMG, it was!"

"Fine," Lisa said, taking a sip of her drink. "But don't spread it around, *d'accord*? Apparently, he had been talking to Nate, who had said something about how streaking was the ultimate distraction, and he was worried—"

"Wait a second," I said, putting something together and staring at Lisa. "How do you know what underwear Dave was wearing last night?" She blushed again and looked down into her cup, a small smile creeping over her face. "Lisa," I said slowly, "do you have something to tell us?"

"What?" Schuyler asked, looking confused.

346

"Lisa," I said, beginning to smile, "did you . . . and Dave . . ."

Lisa looked up at us, still blushing slightly. "Well . . ." she said. It seemed like she was trying to sound casual but was clearly too excited to pull it off. "We did."

"You did?" I asked, not quite able to believe it. "They slept together," I said to Schuyler, who still looked lost.

"You *did*?" Schuyler practically yelled, causing most of the other Stubbs patrons to look in our direction.

"Oui," Lisa said. "In the end, it was actually my idea." She smiled again and took another sip of her drink.

"Well?" I asked, leaning forward. "Lisa! Details!"

She shook her head, giving me a woman-of-the-world smile. "Oh, someday you'll understand, Mad," she said. "But until then, *mes enfants* . . ."

"Oh, come on," Schuyler said. *"One* detail?"

The bell on the Stubbs door rang, and I looked up to see Ruth standing in the doorway, looking a little unsure. I waved her over and saw Lisa's and Schuyler's expressions of surprise. When I'd texted Ruth that morning, I wasn't sure if she'd actually show up. But it made me happier than I'd realized it would to see her there.

She crossed over to us and stood outside the group a little awkwardly. Then Schuyler pulled her wooden chair closer. "Hey," she said, smiling at her.

"Allô," Lisa said.

"I thought that was just for answering the phone," I said.

"I know," she said quickly. "Just trying to see if you'd been paying attention. *Très bien,* Mad."

"Take a seat," Schuyler said.

Ruth sat down and looked around at all of us. "Hi," she said, a little bit of a quaver in her voice as she sat down. She met my eye, and I smiled at her.

"Glad you came," I said, hearing my own voice sound a little unsteady. "So guess what Lisa did last night," I said, trying to get the conversation going again so I wouldn't start crying.

"Oh, mon Dieu," Lisa said. "It's not that big a deal."

"Oh, really?" Schuyler asked. "Then why won't you talk about it?"

"Because I am a mature person," Lisa said. *"Écoute.* Ruth, this is what happened. . . ."

I sat back in my chair and looked at my friends laughing and talking, together again, feeling like something had finally been set right. I took in the sight for just a moment. Then I leaned forward and joined the conversation.

STATUS Q
What's your status?

Madly/
Madison MacDonald

Song: Possibilities of Summer/
Matt Pond PA
Quote: "If my heart was a house, you'd
be home."—Owl City

Age: 16
Location: Putnam, Connecticut

Followers: 50
Following: 50

This user's updates are private. To view
them, you must be one of the user's
friends.

About Me: I heart: my friends, my
boyfriend, iced Stubbs lattes, SUMMER
VACATION. I'm not updating my status
much these days. If you want to know
what's going on with me, give me a call.
We'll talk. ☺

Taken by: N8/Nate Ellis

Madly How many days until school's out?

Glen ➔ Madly 15. I'm counting down . . .

 KitKat ➔ the crew Beach party this weekend? Dave's house?

 Dave Gold ➔ KitKat Um, what?

 KitKat ➔ Madly Mad, we should talk about next year's prom. It's never too soon to plan!

 Madly ➔ KitKat OMG. Yes, it is too soon to plan. Believe me.

 Sarah♥Zach ➔ Dave Gold Okay if Zach and I come this weekend, Dave?

 Dave Gold ➔ Sarah♥Zach Wait a second!

 Jimmy+Liz ➔ the crew Did you guys hear? 10 anonymous donors from Putnam gave $5,000 to the Cinderella Project! Isn't that awesome?

 Madly ➔ Jimmy+Liz, the crew Totally awesome.

Free Brian! ➔ the crew Amazing.

 KitKat ➔ the crew What kind, generous people they must be.

 N8 ➔ Madly Anonymous donors, huh? Hmmm . . .

 Madly ➔ N8 I have no idea what you're talking about. ;)

 La Femme La Lisa ➔ Ruth Rue, are you and Andy coming to the beach party?

 Ruth ➔ La Femme La Lisa We'll be there!

 Dave Gold ➔ the crew Seriously, guys. Stop this.

 Schuyler ➔ the crew So, um, is there a party? Or not? I can't tell.

Dave Gold ➔ the crew FINE. But someone better bring chips this time.

 N8 ➔ Madly So if you're not busy, I was thinking about stopping by at lunch today. . . .

 Madly ➔ N8 I could not be less busy. Can't wait! See you soon.

CHECK IN TO . . .

suite scarlett

BY MAUREEN JOHNSON

Perhaps it sounds like a wonderful thing to be born and raised in a small hotel in New York City. Lots of things sound fun until they are subjected to closer inspection. If you lived on a cruise ship, for example, you would have to do the Macarena every night of your life. Think about that.

There are always tourists in New York. They come in droves in the fall and winter, cruising in through the tunnels in massive out-of-town coaches. Between Thanksgiving and New Year's, the city's population seems to double. There are no tables in restaurants, no seats on the subway, no room on the sidewalks, no beds in the hotels.

But by summer, most of them have gone. The city boils. The subways swelter. Epic thunderstorms break out. Stores have sales to get rid of unwanted goods. Theaters close. Even many of the inhabitants leave. Certainly, most of Scarlett's friends had. Dakota was at a language immersion program in France. Tabitha was doing volunteer work for the environment in Brazil. Chloe was teaching tennis at a camp in Vermont. Hunter was with his father, helping him run a film festival in San Diego. Mira had gone to India with her grandparents to sweep temples. Josh was doing some kind of unspecified "summer session" in England.

Every single one of them was off doing something to beef up their college applications — and set them apart from everyone else. Even Rachel, who was the only other person she knew who had to work, was doing it at a gourmet beachside delivery shop in the Hamptons. They were off being developed, molded into perfect applicants.

Only Scarlett was in the city for the summer, not doing anything to improve herself. It wasn't laziness or lack of ability. She was more than willing and able. The question was entirely one of funding. Hotels make money — but they also bleed it. Especially hotels with fragile decorations and plumbing from 1929 that sit empty much of the time.

This was all part of the reason that Scarlett knew that this "little talk" probably wasn't going to end up being a discussion about going to Paris or bringing a live koala into the lobby to give hugs to all the guests.

"Scarlett," her father said, sitting back down, "you're old enough now to be included in these discussions. I'm really sorry we had to do this today — now — but there's no other time."

Scarlett looked at Spencer nervously, and he tapped his foot against hers reassuringly. His expression, however, was anything but relaxed. He shifted his jaw back and forth, and kept puffing air into and hollowing out his taut cheeks.

"As you may have guessed," her mother began, looking to Scarlett first, "things have gotten a little tight recently. I'm afraid Belinda didn't call out today. We had to let her go."

Scarlett was too shocked to speak, but Spencer let out a low groan. Belinda was the last regular staff member. The others had gone over the course of the last two years. Marco, who handled all the facilities and repairs. Debbie and Monique, the cleaners. Angelica, the part-time front desk person. And now Belinda . . . the last remaining draw to the hotel. She of the spicy hot chocolate and cherry bread that people raved about.

"We'll get by," her father said, "just like we always have. But we have to get serious about a few things. We're going to be counting on all of you. Lola, as you two probably know, is taking a year off to work at Bendel's and to help us out here, especially with Marlene. And we're really grateful for that."

Lola looked down modestly.

"Scarlett," he said, looking a bit nervous now, "we have a big favor to ask of you. We know you plan on looking for a summer job . . ."

It wasn't just a plan — it was a desperate need. A job meant money for clothes, for movies, for basically anything above and beyond eating lunch and getting her Metrocard for the subway. It was the money everyone else in her school just got handed to them in the form of a credit card.

". . . but we're going to need some of your time. Possibly a lot of your time . . . looking after the front desk, answering the phone, cleaning up. Things like that. We'll try to up your allowance a little when you go back to school to make up for it."

It didn't seem like something that could really be argued. The reality of life without Belinda, with no staff at all, was simply too stark.

"It doesn't sound like I have much of a choice," she said.

AND DON'T MISS
THE SEQUEL . . .

scarlett fever

Scarlett Martin is in a frenzy. Faced with her family's new financial woes, she has taken on the job of assistant/indentured servant to a newly minted theatrical agent, professional eccentric Mrs. Amy Amberson. Scarlett ends up at the beck and call of a Broadway star (her own age!), dealing with territorial doormen, and walking a small dog with insecurity issues—all while starting her sophomore year at one of New York's most rigorous high schools.

It doesn't help that Scarlett's brain is clouded with thoughts of Eric, her former sort-of boyfriend. She has thousands of things to say to him, if only he would call. And then there's the new lab partner, the impossible Max, who's on a quest to destroy what little mind she has left.

But somehow Scarlett will prevail . . . right?

To Do List:
Read all the Point books!

Airhead
Being Nikki
Runaway
By **Meg Cabot**

Wish
By **Alexandra Bullen**

Top 8
By **Katie Finn**

Sea Change
The Year My Sister Got Lucky
South Beach
French Kiss
Hollywood Hills
By **Aimee Friedman**

Ruined
By **Paula Morris**

Possessed
By **Kate Cann**

Suite Scarlett
Scarlett Fever
By **Maureen Johnson**

The Lonely Hearts Club
By **Elizabeth Eulberg**

Wherever Nina Lies
By **Lynn Weingarten**

Girls In Love
Summer Girls
Summer Boys
Next Summer
After Summer
Last Summer
By **Hailey Abbott**